An Unforeseen
Motive

A
WINSLOW & FITZGERALD
INVESTIGATIONS
MYSTERY

CHERIE O'BOYLE

Also by Cherie O'Boyle

ESTELA NOGALES MYSTERY SERIES
Back for Seconds?
Fire at Will's
Iced Tee
Missing Mom
Deadly Disguise
The Boy Who Bought It
All Tied Up

DOG MYSTERY
On Scent

WINSLOW & FITZGERALD INVESTIGATIONS
A Preposterous Alibi
An Unforeseen Motive
By Indelicate Means

An Unforeseen Motive

A
WINSLOW & FITZGERALD
INVESTIGATIONS
MYSTERY

CHERIE O'BOYLE

****

O'Boyle, Cherie
      An Unforeseen Motive by Cherie O'Boyle
      ISBN 979-8-9879806-1-3

2023, Cover by Karen A. Phillips, www.PhillipsCovers.com

DEDICATION

This second story in the Winslow & Fitzgerald Investigations series is dedicated to Shireen Miles, a good friend and stalwart supporter throughout my writing career. Shireen has aided at every stage from helping to think a story through, to traveling with me on research expeditions, and then finally posting gracious reviews of the finished work.
Thank you is not enough!

Chapter One

A loud banging on the door caused Evelyn to fear for the integrity of the etched glass window, centerpiece of the handsome entry door. Caught in the middle of setting the table for supper, she dropped a spoon, sending it clattering to the floor.

"Gracious!" she said to her housemate Flora. "You told me Marisol was upset and would be dropping by. You didn't say she bordered on hysterical. Either that or a common criminal bent on evil lurks on our porch."

Full of youthful enthusiasm and heedless of any possible danger, Flora rushed to fling the door open. A weeping Marisol Pacheco-Sanchez threw herself into Flora's arms.

"Oh! Dear me, Marisol. Here, here, come and sit down." One arm wrapped tightly around Marisol's shoulders, Flora escorted her friend to the parlor where the two young women sat on the sofa. Marisol secured a few strands of her long dark hair come loose from the braid down her back, and scrubbed at her reddened eyes with an already soggy handkerchief. Her black coat sparkled where tiny drops of foggy dampness were trapped on the woolen fibers, and smelled muggy. Flora flashed a look at Evelyn, who rose and went in pursuit of a clean hanky and a glass of water. Flora helped Marisol off with her coat and hugged the smaller woman.

After Marisol had a chance to blow her nose and catch her breath, she regaled them with a frightening tale of her effort to travel from the cottage she shared on Cathedral Hill the two plus miles to Evelyn and Flora's house on Green Street. In this third year after the crash of the stock market, labor strikes and deliberate acts of damage to the streetcars could cause any trip on city streets to be a dangerous excursion, but Marisol's journey had proven more challenging than most. After waiting a half an hour on Ellis St. with still no streetcar in sight, she'd been forced to walk the six blocks to the Fillmore line. She'd paid her fare and ridden no more than a mile when the conductor stopped the car right in the middle of Broadway, blocking the intersection in all directions. Then he'd set the brake and simply walked away, leaving the passengers stranded.

Marisol slipped off one shoe and showed them an angry bleeding blister. "I started to walk the remaining distance," she said. "Then realized two disreputable *vagabundos* were following me. The faster I walked, the faster they came after me! I had to run the last three blocks." Marisol whimpered, poking at her bloody heel. Flora gave Evelyn another look. Evelyn sighed and rose again, returning a few moments later with a damp flannel and the box of Band-Aids from the kitchen. She handed those to Marisol. As an experienced nurse, Marisol was capable of cleaning and bandaging the wound herself, giving only small gasps of pain.

Evelyn shook her head. "Gracious, dear, why didn't you let Bernice bring you in her little Ford?"

"She did offer," Marisol said, "but I wanted to talk to you two alone. I'll telephone her in two shakes and plead for a ride home. I don't know how you two manage without an automobile."

Flora moved to her own chair and gave Evelyn a meaning-filled nod. That subject could be sore spot between Flora and Evelyn. She turned back to Marisol. "Thank goodness you're here now. What you have to say must be important for you to have gone to all that trouble to get here. What is it?"

Marisol took a deep breath and launched into another horror-filled tale. "I'm afraid it's more about labor troubles," she said. "I didn't want to say too much over the telephone… and I'd just as soon that Bernice doesn't hear about this before she drives me out to Walnut Creek Saturday. Sadly, like everywhere else, the labor situation in the orchards is ugly. There's brawling and vandalism every day, then last night someone tried to set fire to our Pacheco family barn, endangering the workers who were sleeping there. If the workers hadn't gotten after it, that fire would've destroyed our barn and probably killed our two horses. As it was, our foreman had to be taken to the hospital in Martinez. My aunt is beside herself with fear the family may lose their whole labor contracting business. She even fears for the lives of her sons. I need to get out there and do whatever I can to help my family."

All of them were well-acquainted with the chaos surrounding labor relations in seemingly every sector of the economy in 1932. Neither Flora nor Evelyn were clear on how the situation might play out in the fruit orchards of Contra Costa County, but it was obvious Marisol was overwrought.

"Are you willing to be more specific about what's happening and who might be responsible?" Evelyn asked. She glanced at Flora, encouraging her to ask a question.

"Yes, dear, perhaps you could begin by explaining what you mean by a 'labor contracting business?' I'm afraid I'm unfamiliar with the term." As daughter to the president and owner of Fitzgerald Shipping and Shipbuilding, Flora had roots in that lucrative East Coast milieu, but her privileged upbringing sometimes left her oblivious to the mechanics of working class culture, and she'd certainly never had anything to do with the business end of labor relations.

"Or perhaps," Evelyn said, trying to steer the conversation to matters of more immediate interest, "you could tell us why you came over tonight. You must have something important to discuss to have gone through all that to get here."

Marisol gave Evelyn a pleading gaze, then looked back at Flora. "Labor contracting is the business where my family recruits and dispatches workers to pick fruit for the owners of the orchards. The growers send trucks every day to the Pachecos' barn. The trucks provide transport for the farmworkers to get to the orchards. Each truck driver arrives with instructions from the growers about how many workers are needed. For their part, the farmworkers show up at the Pachecos' barn early each morning to sign up for work. The labor contractors, in this case, the Pacheco family, make the decisions about who are the best workers and will keep the growers happy. The Pachecos load those workers on the trucks.

"My family has been running this labor operation for decades, since the orchards were planted, really. There are always more workers than work, so it's up to us to send the best workers and that's how my family stays in business. The growers trust us."

Flora's brow was furrowed. "But your uncle, *El Jefe*, the big boss, died last year. Evelyn and I went to the funeral."

"Yes, and now his two sons, Rafael and Joaquin, my cousins, have taken over the contracting business."

Flora nodded. "Yes, I remember those young men. We met them at the funeral. Those boys must be, what, in their early twenties?"

"Yes," Marisol said.

"That seems so young," Evelyn said. "I mean, to be responsible for such a large operation."

"That's our first problem," Marisol said. "Plenty of others think Rafael and Joaquin are too young to be running that business. They want to take it over from our family. That's why Tia Rosamaria is afraid we may be in danger of losing the business."

Evelyn's expression grew more serious. "Could these other people simply take over the labor contracting?"

"That's what my family fears. After decades..." Marisol wiped tears before they could fall. She went on to explain about the origins of her family and the other Californios, descendants of the early Spanish explorers of the region. Like many other Californios, the Pachecos had been granted thousands of acres two to three hundred years ago by the Spanish crown. For decades they supported themselves and their families by planting orchards and vegetable fields and by cattle ranching.

"The last few years, the situation has changed," Marisol said. She sighed and wiped her nose again. "This long drought we're in means the trees are not producing as much fruit. There's not so much harvesting work and workers in canneries and food processing plants are being laid off as well."

"But how can the supply of food be decreasing?" Flora asked. "People still need to eat."

"Yes, of course they do," Marisol said, "but with work being scarce, many people can no longer afford to purchase fruit or much of anything else."

"That's true," Evelyn added. "We know how lucky we are to have pork in our bean dinners."

"In any case," Marisol said, "lots of workers laid off from other jobs are showing up at the Pachecos' contracting office wanting to be employed as farmworkers."

"I was just reading about the shipyards and other businesses around the bay that have laid off thousands of men." Evelyn said. "Carpenters and construction workers have lost their jobs, and even clerks and sales people. About the only manufacturing plants still at nearly full employment are the automobile factories."

"Exactly," Marisol said. "Many of those laid-off workers have joined together in their common search for work. Out in the fruit orchards they're calling themselves the Vigilantes, as though they are some band of law enforcers. Mostly Americanos and other immigrants. They show up every morning and demand to be sent out to take the farmworkers' jobs." Marisol shook her head with a look of disgust.

"We heard on the radio the other day," Flora said, "one-third of the American workforce is unemployed right now. One third!. Just a decade ago there was plenty of work for everyone."

"Then there's this other group," Marisol said, bringing the discussion back to the farmworkers' plight. "The people coming to California from Oklahoma and the southwest, escaping from those terrible dust storms. Okies, some people call them." Marisol glanced up, knowing an ethnic slur such as the label Okies would likely ruffle at least Evelyn's feathers. "Anyway, those people are showing up, too, asking for work. All of these new men get angry and cause trouble if the regular Californio farmworkers are dispatched ahead of them. The supply of work and the demand for employment is all out of balance."

Flora shook her head. "Are you saying this labor contracting situation is why someone set fire to your barn?"

"Yes. Previously there's only been rough-housing and rowdiness. Workers pushing and shoving to be first in line. It's like a small riot on workdays. A few days ago my cousin Joaquin had his nose bloodied in a fist fight in his own front yard. And it's getting worse. There were earlier incidents. Vandalism, you might call them. A tire was cut on Rafael's pickup. A window broken. Then last night the situation escalated. A flaming torch was thrown into the barn, setting the straw on fire. Someone could have been killed. My cousins Rafael and Joaquin stay up all night watching out for trouble, but they're both exhausted.

"That's why I've decided to go out to Walnut Creek, to the family hacienda to see if I can be of some help. Bernice will come with me and drive us in her Tin Lizzie.

Evelyn was still patiently waiting to hear how any of this might have any connection to herself or Flora. "And you're telling us this because…"

Marisol shifted to look directly at Evelyn. "I know you're going to Alameda this weekend to housesit for your brother Walter. Alameda is just a hop and a skip from Walnut Creek."

"Yes…?"

"And I know you two sometimes earn extra money in the summers by conducting various types of investigations."

Evelyn gave a curt nod of acknowledgment to that certainty.

6

Fidgeting impatiently, Flora voiced the connection. "And you want us to investigate these acts of vandalism?"

"Yes," Marisol said, and sighed in gratitude. "Yes. I promised my aunt I would visit, and do whatever I could to help the family. Rafael is trying to be the boss, but he's at his wit's end with this labor contracting. He doesn't have time to track down whoever's committing these acts of vandalism, and now the situation is getting more dangerous. If it keeps up, someone is going to get worse than a bloody nose…maybe even killed." Marisol dropped her head and shook it. "And my aunt says Joaquin is such a rascal himself, he's not much help. I told them you two had the know-how and might be willing to find out who's behind this vandalism before it escalates any further."

Flora sighed, and the room fell silent. Evelyn watched another tear slide down Marisol's cheek, then she, too, sighed, feeling more worried than sad. She'd like to help her friend, but not at the expense of her own or Flora's safety. Surely there must be something they could do to help without endangering themselves.

Anxiety clouding her forehead, Marisol asked, "You are still planning to go to Alameda this weekend aren't you? What do you think about investigating? My family would pay, of course."

Chapter Two

"Yes," Evelyn said. "Walter is picking us up on Friday and taking us to his house in Alameda. We had hoped, you know, that you and Bernice would—"

"Yes," Flora interrupted. "You were going to join us on Sunday and we were all going to enjoy the afternoon at the Neptune Beach Amusement Park, remember?"

"I had hoped I'd still be able to join you for that trip to the park," Marisol said, "but now I'm not sure."

Flora glanced at Evelyn, resignation reflected in her eyes. And Evelyn knew, if the troubles in the orchards were as bad as Marisol had described, the frivolous day of fun at the beach they'd planned would likely not happen.

"I'm afraid," Marisol continued, "it's beginning to look as though I'll need to stay with my aunt." She sent a quick apologetic look to Flora.

"That does indeed sound like a difficult situation," Evelyn said. "Did you have something in particular in mind that we might investigate?" Evelyn needed more specifics about circumstances that seemed as though they might be more than simply 'difficult.' The state of affairs might even prove to be dangerous and beyond their skills.

"First," Marisol said, "You two are wickedly clever at figuring out puzzles. You solved the mystery when that unfortunate girl was found in Chinatown. We're hoping you might be able to identify who's behind these serious incidents at our hacienda. If we can stop the vandalism, we might forestall a potential crisis."

Evelyn's face assumed the stern expression she wore when lecturing a wayward student. "Do you mean you'd like us to find out who flattened a tire and tried to start a fire? Is that what you mean?" Even to her own ears, Evelyn feared her words sounded harsh and unhelpful.

Flora gave Evelyn a shocked expression.

Evelyn took a breath and softened her tone. "You've just given us a list of several factions you suspect, and neither Flora nor I know anything about any of them. We simply wouldn't know where to begin."

"Yes, well, when you put it that way, it doesn't sound like so much." Marisol said. "We're concerned though, especially given the threats that have been made. Even relatively minor incidents of vandalism are likely to escalate, given all the other ugliness."

Evelyn took another deep breath and relented...some. "I do understand your concern. I wonder though if your family might be better off simply by keeping a more watchful eye to stop these things before they happen. If Rafael could employ a couple of the farmworkers to keep watch, that might be a better use of your money than hiring us to investigate, don't you think? Especially if, as your aunt suggests, the brother is not going to be reliable."

"Oh!" Flora piped up. "That's a swell idea!"

Evelyn glanced gratefully at Flora and continued. "Though, I do appreciate your confidence in our puzzle-solving abilities."

Marisol nodded, then sighed. "Yes, I see. So you won't help us?"

Evelyn shifted uncomfortably, wondering how she'd managed to get herself into this pickle without even trying. "Let's do this, let's wait until you get out there and learn more. If it turns out there is something specific we might investigate, I'm sure we'll be willing at that time."

Flora rose and went to the library alcove, where she rummaged for moment in the drawer of the desk there. "Here we are," she said, returning with a small box from which she extracted a cream-colored business card and handed it to Marisol. On the card was printed the words "Winslow and Fitzgerald Investigators" with their telephone exchange. "This makes us official," Flora said. "And the truth is, we could use the work this summer, right Evelyn?" Flora nodded pointedly at Evelyn who returned her look with a slightly abashed smile.

"Oh, wait," Flora said. "Give it back." Writing on the card she said, "Here's Walter's exchange. This is the number where we can be reached next week, in Alameda."

Still standing, Flora gazed at Marisol. "Is this vandalism and violence the reason you wanted to see us alone? You're afraid Bernice won't go with you if she knows the truth about what's going on at your family's hacienda?"

"Yes. I mean, no. I'm not helpless, you know. I could get out there on my own, even if Bernice refused to drive me."

"I'm sure, but you did say you took the streetcar tonight because you had something you wanted to talk to us about alone."

Marisol opened her mouth to answer, but was interrupted by Wu Chin Jaing, Flora and Evelyn's housemate, cook, housekeeper, and all-around confidant, appearing in the parlor archway. She clutched at the neckline of her embroidered Cheongsam-style dress and gave a slight bow. "Ladies? Shall I set another place at the table? Your supper is far beyond ready and must be eaten soon. Will you be much longer?"

"Oh, gosh!" Flora said, rising. "I forgot all about supper. By all means, Marisol, please do join us."

Evelyn caught Jaing's gaze, trying to guess whether there would be enough food for another plate.

Marisol saved her from that concern. "No, thank you so much. I must telephone Bernice. She's expecting me home for supper." Marisol made her way to the telephone on the library table.

After her call, she returned the earpiece to its base. "Bernice will be here in a jiffy. Anyway, the thing I need to ask you, and I really hope you will understand…"

Flora glanced at Evelyn, but it was impossible to know if they would understand until Marisol spit out her request.

"As I said, Bernice is driving me out to Walnut Creek on Saturday morning and we had planned to stay overnight. However…" They waited while Marisol organized her thoughts. "Tia Rosamaria told me she'd prefer that Bernice not stay with me in the hacienda. Needless to say, Tia Rosamaria is distressed, what with all that's going on, and she thinks, or she says, that having a stranger in the house will upset her more." Marisol's face took on a contrite expression as she looked at them. "She's asked me not to have Bernice stay, but I've not said anything to Bernice yet. Do you see?"

Evelyn was not sure she did see and was not necessarily sympathetic. Marisol's attitude toward her assumed-to-be beloved housemate Bernice bordered on the disrespectful, in Evelyn's view.

Marisol continued. "Do you think it would be possible for Bernice to stay at your brother's house in Alameda with you Saturday night?" She continued chattering. Without giving Evelyn a chance to respond, she explained that Bernice could drive back to the hacienda on Sunday to pick her up. No promises, but possibly that might be in time for them all to still have a shortened visit to Neptune Beach. Both Bernice and Marisol needed to be back in the city by early Monday morning.

"So," Marisol said, "What do you think?"

"Just so I'm clear," Evelyn said, "your aunt is fine having Bernice drive you to visit but she doesn't want Bernice to stay in her home?"

Marisol had the grace to look embarrassed. "Just the overnight. It's a difficult situation, Evelyn. I'm not prepared to argue with my aunt. Please try to understand."

"Walter and Pearl won't mind if we have Bernice stay with us at their house, will they?" Flora asked Evelyn. "Otherwise she'd have to drive all the way back to the city Saturday night, and back out again to retrieve Marisol on Sunday."

"Oh, I could get myself home on Sunday…if I had to… assuming the streetcars and ferries and trains are running."

"But it's the least we could do, isn't it Evelyn? And surely Walter and Pearl will have no objection. There'll be a bed in one of the boys' rooms, right? Having Bernice overnight with us will be grand fun, won't it?"

Evelyn appreciated Flora's open-minded attitude. She knew Flora occasionally found Bernice's nosy nature to be sometimes meddlesome.

"Of course," Evelyn said, taking one moment longer than necessary for the remainder of her reply. "I'll confirm with Pearl and Walter, and I'm sure it will be no problem." She felt relieved to at last have been asked to provide the kind of help she'd be able to provide.

"Thank you," Marisol said. "At least that's one less thing I have to worry about."

"As long as we're waiting for Bernice to get here and pick you up." Evelyn said, "possibly you could tell us who you think the most likely suspects are in these acts of vandalism. You mentioned the groups vying for the work assignments, but who do you think tried to burn down your barn, for example?"

"Well, quickly because Bernice should be here shortly. First I would say the other farmworker families, the ones who think they should have been allowed to take over the labor contracting when my uncle died. The Alisals out in Danville think Rafael and Joaquin are too young and don't know the business well enough. The Alisals also think we Pachecos are not getting the highest wages for the fruit pickers.

"And then these Vigilantes. They're the scariest, according to what Rafael told me. They think Americanos should have the contracting business, and all the picking jobs too. And those Vigilantes are backed-up by the county sheriff and his men, making them even more dangerous."

"What about those recent arrivals from Oklahoma?" Flora asked.

Marisol thought while Flora helped her shrug back into her damp coat. "What I think about those folks is that they really just want to work. They've come all this way, and most of them with nothing. Someone's been stealing potatoes and other things from Tia's vegetable garden. That might be those people, but only because they and their children are starving. I don't think they care about who does the contracting, only about finding some work and food for their families."

"So your suspects are one, other farmworkers, and two the Vigilantes?"

"Mainly, yes."

Evelyn nodded and said, "And we never want to forget a possible enemy of the Pachecos, someone unknown or who you haven't yet thought about."

Marisol shook her head despairingly.

"Well," Evelyn said, "let's hope last night was the worst of it and the crisis will have calmed down by the time you get out there." She moved the three of them onto the front porch where they could listen for the "toodle-toot-toot" of Bernice's arriving second-hand Ford.

Flora and Evelyn waved goodbye to their friends and hurried inside for a belated supper. The kitchen was fragrant with the scent of slightly overcooked beans. Flora clapped once, and said, "Oh, goodie. What luscious delicacy have you prepared for us this fine June evening?"

Jaing smiled, appreciating Flora's attempt at humor. "I'm afraid it is beans, again, Miss Flora."

Peering into the heavy ceramic bowl on the kitchen table, Flora could see that supper would indeed be beans, this time lima beans, slow simmered and flavored with a bit of ham hock. Nobody's favorite, but filling, and with most of the world locked in economic depression and scarcity, they were glad to have that. Jaing had also baked a batch of cornbread muffins to help the beans go down.

"That's the last of the butter," Jaing said as she placed the butter dish beside the basket of muffins. "The milkman will deliver fresh in the morning."

Although the house on Green Street included a perfectly suitable dining room that Flora had furnished with a Federal-style mahogany table and upholstered seating for six, the three women preferred to eat most of their meals together in the kitchen. The oak table in the center of the room provided ample space while still making cozy conversation possible.

Flora dished out three bowls of beans, each including a small chuck of ham, saving the biggest piece for Evelyn, and slid them around the table. They took a moment of gratitude for the less-than bountiful meal before them, and began to eat.

"I'm sorry we didn't introduce you to Marisol," Evelyn said to Jaing. "Or do you remember her?"

"Yes, I remember your pals Bernice Woodlawn and Marisol Pacheco. Miss Woodlawn is a tall lady, very tall." Jaing stretched one hand high overhead.

"Yes." Flora laughed, gazing upward. "Perhaps not quite that tall. She might come to stay with us at Walter's. Oh, Evelyn, I hadn't thought...do you think Bernice will even fit in one of the boys' beds?"

Evelyn joined in the laughter around the table. She could always trust Flora to keep the mood light.

"In any case," Flora continued, we're taking Spritz with us. She can have a reunion with her brother, Spike." Evelyn and Flora's four-year-old terrier, Spritz, was a handful and her litter mate, Spike, was equally as energetic and in need of entertainment.

"It'll be our vacation, as well, right Evelyn?" Flora said, using a bit of corn muffin to sop the last of her beans.

"Well," Evelyn said, "it will be if we don't get tangled up in a complicated investigation. You should see her list, Jaing. Miss Flora has a whole catalog of adventures made up for us."

"And we want to visit the orchards in Contra Costa as well, and buy fruit." Flora patted Jaing's hand. "We'll bring home nuts for you so you can make those almond cookies we all love."

Chapter Three

Evelyn chuckled at Flora's promise to bring nuts so Jaing could make cookies. "Indeed. Miss Flora is going to keep us busy every day, I'm sure. And we're grateful for your help, too, keeping an eye on this house."

"Will your mother and son come stay here, too?" Flora said. "You all could have a vacation here, if you'd like." Flora smiled in encouragement.

"Oh, no, but thank you," Jaing said, finishing the last spoonful of her beans. "My mother would prefer not to leave her friends."

Evelyn and Flora knew the Chinatown apartment Jaing rented for her mother and young son consisted of two rooms above a bakery on Min Pow Hong Alley, with a bathroom shared by the other apartments on that floor. A three-week vacation in Flora and Evelyn's well-appointed Italianate residence in the exclusive Pacific Heights neighborhood of San Francisco would seem to hold no small appeal. On the other hand, the family's friends and familiar places were all in Chinatown.

"Well, whatever suits," Flora said. She turned to Evelyn. "I do hope Marisol and Bernice will still join us Sunday for our excursion to Neptune Beach...but perhaps not." She adopted a crestfallen expression and ended her sentence in a wistful tone.

Evelyn broke open a hot muffin, used her knife to slip

a tiny dab of butter inside, took a bite, and waited to answer until she had fully savored her mouthful. "We can certainly go, dear, even if our friends are not able to join us."

The two young women settled into their chairs in the parlor after supper for a restful evening. The long school day and eventful visit from Marisol had tired them both.

"Fiddlesticks!" Flora said after an hour of reading, and she slammed her novel closed. She uncurled her slender legs from where they were beneath her in the easy chair, her face a frustrated scowl.

Evelyn tipped down one corner of her newspaper. "What's the problem?" she said.

Flora gave the soft curls of her stylish new hairdo a shake and huffed. "This Faulkner novel, *Light in August*. The narrative style is unnecessarily complex making it hard to follow, and the theme is dark, positively gothic. I couldn't possibly teach this, even with our senior girls. Principal Wendover recommended it but I am afraid I'll have to decline. Something more suitable must be found."

As Vice-Principal at Dorothea Bentley School for Girls, Evelyn Winslow was reluctant to comment on Principal Wendover's curriculum suggestions. She assumed a sympathetic expression, but said nothing as Flora gave another exasperated sigh.

Apparently Flora was finished reading for the evening. She stared until Evelyn laid the newspaper in her lap.

"You know," Flora said, "you gave Marisol's request for help finding their vandal tormenters a less than warm reception. I fear she left here feeling even more discouraged than when she arrived. That's not like you. You always want to help where you can."

"That's just it. It's not that I don't want to help, Flora. It's only, that set of circumstances sounds dangerous, and we don't know anything about the parties involved. What specifically might we do to assist the Pachecos?"

Flora flopped back in her chair beside the fireplace. "We do have a reputation, you know."

Evelyn smiled and gave Flora a wink. "A reputation?"

Flora returned Evelyn's smirk. "A reputation as successful investigators able to solve mysterious puzzles, dear. Besides, our summer recess is about to begin and we need to find a way to earn some extra money. We'll be out there anyway. This could be our ticket."

"That's true," Evelyn agreed. "I'm glad you unearthed those business cards. I was afraid we'd need to launch an investigation just to find those. We'll likely need them if we embark on an inquiry in the fruit orchards. In any case, I had thought we ended the conversation with a promise to wait and see what Marisol learns when she gets there, and decide then what we might do to help."

Flora nodded and Evelyn lifted the newspaper again.

"Look," Evelyn said, tapping the paper. "Right here is an article Upton Sinclair wrote calling for even more labor strikes, and they say he'll be the Democratic candidate for governor in California in the next election."

"That's yesterday's paper," Flora said, leaning to read the page. "Why are you reading yesterday's newspaper?"

"The newsboy was gone by the time I got to his corner this afternoon. I had to stay so late taking care of my vice-principal end-of-term duties, he must have sold out and gone home. In any case, I didn't get the paper read yesterday. Doesn't really matter, does it? Every day is the same bad news gotten worse. The stock market is falling still lower every day. Von Hindenburg disbanded the German Reichstag late last week and called for new elections. The situation there is becoming more ominous by the day." She flipped a few pages back. "Lou Gehrig hit four consecutive home runs on Friday. Good news if you're a fan of the Yanks."

"Which we are not."

"I should say not."

The only sister to four brothers, Evelyn had grown up on baseball diamonds, and the Winslow family rarely missed a Philadelphia Athletics home game. Mama would pack a picnic basket and Papa would load up the Hupmobile with all five children, and a neighbor or two, if they'd fit.

Flora, on the other hand, could take baseball or leave it, even though she'd been among those piling into the Winslows' automobile on a few occasions when she was younger. Although not wild about baseball, Flora was always willing to go along on almost any adventure Evelyn proposed.

"So now that we live in San Francisco, we've become Seals fans?" Flora said.

"That we are. Say," Evelyn continued, "You could have your senior girls read one of those incendiary Upton Sinclair novels. Or better yet, how about that Pearl Buck novel, *The Good Earth*? I see it's still on the best-seller list this week."

"Oh, what a smashing idea, Evie, My girls would rather read something written by a woman anyway, and they might be usefully enlightened about China and the Chinese people, too. Thank you for that suggestion. I didn't even know you were listening to me."

"I always listen to you, dear. I delight in listening to you." Evelyn tucked a chestnut curl into the chignon at her nape, and admired the sparkle in Flora's dark eyes.

"Is there anything more about that poor Baby Lindbergh?" Flora asked.

"No. He was buried two weeks ago, but nothing yet about who might have done the dastardly deed. On a brighter note, our esteemed San Francisco City fathers are considering a proposal to hold a parade down Market Street for Amelia Earhart to celebrate her successful solo flight across the Atlantic last month. First woman to accomplish that."

"Ooh, what fun that would be! Perhaps the streetcar workers would stop rioting long enough to allow us to enjoy a parade. When are they proposing this take place?"

Evelyn nudged reading glasses higher on her nose and peered more closely at the article. "It only says sometime this coming summer." She dropped the newspaper down enough to see over the top. "Say, did I tell you, Bernice almost got herself arrested last week?"

"Do tell."

Evelyn gazed into space while she brought the story back to mind. "According to Bernice, a policeman was chasing after one of the striking streetcar workers and somehow Bernice's umbrella became tangled in his feet, toppling him. He said she put it in his way on purpose but she told him she dropped it accidentally."

"An intentional accident sounds more like Bernice."

"Yes, it does. In any case, he eventually let her go."

At just that moment, Jaing appeared in the parlor archway attired in her black silk dressing gown adorned with her mother's brilliant embroidery on the sleeves. "Ladies? Miss Evelyn? It is after ten o'clock. This is the time I make sure all is locked up and go to bed. Will you be much longer?"

"Ten o'clock!" Flora said, rising. "Evelyn, our electricity bill!"

Evelyn rose and she and Jaing made the rounds checking the house was locked up tight, while Flora rushed upstairs for the quickest of baths before sliding into bed.

The following morning, Jaing knelt on the porch in the darkness before dawn waiting for the milkman's delivery. She wanted to snatch the bottles and parcels and rush them indoors before any hungry scofflaws could get to them. Miss Flora could become quite cross if the milk for her Cheerios went missing.

Evelyn and Flora got a late start on their walk to school, owing to Flora's having overslept. The morning "June gloom" of coastal fog lay close over the rooftops in San Francisco and made it hard to believe that summer was nearly upon them.

"That situation in the fruit orchards certainly sounds like an imbroglio, doesn't it?" Flora said as they began their brisk walk.

Evelyn turned a wide-eyed stare to her companion. She knew Flora enjoyed throwing about grandiloquent words now and then, a result of her love of language. Nevertheless, Evelyn was forced to admit the word Flora had used was a new one on her.

"Do you mean to say it sounds like a mess?"

Flora rolled her eyes and laughed, then continued her thought. "I only want you to know...what Marisol asked you... the idea of you going into the middle of those...labor riots, I find that frightening."

"Yes, and beyond that, even after a good night's sleep I'm still in a quandary as to how you and I might be of any help."

"Although as always, we could make good use of any investigating fees we might earn," Flora said.

The next block was a steep climb up Alta Hill, and the damp and slippery sidewalks under the slick leather soles of their walking shoes required their concentrated attention.

When they reached the top, Flora stopped to catch her breath, her face a mask of sadness. "I find myself thinking about Marisol's poor Tia Rosamaria. First her husband passes away, and now those Vigilantes are trying to take her family's livelihood."

"Well," Evelyn said, "possibly I'm being obtuse about this issue of helping. Do you have some idea in mind as to how we might assist?"

"No. As I said, the idea that we might go out there for the purpose of investigating sounds as though it could be a dangerous state of affairs. Workers are becoming desperate and hungry, and don't seem to care who they hurt. The best we can do is to stay as far out of danger as we are able."

Evelyn thought she heard a bit of a demand in Flora's tone. Surely Flora would not counsel Evelyn as to what she should do.

"Are you forbidding me from going?"

"Ha! When has anyone ever successfully forbid you to do something you wanted to do?"

Evelyn's eyebrows shot upward and she gave Flora a moment to consider before she replied. "I believe, my dear, your memory fails you on that."

Flora gazed at Evelyn in silence, then dipped her head, hiding a smile. "Oh. I wasn't thinking about that."

"No, quite evidently not."

Returning to the previous subject, Flora said. "In any case, it seemed to me you told Marisol you wouldn't go out to Walnut Creek."

"Well, I believe I was clear when I told her I think it's best the Pachecos solve those problems on their own, if they can. If it appears at a later point we might be of some support, we may have to reconsider. And I may be exaggerating the danger. After all, no one's been killed or gone missing...yet." Evelyn tightened her lips at that thought.

And Marisol said her family was prepared to pay for our services," Flora added in an absentminded tone. "Uh-oh."

"What?"

"Look. We must be dreadfully late. The doors are already closed."

A girlish voice rang from behind them and they turned to see a student of about twelve or thirteen rushing to join them, trying to tie her scarf as she ran, book-bag swinging off one arm.

"Oh, Miss Winslow!" she said. "Thank goodness! I can't truly be tardy if I arrive at the same time as Vice Principal Winslow, can I?"

Together the three of them hurried to get inside the school doors before anyone made note of their belated arrival.

Chapter Four

The last day of the term was a jolly occasion, as a rule, with the students at Bentley School excited about the long-anticipated arrival of summer recess. Weeks at sleep-over camps, or family cabins, or relaxing at the beach usually awaited them, followed by promotion to the next grade level in the fall. This year, the third year into a serious economic downturn, the students' usual giddiness was tempered by doubts about what the future might hold for any of them.

The teachers, usually looking forward to weeks to prepare for the following year, were mostly having to seek other employment during the summer months to make ends meet. Worse, it appeared the bleak economic situation would result in a decrease of at least a few teaching positions for the fall term.

Enrollment at the expensive private school had been dropping steadily and no one was willing to hazard a guess as to what the fall term would bring, or if, heaven forbid, there might not be a fall term. Even for the lucky families who continued to have an adequate income, vacation plans were on hold and several family cabins were being offered for sale. This summer of 1932 was going to be unlike any previous summer.

The busy school day passed quickly and ended with a flurry of goodbyes and well-wishes from the bubbling girls. The Mothers Association held a short meeting of appreciation for the teachers and staff, serving punch and fairy cakes at tables set up in the gymnasium. The times being what they were, no gifts were provided to the teachers, although each received a small bouquet of flowers.

Miss Fitzgerald and Miss Winslow bade fond farewells to the others and were among the last to leave. They turned off the lights and waved to the custodian as he locked the heavy doors. Linking arms, they hurried homeward. Reaching the streetcar corner, Evelyn bought the afternoon newspaper. She tucked it into her satchel until the evening when she would have time to read. They waited for the signal to cross.

"I've been wondering," Flora said, then stopped.

"What?" Evelyn said, peering left at on-coming traffic.

"Are you listening to me?"

"Of course I'm listening to you, only the light's changed so let's get across before you tell me what you've been wondering." They scurried to the opposite curb.

"What's that crowd up ahead?" Flora stopped, holding onto Evelyn's elbow.

A few onlookers had stopped on the sidewalk a half a block ahead. The attraction of interest seemed to be a commotion at the site of the construction of a new home. Workmen sprinted away from the building site carrying curious items. One man dashed past them struggling to hold onto a heavy wooden beam. Two others followed close behind juggling several lengths of copper pipe between them. Loud arguments rang out from the ground floor of the house under construction. As Flora and Evelyn drew even with the small group on the sidewalk, a fist fight broke out among several of the men, quickly resulting in more than one bloody nose. Two of the workmen backed away from the fight and joined the group on the sidewalk.

"What's the problem?" Evelyn spoke in a low voice to the group in general.

It was a moment before a workman answered her. "They laid us off," he said. "The bank folded and pulled the construction loan. Foreman says we're done, go on home." In nearly a sob he added, "Go home to the wife and kids and tell 'em we lost our jobs."

"Yeah," the other workman said. "That's bad enough, but folks are getting laid off everywhere. What's really got us riled is they owe us for two weeks wages. They worked us like dogs the last two weeks, run here, do that, an' now they're sayin' they can't pay us for those two weeks. Two whole weeks of hard work with no wages! Guys are mad, stealing everything isn't already nailed down, anything they can sell or use." He gave a disgusted scowl, shaking his head.

At that moment, a chunk of wood came flying, hit the sidewalk with a bang, and the yelling grew louder. Everyone turned when a whoosh exploded in the middle of the construction and flames erupted.

"The kerosene!" The first workman yelled. "Somebody dumped the kerosene. Every one of you better get out of here!"

A general melee ensued with workmen running in every direction, several lugging rolls of electrical wire. Flora and Evelyn and the rest of the group had joined the others fleeing from the fire by the time police sedans pulled up and uniformed officers joined in the chase. Screaming fire engines pulled into the middle of the fracas shortly after.

"You can hardly blame them for being angry," Evelyn said when they reached the relative safety of the next block. "It's not right."

"No it's not," Flora said. "Still, not everyone who loses a job should start a riot." She took a long breath and added, "I thought President Roosevelt was going to fix all these economic problems. Why isn't he doing something?"

"He is, I'm sure," Evelyn said. "You read about all these bills Congress is debating everyday in the newspaper. But the president has limited powers. There's only so much he can do alone. Why, at this very moment there's a banking act working it's way through Congress to insure our bank deposits. Roosevelt says he'll sign it when it reaches his desk, but who knows how long that will take? Before we ran into that brawl you started to say something. Do you remember what was on your mind?"

Flora gave a mirthless bark of laughter. "To be perfectly honest, I was wondering what would happen if Bentley School could no longer pay my salary. So many people are losing their jobs. It's frightening to see all those men lining up on Market Street for a bowl of watery soup and a crust of bread. I worry what might happen to us."

Of the two of them, Evelyn tended to be the more cautious planner, although usually with optimist expectations. Always up for new escapades and a bit of fun, Flora also had a vivid imagination and was quite capable of visualizing dire outcomes. They were a good match in both dreaming up adventures and also keeping one another organized and safe.

"I hardly think we'll end up on a bread line, dear," Evelyn said. "Your father bought the house free and clear and put the title in your name, so we'll always have a place to live. And fingers crossed I'll keep my job."

"I suppose I'll always have Grandmother's trust to rely on for some support. But how do you know you'll always have a job?"

Evelyn gave this a half a moment's thought. Teaching and guiding students brought her joy in life, but she did have a number of other skills. Add to that, her father owned three large office supply stores, the main store in Philadelphia, another in Chicago, and the third, managed by her older brother, Walter, across the bay in Oakland. "Even if Bentley School closes," she said, "Walter can take me on at the store."

"Are office supplies selling so well the store in Oakland could support both you and your brother? Are business people still buying office supplies?"

"Possibly not office supplies per se, but some of his other inventory is selling well." Evelyn was thinking about the line of business machines Papa had taken on several years ago. Calculators and punch card tabulators. He was doing well with those, especially since he was the only supplier in the entire Philadelphia region, and now Walter was also carrying them in his branch. Papa was taking the proceeds from those sales mainly in the form of stock. International Business Machines the company was called, and it was one company that was doing well through this depression. Papa might make his fortune that way. And he'd added radios to his inventory several years ago. Most people couldn't afford much, these days, but everyone wanted a radio, so Winslow's Office Supplies was doing better than some. "Papa also believes in advertising his products and that brings in the customers, too," Evelyn said. "So I expect as long as Papa has his business, I'll have employment. I'm glad you brought it up, though. I might mention something to Walter, just by way of a forewarning. So many people who never expected to are finding themselves in difficult circumstances."

"I know," Flora said. "Sometimes I wake up at night and worry what our future holds. I shouldn't like to end up living in a box on a dirty vacant lot."

"I shouldn't wonder!" Evelyn said, and marveled at how Flora could spin a tale. She seemed especially talented at making up stories with frightening ends. "Anyway, wouldn't your father help if we got into dire straits?"

"Oh, I'm sure Father has plenty of money, however ill-gotten it may be. I got a letter from my sister last week and Mitzi says Father's shipyards are curiously busy even after the military stopped ordering battleships. And cruise companies have even dry-docked their existing liners for lack of passengers."

"That is curious. Who's he building ships for, if not for the Navy or his passenger line?"

"One hesitates to think," Flora said as she slung her book bag onto their porch steps and began digging in her pocketbook for the house key. "In any case, you're right. We'll always have this place to live, and as far as I know, no one can interfere with the income I receive from Grandmother's trust fund."

With supper out of the way, Evelyn sat down in the parlor and searched the newspaper for any reports about labor unrest in Contra Costa County.

Flora laid the latest best-seller in her lap. "Any news about the Pachecos?"

"Not that I can find, although there's plenty of disheartening news, along with a general atmosphere of hopelessness, loss, and fear of the future. It does appear this economic downturn may last many more months, possibly even another year or more."

Flora shuddered. "Only a couple years ago, it seemed, the future looked rosy and prosperous. Hard to fathom how the country has fallen so far in such a short time."

Evelyn tightened her lips. "It says here," she tapped the newspaper, "there've been clashes on the waterfront here in the city with different groups claiming the work of loading and unloading cargo ships."

Flora shook her head. "Remember that transit workers strike last month when we had to stay home from church? Now I've heard there are bombs being planted on the streetcars, too."

"There's another piece here," Evelyn said, "an editorial about the shantytowns. People are calling them 'Hoovervilles.' Desperate people are even building shacks backing up to the slaughterhouses in Hunter's Point. Whole families are living in not much more than paperboard boxes."

"Oh, stop please, Evelyn. I can't bear it. How can people live like that?"

"It is indeed a sad situation."

"Given all the depressing and hopeless news, I might as well go back to reading depressing old William Faulkner."

"Oh, well, never mind that. Shall we listen to the radio instead? Our favorite, *The Ginger Ale Hour* with Jack Benny was

Monday and we missed it. Let's see what the programming is for Thursday evenings." Evelyn flipped the newspaper open to the entertainment page and read, "How about the *The Bing Crosby Show?* That's mostly dance music."

Flora offered to get the playing cards. "We can listen to music and play some gin rummy." Flora smiled and held out her hand. "Unless you'd rather dance?"

Evelyn laughed. "Too tired tonight, I'm afraid." She waved toward the library table where the playing cards were kept.

Flora returned with the cards, shuffled, and began to deal them out. "I hope we don't get too distracted at Walter's house and forget to listen to our programs. We'd especially hate to miss *The Shadow* tomorrow night."

"Good point, dear," Evelyn said. "After we finish this game we should go upstairs and finish packing. We have errands to run in the morning. By the time we get back here it'll almost be time for Walter to pick us up. We'd best get the bulk of the packing done tonight."

"That's very kind of your brother to bring his automobile all the way over here to fetch us."

"Yes, it is, but really, what else could we do? Carrying all our luggage on the unreliable streetcars would be impossible."

"And then there's Spritz," Flora said. "Can't take her on the streetcars." Their tricolored terrier-dog stood when Flora did, and ran up and down the stairs as they climbed, very nearly tripping Flora when she reached the landing.

Friday morning passed quickly, with a stop at the druggist to pick up a prescription for Evelyn's allergies, a visit for Flora at the hairdressers to freshen up her cut, and a last errand at the dry cleaners to pick up their winter coats that had been left off a week ago. They wouldn't be needing those in Alameda where June was usually warm and humid, but there was no sense in leaving Mr. Chin to wonder if they'd abandoned their coats.

They arrived home in time to have a farewell mid-day meal with Jaing who patted Flora's hand and repeated several times that she hoped they would be careful while they were away. Evelyn suspected Jaing had overheard more of Marisol's concerns about labor riots and vandalism than she'd let on at the time.

Making several trips, they got their totes, suitcases, and overnight bags downstairs before Walter's prompt appearance at two in the afternoon. Flora had packed selectively, leaving most of her expansive wardrobe at home. It wasn't as though they would be camped out in the wilderness. The towns of Alameda and Oakland hosted plenty of hat shops, dress emporiums, and shoe stores, should Flora feel the need to supplement what she had managed to stuff into her luggage.

Having set a strict limit on what would fit in his Cheverolet, Walter gazed in despair at the pile needing to be loaded.

"Oh, don't look so sour, dear," Flora said. "We packed very frugally. We've each brought only four serviceable day dresses. Also one pair each of sturdy walking shoes, and one pair for Sunday or dressy. Of course we also had to bring Sunday dresses. Bedroom slippers and beach sandals don't really count as shoes, do they? Because I also put those in for each of us. Oh, and hold your horses." She disappeared upstairs and returned shortly, laden with six hat boxes. "And hats!" she said. "I almost forgot our hats."

"Oh, here now!" Evelyn said. "We surely don't need all of those hats." She the set the hat boxes along the length of the sofa. "Here, dear, you choose three hats, I'll choose a couple for myself, and we'll consolidate those into a single or possibly two hatboxes."

"Three hats! You know I'll need more than three hats." Flora reached for her favorite felt slouch.

"Very well, here, put this one on…" Evelyn pulled the hat over Flora's curls. "And now you'll have four hats."

Chapter Five

Walter loaded himself with as much as he could carry and began moving the pile out to the sidewalk. "What's in these tote bags if your clothing is in the suitcases?"

"Why, delicates, of course," Flora said, with an innocent smile. "We have to have plenty of those. Peignoirs, nighties, and bathing attire. Three Speedos for Evelyn. They're wool, you know, and take forever to dry. And a couple of bathing caps, and let's see…" She peered into the tote she was handing to Walter. "Looks like this one is full of sweaters. Things we simply must have."

Walter grunted as he hoisted the next tote bag. "This one must be loaded with rocks. Surely there are not unmentionables in this one."

"Oh, those are my books. I don't want to run out of reading material. I have to have enough to last me the whole three weeks."

Walter didn't say another word as he shifted and wedged and jammed and finally got everything inside the automobile while still leaving room for three people. At the last minute, Flora dashed inside and reappeared bearing Spritz's favorite saucer, her well-worn dog bed, and the terrier herself on a red leather lead. Spritz had to ride on Flora's lap, there being no other spot left for her.

"Evelyn says we can get our own automobile when I learn how to drive," Flora announced. "She doesn't want us to get stuck if something happens to her. Like that time—"

"Never mind that," Evelyn cut in, feeling no need for her overly protective older brother to know about every jam she got herself into. "I only think it would be best if both of us are able to drive when we go off on an outing. We'll give you driving lessons this summer, Flora."

Walter pulled his collar away from his neck with a gulp.

"Oh, relax, Walter. We wouldn't dream of using your brand new automobile for Flora's lessons."

Walter chuckled. "You could take Pearl's old roadster out. That one's got a few dents and scratches in it already. And truthfully, I'd like if you could take it out once or twice while we're gone anyway. Keep everything oiled up and running smoothly."

Flora squeezed Evelyn's arm in unconcealed glee at the prospect of driving lessons in the roadster.

They set off on time, but their wait in line for the ferry was longer than usual, as many others were leaving the city on that Friday afternoon. Flora got Spritz out for a walk while they waited.

Evelyn turned to her brother. "Do you know anything about that labor unrest in the orchards east of you?"

Walter pulled on his chin. "In Contra Costa, you mean? I know there've been some problems out there. I know more about the longshoremen and dock workers at the shipping ports in Oakland. Every once in a while I get a shipment held up and can't get the stock I need for the store. There's been a fair bit of violence on the docks. Couple of fellows even got themselves shot. The reporter said those longshoremen were doing nothing more than carrying picket signs. After a bit of a scuffle, evidently, between the longshoremen and some scabs—strikebreakers—the cops got overexcited and started shooting. Injured a couple of 'em, too."

"Good grief! The police shot workers for no more reason than carrying signs?"

"Well, it's desperate times, Evelyn. Men have got to work, provide for their families. I try to stay far away from that kind of trouble. I hope you do, too," he added as an afterthought.

It was late, nearly time for supper when they pulled up in front of Walter's comfortable home on the west end of Alameda Island. Evelyn's nephews, Wally Jr., eleven, and Warren, nine, were beyond excited. Not only were they thrilled the school term had finally concluded and their aunts Flora and Evelyn had come to visit, they were also eager to board the train the following morning for the journey to visit their grandparents and cousins in Philadelphia. The boys made so many trips running up and down the stairs unloading Evelyn and Flora's things there wasn't much left for Walter to carry in. Meanwhile, Spritz and Spike ran circles around everyone as the dogs got reacquainted with one another. Flora and the boys eventually made their way to the large backyard to play and get out from under Pearl's feet so she could get supper on the table. Evelyn went through the drawers on the sideboard pulling out flatware and setting the dining table for six.

While she and Pearl worked, Evelyn explained about Bernice's need for a place to stay and asked for Pearl's approval. They got sidetracked talking about the labor unrest in the orchards.

"We heard about that on the wireless yesterday," Pearl said as she placed slices of boiled beef tongue onto the plates and disguised each with a pile of sauerkraut and potatoes. "Yesterday the sheriff's deputies rounded up almost two hundred Californios and Mexican farmworkers like cattle. They were detained to prevent them going to their harvesting jobs and the work went to others."

"What a shame!" Evelyn said, shock registering in her tone. "And I'm confused. How can they be arrested and prevented from going to work?"

"That all has to do with them striking, don't you know? The growers keep lowering their wages and cutting their hours. The farmworkers go on strike, but they're not organized, you know, in a union, and there are plenty of scabs to take their jobs, and next thing you know there's a big fight and a bunch of folks get arrested. Although it always seems to be the farmworkers who are the ones getting arrested and not the strikebreakers.

"And you know there's less produce overall, what with the drought. We already have a hard time finding vegetables, between that and the riots." Pearl pulled a bowl from the refrigerator and began adding coleslaw to each plate. "Yes siree, my shredder got a workout with this meal. Do you girls like coleslaw? I make it fresh from cabbage in my garden.

"Oh, and you know what else? You might not have heard this, living in the big city as you do, but with this drought, the growers are having to pump irrigation water from underground and what's coming up is so high in salt, it's killing the trees. There just isn't enough fresh water for the orchards and now on top of all that there's this labor unrest too." Pearl hardly took a breath before announcing supper.

"Boys! Everyone! Supper's on! Come in and wash up!"

Evelyn was shocked into silence with all of Pearl's chatter and Walter' s talk about shootings. She found herself almost wishing she and Flora had stayed in their safe home on Green Street. At the very least, she'd try to avoid getting involved in Marisol's family troubles.

Gratitude for the meal was expressed and everyone commenced eating. Evelyn was a bit fearful that Flora might turn her nose up at the lesser cut of meat on her plate, but what with Pearl's constant prattling, the squirming boys, and the two dogs racing around under the table, supper seemed over in a flash. Little Warren did get caught trying to slip an unwanted bit of sauerkraut under the table to Spike. The dog took the bite, then dropped it at Daddy Walter's feet. Spike didn't want the sauerkraut either. The incident resulted in the weeping boy being sent to his room. As Pearl explained to her boys, the Winslows were not ones to waste perfectly good food when so many others were going hungry. She reminded them about the starving children in China.

After supper, Pearl kept up her steady chatter, explaining to Evelyn where to find everything they might need during their stay. She demonstrated the operation of her brand new Sears & Roebuck washing machine. Her new model featured a disturbingly efficient wringer arm operated by an electric motor, which gave Evelyn pause. Their hand-operated wringer at home got most of the water out of the clothes without risking the accidental loss of an errant hand in the process.

"Oh, you needn't be concerned," Pearl said. "Simply be certain to have all your laundry downstairs on Thursday mornings. The woman who does for me, Lolly, will be here bright and early to get it done."

Walter showed them how to run the lawn mower with a minimum of effort. He kept the blades sharp and the machine well-oiled so that even his youngest boy could push the mower and complete the job in an afternoon. Pearl had various planting beds around the edges of the backyard, filled with vegetables. Even a few strawberries remained. That area would need regular watering, as she explained.

Flora remembered about *The Shadow* in time to get the broadcast tuned in and everyone finally settled down for the evening. When the program ended, Flora announced she was exhausted and would retire to bed. Evelyn knew it likely would be an hour or more before Flora gave up her reading and was ready to turn out the light. Still, heading off to bed for a restful night's sleep sounded good to everyone including the worn out dogs.

The boys were too excited to eat a full breakfast in the morning. The Chevy was loaded and everyone piled in for the trip to the railway station, which turned out to be a mad-house. With a hundred passengers or more boarding all at once for the trip east, heavily laden luggage carts wheeled by running porters threatened to mow over distracted travelers.

"We'd best get out here and unload," Walter said.

Evelyn had anticipated a longer goodbye and time to send hugs to Mama and Papa, but this was precluded by the confusion at the station. The best she could manage was a quick buss on the cheek for Pearl and a wave as the parents got the two exhilarated boys headed in the correct direction. Flora searched the Chevrolet quickly, looking under and around for anything that might have been missed.

"Hop in and off you go!" Walter said with a last wave.

Evelyn gripped the wheel and steered the automobile away from the station.

"This is something, isn't it?" Flora admired the interior of the royal blue Chevrolet Confederate. "What goes in this hole here?" She pointed at a gaping rectangular opening in the dashboard.

"Walter had them leave an opening there for when an automobile radio becomes available. He said this year the radio is roughly a third the cost of the whole automobile. He's hoping the price comes down and the quality goes up next year, and he'll get one then."

"He must be doing very well indeed to afford a brand new automobile every two or three years," Flora said.

"You know, there is that to consider, my friend. Every year automobiles are improved in important ways, and now with this economic downturn, they're less expensive every year, too."

Flora settled for a quick but pointed look at Evelyn over the top of her dark glasses. Words were no longer really necessary on the topic of purchasing their own automobile, and neither was in the mood for a quarrel.

Waiting at a stoplight, Evelyn gazed with admiration at the interior of the Chevrolet. "Walter says they call this model a 'Baby Cadillac' because it has so many features in common and even looks like a Cadillac." Evelyn practiced with the brake pedal, and turned the steering wheel a bit right, then left, getting used to the feel of it. It would not do to have Walter come home and find his precious new automobile damaged in any way. Especially not if the damage had been on account of any sort of careless driving.

"Did you see the running boards?" Flora said. "Remember that movie…the one where the actor…must have been John Barrymore? He jumps on the running board of that moving automobile and climbs through the window…Oh, what was that movie…?"

"I'm afraid I don't recall."

"Oh, well. Anyway, he was so swashbuckling. Made me want to run right out and try it."

Evelyn gave a hearty laugh. "My dear, I do believe watching that movie is supposed to cause you to swoon over John Barrymore, not to want to attempt that stunt yourself. Possibly you could try a practice run in the privacy of the garage."

Flora scowled at Evelyn. "You know you are in some danger of turning into an old fuddy-duddy. I mean, for a girl who leaps into the Bay for an open-water swim at the drop of a hat, when did you ever pass up the chance to try a dangerous sport?"

Evelyn had to laugh again. "You may be right, dear, although leaping onto the running board of moving automobiles and diving through open windows hardly qualifies as a sport."

"I beg your pardon! I believe I read recently that sport has been submitted for inclusion in the upcoming summer Olympics in Los Angeles next month."

"Oh! Well, pardon me. I must have missed that announcement. Are we going to see those Olympic games? Shouldn't you be in training by now?"

"Humph. Where are we?"

Chapter Six

All the time they'd been conversing and laughing, Evelyn had been driving south on San Pablo Boulevard into downtown Oakland. She slowed a few doors from Winslow's Office Supply and cruised past the plate glass windows displaying office furniture and desk appointments at the store's entrance.

"Quite a handsome store it is," Flora said as she admired the wide corner location. "Let's stop for a moment. I'd like to pick up a few items."

They crossed the threshold and were greeted by a smiling young man in a handsome suit and tie. Evelyn started to introduce herself, but the young man interrupted.

"Oh, you must be Mr. Winslow's sister!" he said. "I knew you immediately by the family resemblance."

Flora smiled. It was true. Every one of the Winslow children could have been a twin to the others, especially when they smiled and those dimples appeared.

The man introduced himself as the store manager and gave them a short tour of the premises and its inventory, keeping one eye on the entry door at all times. The section displaying the latest models of radios from large furniture consoles to compact table top designs took up a good part of the floor. Flora selected a new fountain pen, a lined tablet in which to continue drafting her novel, and a small notepad. She placed them on the counter and began digging through her pocket-book for her coin purse.

"Please," the young man said, "allow me to treat you to those items. We're so happy you dropped by to see us."

Flora handed the notepad to Evelyn. "In case we decide to help the Pachecos out with an investigation," she said. "We'll need to keep notes."

The front door opened, admitting a well-dressed older man with a much younger woman on his arm.

"We do hope you stop in again soon," the manager said, nodding politely to Flora and Evelyn. He rushed to greet the new customers before Flora even had a chance to say thank you.

"'Customers come first' was always Papa's byword in his stores," Evelyn said.

Flora waited until they reached the privacy of their auto-mobile before she asked, "Did you see the chassis on that dame? I bet that Sugar Daddy's buying her a radio to pay for services rendered."

Evelyn glanced at Flora and winked. "My, my, dear. When did you take up speaking like a gangster's moll from the movies?"

Flora giggled. "I'm practicing for a scene in my novel."

"I thought you said your novel was about us?"

"It is, but we're not the only characters in it. We might get mixed up with some gangsters later on. It is fiction, you know. Who knows what might happen?"

Evelyn chuckled. "I can hardly imagine anything less likely." Then she remembered about the dangerous situations and uncertainty surrounding them. "You could be right though, Flora. We have no idea what might happen in the days ahead."

A few blocks after leaving downtown they reached the Posey Tube entrance. Completed only a few years before, the narrow tunnel carried automobile traffic under the waters of the estuary and onto the island of Alameda. As required,

Evelyn turned on the Chevrolet's headlamps. Flora sat very straight as their automobile dipped down into the darkness.

"Don't hold your breath, Flora," Evelyn instructed. "It's too far. You'll faint dead away."

"I can hardly help it. We're going under the water."

A few moments later, they pulled up into the sunshine, safely through the Tube.

"Ha!" Flora said, "and we didn't even get wet."

They fixed themselves beef tongue sandwiches on the pre-sliced bread Pearl had stocked. Evelyn placed the sandwiches on plates and added homemade pickles.

"Sandwiches made with pre-sliced bread look less substantial than our hearty home sliced," Evelyn said. "Do you think that'll be enough?"

"It certainly is nice not to have to hack at a loaf, though. I think I'll not complain."

"No, not complaining at all. It's just different to open the bread box and find the bread already sliced. Jaing wouldn't hear of it, you know. Oh, drat! Is that the telephone ringing?" Evelyn cocked one ear.

"Not very likely anyone is calling us is it?" Flora said, biting into her pickle. "We could just let it go."

"Better not. Mama might be calling to see if Walter and the family got off as planned." Evelyn scampered through to the telephone in the entry hall and caught it on the fourth ring.

Evelyn's conversation was an animated one. In short order, she bustled into the dining room. "Eat up, Flora. We need to go out again. That was Bernice on the telephone, calling from out in Walnut Creek. She's just dropped Marisol off and wants us to come pick her up immediately. We need to get a wiggle on."

Flora raised her eyebrows at the abrupt nature of the command. "What's the emergency, Evie? Has there been more trouble in the orchards? Or is Tia Rosamaria sending Bernice away, now that she's delivered Marisol? And why do we need to collect Bernice at all? She drove herself out there didn't she?

Did something happen to her old flivver?"

"Oh…you know how Bernice is. I suppose it's not really an emergency at all, but she is distressed and wants us to collect her as soon as we can. She wasn't specific about any trouble. I'll explain why she can't drive herself here once we get on the road. In the meantime, chop, chop"

Evelyn began poking through the cupboards while chewing the last of her sandwich. "Pearl said she'd left a plate of cookies here somewhere. Do you remember where she said…?"

"No, I'm sorry I don't. They must be here. Cookies don't just get up and walk away on their own." Then they both remembered about the young boys who lived in that house. "On the other hand," Flora said, "it is possible that particular plate of cookies did indeed walk away. Oh, well, perhaps we can ask Pearl's housekeeper to make us some more when she's here. Speaking of housekeeping, shouldn't we put clean sheets on the bed Bernice will sleep in tonight?"

"Good thinking, Flora. I'm sure she would appreciate that effort, but possibly we can do that when we return. We need to get on the road quick." Evelyn hurried around the kitchen putting food items away in an agitated manner.

"Are you sure there's no emergency, Evie? You seem concerned."

"I'm sure it'll all be fine. I'd just like to get going, as I said."

Flora quickly rinsed the dirty dishes, leaving them in the drainer to dry. "How far is it?" she asked as she returned downstairs with sweaters for each of them against the chilly fog beginning to roll in across the bay. "How long will it take us to get there? Should we take the dog? Or both dogs? Will we need to go through Posey Tube again?"

Evelyn popped on a dark purple slouch hat, thought about and then discarded the idea of a heavier coat, pulled her pocketbook onto her arm, and waved a slip of paper toward Flora. "Here are the directions. Bernie says it's about twenty miles and should take us no more than an hour to get there, as long as we don't have a flat tire. No, I don't think so on the dogs. Yes on the Tube."

Flora gazed with sad eyes at Spritz until the dog began to whine, but Evelyn reminded her how much Bernice was not fond of even small dogs. In any case, Spritz had Spike for company. The plan was for them to return to Alameda well before dark.

"The dogs have their beds in the basement, and can get to the yard from there. They'll be fine on their own."

Flora wasn't so sure. "Spritz isn't used to being left alone, Evie, and this isn't even her house. Won't she wonder where we've gone?"

"You know how dogs are, dear. The minute you leave they fall asleep and stay asleep until you return. We'll zip out to Walnut Creek, gather Bernice, and have her back here before supper. Spritz will hardly know we've gone." They took the back stairs to the garage and pulled the double door open. "You know," Evelyn said, "I expect we'll need to drive Bernice out there again in the morning so she can retrieve her automobile and pick up Marisol as soon as church is over. If that turns out to be the plan, possibly we'll still be able to spend tomorrow afternoon at Neptune Beach, as you'd hoped."

In no time, Walter's Chevrolet was rolling west along Broadway and began to climb the narrow road that wound its way over the Berkeley Hills.

"What you said before, Evie…about the flat tire? We're not going to have a flat tire, are we?" Gazing at the trees hanging over and darkening the empty road ahead, Flora chewed on her lower lip.

Evelyn chuckled. "I sincerely hope not, dear. This is a spanking brand new car so the tires are new, too, and in any case, the quality of automobile tires is improving every year. I'll try to avoid the pot-holes."

"Very well. Now will you tell me now why we need to collect Bernice? If she drove Marisol out there in her Ford, can't she simply drive her own car to join us in Alameda? After all the fuss we made about not wanting to go out into the middle of those labor riots, I am a bit surprised we've consented so nonchalantly to Bernice's request."

Evelyn hesitated. Flora usually did her best to steer clear of any sort of unpleasantness, and here was Evelyn driving her friend right into the middle of a decidedly frightening-sounding scene of riots and vandalism.

"Bernie's Tin Lizzie is fine…" Evelyn said, then paused. "At least as far as I know it is. The thing is, Bernice said the Pachecos' automobile had been…" Evelyn searched for the word with the least potential to cause upset. "Well, she said the Pachecos' automobile was disabled last night. As a consequence, Marisol asked if Bernice would leave her Ford at the hacienda so that Marisol and her aunt could use it to get to church in the morning."

Flora scowled. "Let me see if I understand. Tia Rosamaria doesn't want Bernice to stay at the hacienda with Marisol but she doesn't hesitate to ask Bernice to leave her Ford for their use, is that right?"

"Yes, that's about the size of it."

"Well, doesn't Tia Rosamaria have her nerve. What happened to their automobile last night? Overnight, you mean? What happened to it?"

"I only know what Bernice told me over the telephone."

"Yes?"

"Well, apparently there was another big fight yesterday and then early this morning the Pachecos went outside to find their Plymouth had been set on fire. 'Disabled' was the word Bernice used. They still have a truck to get around, but Tia can't get herself up into the truck. That's why they need Bernice's automobile to get to church tomorrow morning."

"Good grief! How does Bernice know those ruffians aren't going to disable her jalopy if she leaves it there?"

"That's a good question to which I'm sure I don't know the answer. And, of course, we don't know who it was who did the deed." Evelyn took one turn a little too wide and went back to focusing on her driving. "This would be a good place for a center line marking," she mumbled. "I'd prefer to avoid a head-on collision if I could."

"Every street could do with a center line marking, in my opinion."

"Yes, you're right about that. The days of horse-drawn carriages meandering from side to side are long gone. It's high time for a good many more traffic signs, too."

Evelyn was still a bit distracted wondering where, exactly, she was taking them and if they would end up in the middle of another imbroglio.

"We're not driving into a riot, are we?" Flora asked.

Evelyn took a half second to give Flora what she hoped was a reassuring smile that did not reveal her own increasing anxiety. "We're only going to pick up Bernice and go directly back to Walter's. There's no need to worry."

"As far as you know."

"Yes, as far as I know."

Chapter Seven

Evelyn's assurance their day would remain peaceful seemed to placate Flora for upwards of five minutes. Then she began chewing on her lip again and went back to puzzling aloud over the labor situation. Evelyn had learned that if you gave Flora a few pieces of a puzzle, she immediately felt compelled to work the pieces together into a whole picture.

"Say Evie, if, as Marisol said, the Pacheco family was granted that land a hundred years ago or more, thousands of acres, how did they lose it?"

"I don't know the complete story, but I do know most of those land grants, even the ones being actively farmed or ranched, were nullified when the United States Army invaded several western states in the middle of the last century. Many of the Californios were pushed out and American immigrants moved in and took over the land, just like what happened with the native Indians across the rest of the country."

"Marisol said her family still owns the land around their hacienda."

"Yes, that must be true, and they were also somehow able to establish and hold onto the labor contracting in the fruit orchards around the town of Walnut Creek."

"Sounds like that's turning into a big headache."

"I suppose, but the family has to make a living like every-one else." Evelyn jerked the steering wheel back to the center again, as the automobile drifted left. "I wonder if road builders could possibly have put a few more curves in along here."

"I don't see how they might have managed more, and the way the road drops off on both sides into steep canyons is positively terrifying."

Evelyn gritted her teeth, and Flora sat taller, her eyes shifting from one canyon to the other.

"Why is this road called Tunnel Road?" Flora said. "I just saw a sign that said 'Tunnel Road.' Is there going to be a tunnel on this road?"

Evelyn shrugged. She had not noticed any tunnel marked on the map she'd tried to memorize before they set off. "We'll cross that bridge when we come to it, won't we?"

"Amusing, Evie. Very droll. It's a good thing I'm not the worrying sort." Evelyn raised her eyebrows, but wisely held her counsel.

They rode on in silence for a time, and before long, sure enough they came to the dark and constricted entrance to an ancient tunnel.

"What is this?" Flora said. "It looks like the opening to a mine shaft. It's hardly wide enough for a horse carriage."

"Most definitely not wide enough for two autos to pass inside." Evelyn said quietly. She let the Chevy roll to a stop while they peered into the blackened entrance. "I did read there are plans being made for a new modern twin bore tunnel way down below us. That one will eliminate the need for driving this winding and dangerous road altogether, and cut down on the number of serious accidents."

"That seems wise."

"There's going to be one bore for westbound traffic and one for eastbound. They're currently working on the surveys."

"Hmm. Doesn't help us now, does it?" Flora said still looking ahead.

"No, it does not. Well, if I'm not mistaken, this is the tunnel the sign referred to and we should go on through. Are you all set?"

"I'm fine. As you know, I love a good adventure. If it's all the same to you I do believe I'll close my eyes though. Just until we've gotten to the other side."

Evelyn gulped hard, then goosed the automobile slowly forward. A rusted sign beside the tunnel opening showed an arrow pointing inside with "Walnut Creek" lettered below. There was nothing for it but to drive ahead at a snail's pace. Evelyn was torn between wanting to hurry through and not wanting to run head-on into a vehicle coming from the other direction. She glanced at Flora, sitting ramrod straight, her eyes squeezed tightly shut.

"I could use your help," Evelyn said. "Watching out for on-coming traffic."

"Very well." Flora pried one eye halfway open. "Did you remember to turn on the headlamps? Is that round light up ahead the other end of the tunnel or an on-coming automobile?"

"Yes, dear, the headlamps are on. I can't say what that light is ahead."

As it turned out, the light was indeed the other end of the short tunnel. Upon safely navigating through, Evelyn pulled to the side of the road so they could each breathe a silent prayer of gratitude for their safe delivery.

"Whew!" Flora said, cranking down her window. "Why's it so hot in here all of a sudden? Has something gone wrong with the automobile?"

Evelyn rolled her window down as well. "It must be ten degrees warmer on this side of the hills. Guess we won't be needing these," she said as she struggled out of her sweater.

They continued, cruising through the small verdant valleys on the eastern slope of the Berkeley Hills.

"Look how beautiful the orchards are," Flora said. "Leafed out in their lime-green finery. They make such a stunning contrast with the yellow golden of the grasses beneath them. Those trees look like walnut trees. If you look closely, you can see the green nut shells."

"Oh?" Evelyn nodded and smiled without taking her eyes off the road.

Flora chattered on about the passing scenery. "What a darling creek here alongside the road. Later this week we could bring a picnic and sit beside this babbling creek. Away from the road, I mean, but wouldn't that be so restful?"

"Smashing idea, Flora. That would indeed be lovely. You could bring your paints and create a delightful memory. You know how much I love that one you did of the cabin near Muir Woods. What happened to that slip of paper I gave you with the directions?"

Flora rummaged through the pocketbooks, hats, and snacks cluttered on the seat between them while Evelyn kept her eyes on the road ahead.

"Oh, here it is," Flora said, extracting the crumpled paper from the pocket of her day dress.

"Good. Read it to me, please? Where's our next turn?"

Flora read the directions aloud and Evelyn slowed the automobile, searching the road ahead for signs.

"Ooh, look!" Flora said. "Up there on the right. Is that a fruit stand? Could we stop and get fresh fruit, and right from the farmer, too? Oh, drat, it looks like it's closed already."

"Are you watching out for our turn on the left?"

"Oh, sorry."

They went on another couple of miles, deciding at that point they had missed their turn. Evelyn waited for a wide enough spot that wouldn't have them ending up in the creek, reversed the automobile, and started back.

"There it is," Flora said, "ahead on the right. It's across from the closed fruit stand. That's why I missed it. See? Acalanes…or however you say that." She read more from the note. "And then we look for a driveway about two miles on the right. Then go up the hill to the adobe house at the end. How exciting! Do the Pachecos live in a house made of real adobe? I should have brought my Kodak. Wouldn't your Mama get a kick out of seeing that?"

The Chevrolet's nose crested the hill and Bernice came into view, sitting on a small suitcase in the driveway of the rambling and handsome vine-covered adobe brick home.

Marisol stood beside Bernice, her arms crossed tightly over her chest, her eyebrows lowered in a frown. She caught sight of the arriving Chevrolet and came forward, making her way to the driver's side window. Her voice lowered to a whisper, her eyes shooting darts in every direction, she spoke to Evelyn. "I discussed it with the family, Evelyn. After the destruction of their Plymouth, Tia Rosamaria and my cousins are willing to pay you any fee you might charge to investigate that crime. Any amount."

Evelyn drew her eyebrows together in a worried frown. Perhaps she should consider helping the Pachecos, despite her misgivings. "Give us some time to think about it," she said, hoping to reassure Marisol. "And in the meantime you could write down everything you know about these crimes. Dates, times, people or parties you suspect."

Marisol spun toward the house, sending a small wave to Flora before disappearing under the entry arbor. She pointedly ignored Bernice as she passed. Bernice stood, snatched up her case and a large paper sack, a black expression clouding her face.

"Oh, dear," Flora said in a whisper. "Bernice looks upset. I hope she doesn't take her anger out on us." She waved gaily to Bernice, and climbed out the passenger side. "Here, Bernice, why don't you ride up here next to Evelyn and I'll get in back?" Flora scrambled onto the middle of the rear seat and Bernice set her suitcase and the paper bag beside her.

As Evelyn made a wide turn in the driveway, the burned out shell of an automobile came into view a few yards from the hacienda.

"Gracious." Evelyn said, stopping the Chevrolet. "That Plymouth is beyond disabled. Why, it's been completely destroyed. Burned to a crisp. That must have been some fire, and so close to the house. It's a wonder the whole place didn't burn down with it."

"Sorry," Bernice confessed. "I didn't want to shock you so much you wouldn't come for me. Rafael thinks the auto was firebombed. He says the hacienda is probably next. Everything out here is in such an uproar. I tried to talk Marisol into coming with me tonight because I don't think it's safe to stay here, but you know how stubborn she can be."

Evelyn nodded, and caught Flora's gaze in the rearview mirror. The look they exchanged said something very much like "pot calling the kettle black," but neither said a word aloud.

"And every morning now," Bernice continued, "when the farmworkers line up, evidently there's another riot. See here? In the barn here to the right? That's where the labor office is, right here only fifty yards from the house."

Evelyn took in Flora's startled gaze in the mirror. "Is that the barn someone threw a torch into and tried to burn the other night?"

Bernice nodded slowly as they drove past the farm building.

"Where's your Ford?" Flora said, searching the shade under the overhanging branches.

"Rafael parked her inside the barn," Bernice said. "Last week someone set fire to the few little houses they had for the farmworkers up behind the hacienda, so Rafael is letting several of them sleep in the barn. He says whoever is setting these fires learned their lesson and won't try to burn the barn again. My old Ford should be safe in there, and anyway no outsiders even know the jalopy is there. If there's going to be more trouble, he hopes that won't happen until Monday morning when the orchard owners send more trucks to haul the harvest workers. Sunday should be peaceful. That's really the only reason I gave up arguing for Marisol to come with me."

Bernice turned to Evelyn. "I know this is not your problem, but Marisol and her family could really use your help. They don't know if it's the Vigilantes committing this vandalism, or the Okies, or even some disgruntled farmworkers trying to take over the contracting business."

"What about law enforcement?" Evelyn asked. "Can't the sheriff out here do something to stop the vandalism?"

"Ha! The sheriff looks the other way when it's Vigilantes against Californios. Half the time, the sheriff's deputies join in with the Vigilantes. They may not wear white sheets and hoods here like they do in the South, but they're klansmen all the same. And you know how terrifying those fellas can be."

"Horrors." Flora shuddered. "And to think, right here in California in 1932." She gazed in apprehension at the passing bucolic landscape.

Bernice looked over the back rest and she too shuddered. "Now that I've been telling you about it, I'm getting the hee-bie-jeebies myself. I wish I hadn't left Marisol there."

"We've not even made the turn onto the highway yet," Evelyn said. "Do you want me to go back for her?"

"She wouldn't come anyway," Bernice said. "She's furious with me for arguing with her to come away, and her aunt is being ugly to me. Do you know what the word *bruja* means? Tia calls me a *bruja*."

Flora shot a quick look of horror to Evelyn in the rearview mirror. "I do know what that means," she said. "It's not a very nice thing to call someone. Why on earth would she say such a thing?"

"I'm sure I don't know," Bernice said, as she looked away, out the window. "Anyway, Marisol's going to take Tia to church tomorrow and we'll pick her up right after that. I know she's looking forward to our afternoon on the beach as much as you are, if it can be managed. She doesn't have to start her next shift at the hospital until Monday morning.

"Look," Bernice continued. "Speak of the devil and up he jumps. Here's some coppers now." Bernice pointed at a dark vehicle parked beside the closed fruit stand at the junction with the highway. Two uniformed men stood in front, sending glowering looks toward the Chevrolet. One man slapped a billy club against his palm. "Quick," Bernice said, "try to look innocent."

Chapter Eight

Evelyn made a deliberate stop at the sign, looked carefully in both directions, and eased the automobile into the right turn. Flora leaned forward from the rear seat, gazing with wide eyes at the men who glared at them.

"How does one 'look innocent'?" she asked in a quiet voice.

Evelyn laughed despite her concern. "You don't need to try to 'look innocent,' dear. You are innocent."

Bernice lifted her eyebrows as though she hoped to get a bit more information on that topic, but she waited in vain.

A hundred feet farther along the highway, two more deputies appeared beside another sedan sporting a sheriff's decal. The law enforcement automobile leaned into a ditch beside a narrow dirt road disappearing into a walnut orchard.

"Looks like something's happened up that-a-way," Evelyn said, slowing, her curiosity getting the better of her. "I wonder what's going on. Should we pull over and ask?"

"Oh, don't do that!" Bernice nearly squealed, setting Evelyn's teeth on edge. "Let's get out of here!" She stared up the dirt road as Evelyn rolled to a stop. "From what I hear, we don't even want to know what's going on." She turned back to the others. "You know, I don't trust those sheriff's deputies as far as I can spit. They sure don't seem to be in any hurry to help Marisol's family with this labor situation."

"Oh, my. Who are these people then?" Flora said, putting one hand over her mouth. Surrounded by several uniformed deputies, a group of eight or ten mostly barefoot people dressed in rags shuffled toward the highway. Each carried what appeared to be a bedroll or bag of belongings. "There are women and children, too," she said in a hush.

"Yeah," Bernice said. "They sleep in those orchards. Well, the truth is, they live on the dirt between the trees. They eat, sleep, and do their business out there. Those are the people who used to be the farmworkers. They had a few shacks up behind the hacienda but those were all burned to the ground a couple of weeks ago."

"Gracious," Evelyn said. "Of course I didn't imagine anyone would provide them with housing, but still. I guess I just didn't think about it."

"Nope, no housing, no bathrooms, and no sooner do they find some hidden nook to camp in than the law shows up to clear 'em out."

Evelyn accelerated and continued the drive toward their own safe haven and warm beds. Her lips were tight.

"Thank goodness we're away from there," Bernice said.

Evelyn frowned. Bernice's nervousness was contagious. She started to form a question, but Bernice was in a hurry to change the subject and she interrupted Evelyn's thought.

"Look in there," she said to Flora, and pointed at the paper sack beside Flora on the rear seat.

"What's in the bag?" Flora pulled the edge closer and peered inside. "Ooh, peaches! These look beautiful, Bernie. Are they for us?"

"It was the least I could do, what with you gals coming all the way out here to collect me and put me up for the night." She turned to Evelyn. "If you'll take that left turn at the sign to Orinda, we can stop at the Shell service station there and I'll fill your tank. A dollar should take care of it, I think."

"Taking the turn to Orinda then," Evelyn said, as she turned the wheel and drove the automobile across a bumpy bridge.

"These peaches have a fragrance like ambrosia," Flora said. "Can you smell them, Evie? We can make jam with a few of them."

Bernice laughed, which Evelyn took umbrage at, thinking Bernice didn't believe Flora knew how to make jam. "There's only a few in the bag, sweetie," Bernice said. "Enough for fresh fruit on our cereal in the morning and a snack or two, but not enough for a whole batch of jam."

"Oh, well," Flora said. "Perhaps the fruit stands will be open the next time we drive out. We can buy bushels of peaches. Don't you think, Evie?"

Evelyn did not reply, distracted by needing to follow the signs into the town of Orinda.

Flora scooted forward. "She's listening to us, Bernie. She's just like that when she's driving. She gets preoccupied."

"Preoccupied with staying on the road and not driving us into a wreck in Walter's new automobile, you mean," Evelyn said.

"Yes, I know, and I do appreciate your concentration."

The Chevy rolled into the Shell service station. Evelyn lowered her window and greeted the uniformed attendant. Being an automobile owner herself, Bernice knew just what to do. She leaned across Evelyn's lap, handed him a bill, and asked him to pump one dollar's worth of fuel. Evelyn watched in fascination as he filled the tank, then dug in his pocket and handed fifteen cents in change through the window.

"I should have known," Evelyn said. "Walter probably left us with a full tank." She pulled away and back-tracked to the highway heading west.

Flora bent closer to Bernice. "So tell us what happened? The Pachecos' automobile was set on fire last night and you didn't find out until you and Marisol arrived this morning? Why would anyone burn their auto?"

"I know!" Bernice said. "Shocking isn't it? Every week, more men are desperate for work, and the situation gets more violent."

Evelyn felt disgusted. "If those people don't stop all that nonsense, someone's going to get hurt."

Flora chuckled from the rear seat. "Evie, just then, you sounded exactly like your Papa when the boys get to rough-housing. I know you're right, though. Someone is going to get hurt. I should think you'd be petrified to leave Marisol out there, Bernie. What if something happens tonight?"

"Not my choice, Flora. Marisol said no and that's the end of the discussion." Bernice changed the subject. "You gals have known each other a long time, haven't you? I mean, for you to know so much about Evelyn's Papa, and her family, and so on."

"Almost ten years," Flora said, gazing at the passing scenery. "Ten years in December. Oh, look. Here we are back at the tunnel again. Headlamps, Evie."

They returned safely to Walter's and the pair of hungry dogs awaiting them. The evening passed with supper at a tiny Russian tea room on Webster Street and a walk home in time to catch a few favorite programs on the radio. Even with the diversions, Bernice complained of feeling agitated and said she was sure she wouldn't be able to sleep. Her anxiety was beginning to get on everyone's nerves.

"How about we play a game?" Flora suggested.

"What do you two like to play?" Bernice asked.

"Hmm…" Flora said. "Evie and I work crossword puzzles and the like. Most of the games we play are games for two."

"I shouldn't wonder," Bernice said, letting her eyebrows jump, and causing Evelyn to smirk.

"I'll go look in the boys' room," Flora said. "I'm sure the boys have some games." She returned ten minutes later bearing a box containing a board game and an empty plate. "Evelyn, look what I found under Wally's bed when I put on the clean sheets."

Evelyn pulled her reading glasses down her nose and

folded her newspaper, looking at the plate. "That solves the mystery of the cookies that walked away then, doesn't it?"

The board game was called *The Landlord's Game*, and required that players use pretend money to buy and sell cards representing the titles to properties. After an hour, Flora had completely lost interest, and suggested they retire for the night.

"You gals don't listen to that Walter Winchell news broadcast then?" Bernice asked.

"I should say not!" Evelyn snapped. "And his clap-trap isn't news anyway. It's pure sensationalism, strictly for entertainment."

Bernice grumbled all the way up the stairs about being too nervous to sleep, but the long day and brisk walk from the tea room had worked their magic. Once she closed the door to Wally's bedroom, not another sound was heard from her.

As she readied herself for bed, Flora spoke quietly to Evelyn. "You've not said, Evie, but we'll need to take Bernice back out to Walnut Creek tomorrow, right? We agreed we'd stay clear of those troubles and here we are driving straight into the middle of them two days in a row."

Evelyn sent Flora an apologetic smile. "I know, but what choice do we have?"

The trip to take Bernice back out to the valley would be made on Sunday. Evelyn hoped the various factions involved in the labor disputes would all be in church, or at their homes having Sunday dinner tomorrow, making for a safe trip. "We'll go, then turn around and come right back. I can't think of a single reason we might get ourselves tangled up in those troubles."

Sunday morning they had settled down in the bright dining room for a breakfast of poached eggs, buttered toast, and sliced peaches when the telephone in the entry rang.

"Who would be calling at eight in the morning on a

Sunday?" Evelyn wondered aloud on her way to catch the call. The obvious answer was that it was someone in the Winslow family back in Philadelphia, but she returned a moment later. She nodded at Bernice and said, "It's for you, dear. It's Marisol."

As Bernice left the room, Flora leaned in to Evelyn's shoulder. "How did Marisol sound? Did she sound upset? Did she tell you why she's calling?"

"I'm afraid she did sound upset. I didn't ask why as it's really none of our business." Flora stopped chewing and they grew quiet, listening to the low murmur coming from the other room.

When Bernice returned, her expression was dark and troubled. "Marisol's cousin Rafael has been arrested," she said without prompting.

"Oh, no." Evelyn said. "Will this labor trouble never end?"

"That's just it," Bernice said, her voice shifting into a higher and more anxious pitch. "It wasn't the labor troubles. He was arrested on suspicion of murder."

Flora sat back hard in her chair, and dropped her toast onto her plate. She sent Evelyn a horrified expression.

"Murder?" Evelyn whispered. "Who was killed?"

"That's just the thing, you see. No one knows what's going on. Yesterday evening her cousin Joaquin went out. Told one of his pals he was going to see a man about a horse, but he wasn't specific. Then he didn't come home at all. His brother, Rafael, went out later, after midnight, to look for him. Rafael was gone for a couple of hours. Of course, now questions have come up about what he did while he was gone. He got home in the wee hours. Marisol was waiting up for him, but he told her he hadn't been able to find his brother. Rafael was in his own bed asleep, they were all asleep, early this morning when the sheriff's deputies showed up and, out of the blue, they arrested Rafael."

In a hushed voice and with one hand at her lips, Flora said, "Sounds like a frame-up to me. Marisol must be simply beside herself."

"Indeed," Evelyn said. She immediately had another thought. "Surely, Joaquin has returned by now? Marisol and her aunt can't cope with this situation all on their own. Joaquin came home eventually, didn't he?"

"No," Bernice said. "Marisol says Joaquin has simply vanished into thin air. He's somewhere, of course, but they still have no idea where he could be."

Evelyn's brow furrowed. "Doesn't 'go see a man about a horse' mean going out to find whiskey? If he went out drinking, possibly he's simply passed out somewhere and will return home when he wakes up. It's early yet."

Bernice absent-mindedly scooped up a bite of her cold poached egg. "Maybe. Marisol and her aunt are going down to the barn to get in my Ford and go to church. Joaquin may be sleeping in the barn. Or if he's not there, might be they can talk some of the farmworkers into tracking him down. He's younger than Rafael, and a bit of an idle rascal, but the family needs him now. Rafael's old hayburner of a pickup truck is still at the house, so they think wherever Joaquin went, he must have hoofed it, or caught a ride. That means he'll be on foot getting home and that would slow him down."

This pronouncement was followed by a long silence, the eggs and peaches forgotten on their plates, their coffee growing cold. Evelyn turned to find Flora already staring at her, and probably even sharing her thoughts. Who was Rafael supposed to have murdered, and where was his missing brother Joaquin?

Chapter Nine

Still at the breakfast table, Bernice heaved a deep sigh. Marisol's telephone call announcing Rafael's arrest had put an end to the plan of the four of them having a fun afternoon at the amusement park. She turned to the others. "Marisol said we should go ahead and have our day, then pick her up late this afternoon. She's decided she needs to stay as long as she can with her aunt. I have to get her back to the city tonight so she can get a good night's sleep before her shift in the morning at the hospital, but she says she needs to be with her aunt as long as she can today."

Flora sighed too, picked up the crust of her toast, and began munching on it again. "I suppose we should at least finish breakfast." Evelyn moved next to Bernice and wrapped a comforting arm around her friend's shoulder.

With a watchful eye on her inattentive human companions, Spritz hopped up on the chair in front of what was left of Evelyn's poached egg and pushed her snout toward the enticing left-over. Flora stood and removed the uneaten remains of breakfast.

"No, no Spritz. What's left on our plates will be scraped into your dish anyway, but there's no point in letting you get in the habit of stealing food off the table. Heaven only knows what Jaing would think if she ever caught Spritz at that."

Evelyn stayed with Bernice as Flora fed both dogs, then took them into the backyard for a rousing game of fetch-the-sticks. Bernice's shoulders shuddered in a quiet sob and Evelyn patted her back.

"There, there. We can't do anything more for Marisol and her family right now. What do you think? Should we go ahead with our visit to Neptune Beach? Just the three of us? A good long swim might be just what you need."

"I suppose that'd be best, although I'm not much in the mood for Ferris wheels and rollercoasters. Swimming does sound calming."

With an absentminded gesture, Evelyn swept a few crumbs off the tabletop, and began quietly chattering. "There's a massive swimming pool almost as large as Fleishacker Pool, although the pool is often crowded beyond belief. They've also built a sandy beach along the bay for sunbathing and swimming. I've heard it's even possible to do an open-water swim around the entire island of Alameda. That's fourteen miles, but one is never more than a few yards from shore the entire distance. That's not for today, but you and I can put in a couple of miles going safely back and forth in front of the beach. After all, we both need to get into shape for that Alcatraz swim that's coming up. Flora might like to spend her time sunbathing, and we'll find something for lunch along the midway."

Bernice's eyes softened and she hugged Evelyn. "Right-o then, let's do that. Flora won't be too disappointed to miss out on the rides, will she?"

Evelyn smiled. "In view of the upsetting news about Rafael's arrest, I'm sure Flora will be quite content to sit on the beach in the sun this morning and read. Besides, of late we find ourselves attracted to more sedentary thrills than rollercoasters."

Bernice let her eyes widen and she smirked. "Oh?"

Evelyn laughed and shook her head. "Poor choice of words on my part, Bernie. I meant to say we've come to prefer amusements such as reading good books and an occasional afternoon at the movies."

Flora was amenable to a morning spent lounging in the sun, a rare opportunity afforded in the usual summer fog of San Francisco. She packed up towels and they borrowed sun hats from Pearl's large collection. Evelyn and Bernice hid bathing suits under day dresses, and carried totes with their belongings. Beach chairs could be rented when they arrived.

Evelyn slipped three dimes into her dress pocket so she could pay their entry fee into Neptune Beach with a minimum of fuss from Bernice about paying her own share, and they were off.

"I don't like to keep going back to this," Bernice said as they strolled toward the park, "but what do you think about helping Marisol figure out these mysteries, especially now the situation has become more serious. At least maybe you could talk to her later today? They've got the vandalism to deal with, and now there's Rafael being arrested. We have to hope that'll be settled quickly. He's not the kind of young man to go around murdering people. There's still the question about who's causing trouble for the Pachecos. If you don't want to help, I'll stop making a pest of myself, but you have solved trickier mysteries before. And there is the money to consider. Marisol says the Pachecos make a good living from the labor contracting and can afford your fees."

Evelyn considered the question in silence. They watched for traffic when they got as far as Webster Street and made the crossing. Finally she said, "It's not that I don't want to help, Bernice. It's only that I can't see what I might do that someone else couldn't do better. For example, that burned out automobile. Surely the sheriff's deputies should be the ones to investigate that?"

"Huh! Marisol said they told Rafael the auto must have had a faulty electrical device and that started the fire. They'll be no help with that, or anything else. They're on the side of the Vigilantes."

That's not good," Evelyn agreed, "but I might equally steer the investigation in the wrong direction, given my own prejudices. Here I've been assuming all along the Vigilantes started the fire, when it could just as easily have had an electrical cause."

Flora linked her arm with Evelyn's as they approached the entrance gate. "Surely there must be something we can do to help Marisol that doesn't involve sticking our noses in where they don't belong?"

"Yes, I suppose that's true. In any case, I did promise Marisol we'd think about it," Evelyn agreed.

"Look," Flora said. "There's the giant roller coaster. Do you girls know the roller coaster here at Neptune Beach is the same one built for the 1915 Panama-Pacific International Exposition in San Francisco? The exact same one."

They had arrived early enough to snag a wide empty space on the sand and three beach chairs. Evelyn and Bernice shed dresses, shoes and hats, revealing not-very-fashionable woolen racing Speedos. Unable to resist one more second, they trotted to the water's edge, trailed by Flora.

"So, Flora, dear," Evelyn said, "we're going to swim north, to just even with whatever that tall thing is there, do you see?"

"Um-hmm."

"And turn and come back south. How far do you think south, Bernie?"

They continued mapping out their route while Flora nodded and smiled. There were too many arms and hands waving about pointing this way and that for her to make much sense of the plan.

"How long do you think?" she said.

Bernice popped her eyes open in mock horror. "Do you mean to say you'll not be watching us every minute? This is a race, you know. I thought you would time us."

"A race," Flora said. "That's hardly fair, is it? Look at your long arms and legs, Bernie. Surely you will win any race."

Bernice laughed. "Have you taken a good look at your friend here? She may be shorter than I, but she's a good five foot five of pure muscle. Why, Evelyn has a body built for swimming."

Flora let her gaze slide to the distance. "I thought I would get us some lunch while you two are racing. Are hot dogs with all the fixings and lemonade good for everyone?"

"That sounds swell," Bernice said while pulling on her bathing cap.

"Chop, chop, then!" Flora said. "Goggles on and off you go! Ready, set, go!"

Bernice and Evelyn splashed into the bay waist deep, dove under and came up racing. Flora watched the first lap, which Evelyn easily won. In fact, Evelyn won every lap, including the ones Flora wasn't watching. Her athletic body was indeed built for the open-water swimming she loved, and even Bernice's strongest stroke was no match for Evelyn's practiced crawl, propelling her like a bullet through the waves. Evelyn arrived back at their beach chairs at least ten full minutes before Bernice, and Flora handed her a large towel. When Bernice appeared, the three of them settled into their chairs for some sun and a snack.

Flora unwrapped hot dogs with mustard stripes, pickles on the side, and passed those around. She handed each a curvaceous bottle of cold Coca-Cola, the caps popped off by the vendor. They ate and watched the other sunbathers around them.

Spreading her now-damp towel on the hot sand to dry, and cutting a sly glance at Flora, Bernice sat back in her beach chair. "So tell me, Evelyn, how did you and Flora meet, anyway? I know you came from Philadelphia together, so you must have known one another there. How did you and Flora get to know each other?"

Evelyn shifted uncomfortably, and tried to catch Flora's expression to gauge just how much she should reveal. Evelyn's out-going and honest nature sometimes clashed with Flora's desire for privacy and the need to be more reserved about their personal lives. Evelyn didn't want to put herself in the dog-house. Not helpful for Evelyn's predicament, Flora had covered her face with a beach hat.

"Well, now," Evelyn started. "That would have been December of 1922, I believe." She glanced again at Flora's immobile wide-brimmed hat, gleaning no clues as to how much to go on from there. "Philadelphia had a heavy snowfall the day before. My brothers and I and some of my students were tobog-ganing on the hill surrounding the Marsten mansion."

"Humph," Flora said from under her hat. "Hill? That was more like a precipice."

Evelyn chuckled, feeling a bit relieved that she hadn't said anything unacceptable—yet. "That is quite a steep hill, I agree. Sledders have been known to break limbs on that hill. Anyway, we were all having a wild time, when along came this group of snooty young people from the adjacent neighborhood, and one of them, this one," Evelyn slung a thumb at Flora's hat, "said it looked as though we were having such fun and she would like to try it. I invited her to share my toboggan…" Evelyn paused, and decided to cut her tale short, thus saving herself from the dangers of indiscretion. "She accepted my invitation, and here we are, all these years later."

"Still sharing a toboggan, eh?" Bernice laughed.

"You might say," Evelyn said quietly, glancing at Flora's hat again.

"That's a darling of a story," Bernice said.

Flora swept the hat off her face and sat up straight. "And how did you and Marisol meet?"

"Not in nearly such a fun way." Bernice chuckled. "I broke my ankle in a rugby match. Or rather, another player got angry, stomped on my ankle while stealing the ball, and broke my ankle in three places. When the docs finished with my surgery they wheeled me into the ward at the hospital where Marisol was working. I was there for two weeks. Despite all my complaining and whining, the two of us managed to become friends anyway."

"How long ago was that?" Evelyn asked.

"See that right there?" Bernice showed them the shiny white lines on her ankle. "Eight years after the surgery and you can still see the scars. No matter. I went right back to work after it healed, and I can still swim. What's a few scars? Marisol says they only enhance my delicate beauty."

Flora had to stifle a giggle at that satirical comment, and Evelyn smiled. Bernice's broad shoulders and narrow hips made her a gangly triangle, far from a shape anyone would describe as delicate.

"That would have been '24, in the spring," Bernice concluded. She scrunched her forehead. "So, after the snowy day of tobogganing, what did you two do to get acquainted?" She gave Evelyn a wink that could only be described as lewd.

Flora missed the gesture because she was busy standing up. "Oh, for the love of Pete," she muttered as she gathered their food wrappers. She called over her shoulder as she headed for the trash can, "Anyone want anything else?"

Chapter Ten

"Now you've done it," Evelyn told Bernice as she watched Flora walk away.

As was often the case, Bernice seemed oblivious to her social gaffe. She held onto Evelyn's elbow, detaining her in the beach chair, and whispered urgently. "Really, my friend, it's obvious you and Flora are close. Why is she so reluctant to discuss anything of your lives together? She comes across as a bit of a bluenose, don't you know?"

Evelyn extracted her arm and stood, preparing to follow Flora. She shook out her damp towel and draped it neatly over the back of her chair. "You're making some unwarranted assumptions, Bernice. I suspect you're only curious."

"Humph!" Bernice looked away, then back. "Dr. Freud describes excess prudery as a psychological problem, you know. He calls it repression."

Having reached the trash can and deposited their waste paper, Flora glanced back, her eyes narrowed in a black look, almost as though she could hear the words being spoken.

Usually unflappable, Evelyn felt herself becoming perturbed. Gazing over Bernice's head in barely controlled exasperation, Evelyn said, "What makes you think..." She stopped. "Oh, never mind." She bent close to Bernice's ear. "She's a minx," Evelyn said in a voice only Bernice could hear.

"Really! A minx, you say?" Bernice shifted her sly grin in Flora's direction. "Tell me more…"

"That's all you're getting, Bernice, and more than you deserve." Evelyn threw the words over her shoulder as she went to join Flora.

By shortly after noon they'd all had enough swimming, sunbathing, and more than enough Coca-Cola and hot dogs. Their shared anxiety about Marisol and her family had also gotten the better of them. They decided if they left as soon as they'd changed clothes, their arrival in mid-afternoon at the hacienda might coincide with the maximum opportunity to be of help. They packed their things, returned their rented chairs, and stopped at the ice cream cart for Dixie cups of vanilla with tiny wooden spoons attached to eat on the walk back to Walter's.

Bernice and Flora were downstairs waiting for Evelyn to finish getting changed when the telephone rang in the entry hall. Being the closest thing to a Winslow in the room, Flora went to answer it, then immediately called to Bernice and handed her the receiver. A hysterical Marisol was on the other end of the line.

Bernice returned to the parlor less than three minutes later. "We really need to go, and right now," she said. She called up the stairway. "Evelyn? We've got to go now. There's a…another problem."

"Oh, no," Flora said. "What happened? More trouble with Rafael?"

Half way down the stairs and tugging on a sweater, Evelyn sent Flora an alarmed glance, but they both kept quiet, fearful they had already deduced what had prompted Marisol's telephone call.

Bernice dropped into a chair, her face drained of color. "Joaquin has been found but he's dead. His body was in an orchard, beaten to death. The deputies took him to the coroner's. He was found earlier this morning but they didn't know it was Joaquin. The sheriff is only now telling the Pachecos they think it's him. They're asking Tia Rosamaria, his mother, to go to the coroner's and identify his body."

"Oh, dear!" Evelyn glanced at Flora, who gazed back in horror. Their worst fear had been that Joaquin's disappearance would in some way be related to Rafael's arrest for murder. "Are they suggesting Rafael killed his own brother?" Evelyn asked.

"I only know what Marisol told me. She says Tia is in hysterics, and Marisol didn't sound much better. Tia wants Marisol to take her back to church. She's hoping the priest will go with them to see the body."

"Where's Rafael?" Flora said in a small voice. "I suppose he's still in jail? His mother needs him now. Can't they at least let him go to the coroner with his mother?"

Bernice appeared to have not understood the question. She stared blankly at Flora for several seconds. "The deputies are waiting at the hacienda now, wanting to take Tia to the coroner's, but she's in hysterics and won't go. The sheriff hauled Rafael away and arrested him this morning, remember? And yes, Evelyn, the deputies said Rafael is being charged with his brother's murder."

Shock settled in as each of them grasped the full significance of the news. No one managed even a few words of comfort for Bernice.

In a shaky voice, Bernice said again, "We really need to go, and right now. I'll put my things in the auto and we can be on the road in a jiff."

The minute Bernice disappeared down the stairs toward the garage, Flora whispered urgently. "What did you decide about helping? I know you said we wouldn't be much help in finding the guilty parties involved in the acts of vandalism, but this is different. Now there's been a murder. You do have some expertise in solving murders."

"We," Evelyn said. "Together we have some experience puzzling out mysteries. And usually we know most of the people involved. I still don't see how we can investigate this very different situation." Evelyn rarely struggled with self-doubt, but this was a puzzle where she couldn't even see the edge pieces. Who was she to investigate a murder in the fruit orchards?

"Think about it though, Evie. I know I said I thought it might be dangerous for us to get involved, but now, without our help, Tia Rosamaria will lose both sons, one to murder and the second to being framed. If we don't help her and Marisol, who will?"

"You're right about that, dear. It's simply, I don't want us to get in over our heads, especially if we take this investigation on as a professional matter. What do we really know about the situation? Even so far as what you just said about Rafael being framed. Do we know that to be true?"

"Yes, I suppose you're right about that."

"How about if we take this one step at a time, shall we? We'll take Bernice back out there today, and if something comes up we feel we might be able to help with, we'll decide then whether to go ahead with the next step."

"One step at a time?"

"Yes, and we'd best be getting out there before the afternoon gets any later."

Bernice sat quietly, wringing her hands, while Evelyn negotiated the traffic through downtown Oakland. They'd begun the climb into the hills before she spoke. "You know, Evelyn, I'd do everything I could to help Marisol, but right now I'm afraid she doesn't want any help from me. I'm not even sure she'll come home with me this afternoon, given what's happened. I have to go or I'll lose my job, and so will she if she doesn't show up for her nursing shift in the morning, but maybe she doesn't care about that any longer." Bernice sighed deeply, wiped a tear from one cheek, and went back to wringing her hands.

"We'll see what's needed when we get there," Evelyn said. "At the very least, I can drive Marisol and her aunt to the coroner's. That would probably be helpful."

"Yes," Flora said, "and Evelyn could even go in with Marisol and Tia at the coroner's. Evie has experience in seeing bodies, you know. She has a college degree in physiology."

"Yes, thank you," Bernice murmured, and wiped another tear. After a shorter silent spell, she said, "Say, what's this gaping hole in Walter's dashboard?"

Flora managed a smile. "That's his radio. I'll show you..." and she broke into a soothing version of *As Time Goes By*. Evelyn and Flora together managed to make a crooner out of *All of Me*, and the three of them joined in for *A Closer Walk With Thee*. Only Flora was able to finish that one without her voice cracking in unshed tears.

Evelyn sent a quick but kind smile to her companions as they neared the turnoff. "I daresay, Flora, who needs a radio when they have you along to pass the time?"

All appeared quiet when they arrived at the hacienda just after two. Bernice's Tin Lizzie was parked in front, so it did seem likely the silent house was occupied. The sheriff's vehicles, reported to have been there earlier, were gone. Bernice disappeared by herself under the arbor to the front entry. A few moments later, both she and Marisol appeared and gestured for Flora and Evelyn to come inside the adobe house.

Flora gave Marisol a comforting hug under the arbor, and they expressed their sorrow at the loss of Marisol's young cousin.

The low-ceilinged sitting room where Marisol settled them was cool even in the hot afternoon and had an expansive view out to the verdant yard in the rear and the patio there. Marisol brought tea on a tray.

"My aunt is taking a nap," she explained. She didn't comment on her own reddened eyes and puffy face. "Father Bertrand won't accompany us to the coroner to see Joaquin. Or rather the deacon said he couldn't find the Father. Sounded a bit frantic, too, as Father Bertrand has a wedding scheduled for four this afternoon.

"Personally, I think Father is just afraid of the Vigilantes, as everyone is afraid. I'm hoping you'll come with us." She drew her eyebrows together in a pleading expression and looked at Evelyn, then Flora. She appeared to be ignoring Bernice. "If you won't come with us, I'll have to take Tia myself, when she awakens." Again, no mention was made of Bernice, whose automobile would apparently be used for this sad errand.

"Of course we'll go with you," Evelyn said. "All five of us can easily fit in my brother's Chevrolet." She wanted to say more, something along the lines of how happy they'd be to accompany Marisol and her aunt, but that hardly seemed appropriate.

"We're glad to be able to be of some assistance," Flora said, finishing Evelyn's thought. "Why is everyone so afraid? Does the priest think Rafael is really to blame, and he doesn't want to get in the middle? Or does he believe it was the Vigilantes who...who hurt Joaquin and..."

"And he's genuinely afraid of incurring their wrath himself?" Evelyn concluded. "Seems unlikely to me the deacon doesn't know where to look for the priest on a Sunday afternoon."

"Here, let me pour more tea," Bernice said, her hands shaking. In her zeal to make herself useful, she nearly knocked over the teapot. Tea splashed onto the tray, and she sopped at it with her napkin.

Without breaking her warm gaze directed at Marisol, Flora stayed Bernice's hand and cleaned the tea tray herself while still talking.

"What are they afraid will happen?"

"Truthfully," Marisol said, "it's hard to believe those men would resort to outright murder. From what I've seen here, what the newspapers are calling labor riots are mostly a lot of yelling, with some pushing and shoving, although Joaquin did come away with that bloodied nose the other day, so possibly there's some special grudge against him.

"When I talked to the medical examiner on the telephone, he told me Joaquin had been killed by..." She paused, and her voice trembled. "By a crushing blow to his face using a large rock. They found the rock beside him." Marisol stopped, gulped, and steadied her breathing. "He was left dead in the walnut orchard. That's a ways away from the barn here on our property where the disturbances have been happening."

"That does sound more like a deliberate murder than a labor riot gotten out of hand," Evelyn said. Flora sent her an encouraging and supportive expression, as if to say, "See, I knew you would be helpful." Evelyn turned her gaze back to Marisol.

"That's exactly what I thought," Marisol agreed. "The sheriff's deputies said Rafael killed Joaquin because of a labor dispute, which makes no sense whatsoever to me. And they had no witnesses or evidence to support their ludicrous theory.

"This morning, when they came for Rafael and said he was being charged with murder, they had no idea whose body it was they'd found...because of how badly damaged Joaquin's face was, you understand? Even so, they were sure Rafael must have done it. That shows you how the deputies have it in for us Californios.

"Then, when they decided the body was Joaquin—I think they found his identification or something, and they heard Rafael had been out last night looking for his brother, that only confirmed their belief they'd already arrested the killer."

"So, let me understand," Flora said, evidently ready to put a few pieces together. "The body was found early this morning, and right away the deputies came to arrest Rafael for the murder, before they even knew whose body it was?"

"Yes. They knew the body was a farmworker, and made the assumption that, as the labor contractor, Rafael was the most likely suspect."

"I see," Flora said, in a tone that suggested she didn't. "Then later, after they learned it was Joaquin—"

"And after they'd already arrested Rafael?" Evelyn interrupted.

"Yes," Flora continued. "Then the deputies started lining up evidence to support their theory and justify Rafael's arrest?" Flora gave Evelyn a knowing gaze.

"Backwards, huh?" Evelyn said.

"Elementary, my dear."

Chapter Eleven

The room became quiet, leaving the four of them to think through the implications of everything that had happened. To Evelyn, the conclusion that she and Flora might indeed be needed to help this family was becoming clearer by the moment.

"And you're sure they arrested Rafael on suspicion of murder?" Evelyn asked. "Not for participating in any riot, or instigating one, or something less serious than murder?"

Marisol turned a confused expression to Evelyn. Her eyes filled with tears again. Bernice stood and draped an awkward arm over her friend's shoulder which Marisol barely acknowledged. Evelyn and Flora exchanged a quick glance.

"I'm sorry, Evelyn," Marisol said. "It's all very confusing. You can see now, can't you, why we need your professional help? We can afford whatever your fees."

Evelyn sent Flora a quick glance. Flora gave a slight nod, and the deal was struck. "Very well," Evelyn said. "We'll help where we can, and we'll keep a running tab. You know though, we can't make any promises."

"Yes, of course." Marisol said. "With Joaquin's death, whatever you might be able to do, you know, if anything, to clear Rafael of these bogus charges of murder. We would be so grateful. And just knowing we have your help. That alone will be reassuring.

"In any case, my aunt wants to take Joaquin to the funeral home, but the coroner won't release his body until she identifies him. He'll need to be identified from birthmarks because his face is...you know... After we take care of that, possibly we can go to see Rafael and he might be able to answer a few of your questions. That is, if you are willing to drive us around today?"

"As Flora said, we're glad to be able to help."

The sounds of Tia Rosamaria up and about in the bedroom wing of the house heralded her imminent arrival in the sitting room.

Marisol leaned forward as though not wishing to be overheard. "Our family has simply never been in the middle of something like this. You at least know the right questions to ask, *verdad*? True?"

Marisol's plea was so heartfelt, Evelyn couldn't bring herself to say anything that might be interpreted in the negative. At the same time, she remained reluctant to make promises she'd later be unable to keep. Already she was concerned she might have gotten in over her head. She nodded. "We'll see what can be done, dear, of course."

Marisol rushed out of the room, on her way to help her aunt. Evelyn looked at the others in silence, not knowing what to expect of the afternoon ahead.

"You know, Evie," Flora said in her quietest voice, "one way you might really be of help..."

"What's that?"

"At least you and I won't be as afraid of those Vigilantes as everyone else seems to be. We won't refuse to help on that account, at least. What could they possibly do to us?"

Short, round, and dressed from head to toe in black, Tia Rosamaria bustled into the sitting room, still pinning on her hat.

Marisol handed her aunt the business card Flora had given her showing Winslow and Fitzgerald, Investigators.

"These are the investigators I told you about, Tia. Evelyn Winslow and Flora Fitzgerald."

"How do you do, ma'am," Evelyn said, standing and extending her hand.

Tia stared at the card, then looked up at Evelyn. "Girls?" she said to Marisol. "The investigators are girls? Where is this…" She tapped the card. "Where is this Winslow and Fitzgerald?" She turned to Evelyn. "Where is your husband, *chica?*" Without giving Evelyn a chance to answer, Tia let fly a string of Spanish that caused even Marisol to look confused.

"*Terminemos con esto,*" Tia concluded. "Let's get this over with."

The five of them went out to the Chevrolet and sorted themselves inside. Shifting her ample behind from side to side, Tia made it clear that Bernice would not be permitted to sit on the rear seat next to Marisol and herself.

"We could tuck Bernice back in the struggle buggy," Flora said in a whisper only Evelyn could hear, pointing at the rumble seat at the far rear of the Chevrolet.

"Wouldn't be much of a struggle with her all by herself back there. Let's let her sit up front with me. Tia Rosamaria can't object to you sharing the rear seat with the two of them, if that suits?"

Almost before the doors had slammed shut, Marisol's aunt began a steady jabber.

"Do you girls know about the disturbances here in the orchards? Such a shame. We know everyone is desperate… searching for work, but why do those Americanos think they can push our people out? Our farmworkers are being forced out of their jobs. And sometimes even our homes where we've lived for generations. Do you know they are packing us onto buses and sending us to Mexico?" Tia's tone had become shrill, tears threatening to fall. "My own nephew, Felix, in Los Angeles, put on a bus to Mexico. He was born right here! Our *ancestros* were Spaniards, not Mexicans, but it doesn't matter. If your name is Spanish, they send you to Mexico and steal your job. You know they would never hire us Californios on those assembly lines, at the shipyards, and in the automobile factories. Huh! They wouldn't have us. Now those factory workers come here and try to take our jobs!"

Evelyn leaned to the side and caught Flora's gaze in the rear view mirror. Tia Rosamaria was speaking more and more rapidly. Evelyn knew the woman was probably trying to distract herself from the dreadful errand they were on, but Evelyn was afraid she was spinning out of control.

Flora reached across Marisol's lap and patted Tia's hand gently. "It is a terrible situation, I know. Simply terrible. I'm so sorry your family has been dragged into the middle of this." She squeezed the older woman's hand.

"Up here," Bernice said, pointing. "Turn left onto the highway, and then another left when you get into town. Isn't that right, Marisol?" Bernice hitched herself around and made eye contact with Marisol, who leaned forward.

"Yes. The coroner's office is at the far end of town a few miles ahead on the left."

When Marisol sat back, Tia began her insistent chatter again, only now in Spanish, and quietly so that only Marisol could hear much. After a few moments, Flora sent Evelyn an alarmed expression in the mirror.

Tia leaned around her niece to catch Flora's gaze. "You didn't say, dear, where is your husband?" she asked.

A momentary confusion silenced the other occupants and they sent perplexed and mildly amused glances to one another, all except Flora. Flora kept a polite smile pasted on her face and maintained eye contact with Marisol's aunt. Keeping the peace was of overriding value in Flora's interactions, sometimes at the expense of the truth. Almost without missing a beat, Flora adopted a sorrowful expression and said, "I'm afraid my erstwhile husband is buried under a poppy field in Flanders, ma'am."

"Oh, my word. I'm so sorry to hear you say that. I am a widow myself. I understand your sadness."

Flora nodded with a grave expression.

"What about children?" Tia asked Flora. "Do you have any children?"

"Oh, no." Flora conjured up an even more intensely despondent expression. "No, we were hardly more than children ourselves when he was...you understand..."

The total silence and frozen expressions on the other riders spoke volumes, but Tia was intent on believing what she wanted to believe. They rode on in silence until Marisol pointed out the low brick building on their left. Evelyn steered into the gravel lot and parked.

She glanced into the rear seat as she pulled the parking brake. Tia's crumpled body formed a woebegone and unmoving lump. "I'll go in with you, shall I?" Evelyn offered. She softened her eyes at the older woman. "I've done this before. It's dreadful, but it's over quickly."

Tia's eyes filled with tears that spilled rapidly down her face. "My boy Joaquin, I always knew he would come to a bad end. He always, from the time he was little, he defied God's will." Her voice caught in a sob. "Any more, do you know, he wouldn't even come to church with me?"

"Here," Evelyn said as she stepped out the driver's side and walked sedately around to open the door for Marisol and her aunt. "Let me help you."

Still, Tia didn't move. "I cannot do it," she said. "I cannot. Not my baby boy. I cannot." She shook her head from side to side, tears streaming down her softly wrinkled cheeks. "Marisol, you must go."

Marisol's face had paled to an ashen gray. "Will they take my word, Tia? The coroner said on the telephone it had to be family who identified him. I'm not sure they'll let me do it."

"He has a scar here, on his arm, where he broke it," Tia said, and pointed to her own arm. "He was a baby. Even then, he would not do as he was told. He climbed out of his crib. The bone, it poked through just there, and left a scar. You can identify him that way."

Flora opened her door, letting Marisol slide out, then climbed back inside and patted Tia's hand.

"And he has the tattoo," Marisol's aunt said. "The snake. Here, on his shoulder. He was only thirteen when he got that. His papa was so mad." She gestured to her own shoulder. Marisol nodded, stumbling forward. Evelyn hurried over and steadied her friend.

In the end, only Evelyn and Marisol went inside, leaving Flora and Tia in the automobile. Bernice walked listlessly toward the entry, but stopped and stood alone on the concrete porch after the others had entered.

Once inside, the intense odor of bleach made Evelyn's eyes water. She pinched her nose to stop the stinging and sat on a low bench with Marisol where they had been told by a sour-faced receptionist to wait.

"It's not seeing a body that I mind, you understand," Marisol said. "I see plenty of bodies as a nurse, but this is my cousin and they said his face... I'll just make the identification and then we can leave. The less I see, the less I'll have to remember. I'll want to tell Tia her Joaquin is beautiful no matter what."

"I understand," Evelyn said, and sighed, then noticed the tight-lipped receptionist staring at them.

"Which one of you girls is family of the deceased?" the receptionist said. "Only immediate family is permitted to view the deceased. The doctor is far too busy to take time with anyone who's not family."

Without batting an eye, Marisol spoke up. "We're both family. I'm Marisol Pacheco, Joaquin's sister and this is our cousin Evelyn. Her father is married to my mother's sister's brother-in law."

The receptionist opened her mouth, scowled, and closed it again.

Evelyn turned her attention away from the woman who might have been jealously guarding her employer's time, or possibly just feeling jealous.

She turned to Marisol. "Have you learned anything more about how Joaquin died?" Evelyn said. "Where, exactly, he was found, for example, or why he might have been killed?"

Marisol stared at her lap, and for a moment, Evelyn feared she wasn't going to answer.

"Everyone is assuming it was something to do with the labor riots," Marisol finally said. "The growers keep lowering the rate they'll pay. One grower is down to fifteen cents for a whole bushel of peaches. That's over an hour's work! So the farmworkers get together and refuse to work, but then these Vigilantes go to the growers and offer to take the jobs, and the growers pay the scabs more! That's what starts the fights, but it's usually just a lot of pushing and shoving, name-calling. One Californio got beaten up badly out near Antioch a week or so ago. Someone heard gun shots at another orchard, but they said the grower was trying to restore order. No one got hurt."

"Something more happened to Joaquin, though. He was beaten?"

"That's what the sheriff said. Some pickers found him early this morning when they went to work. He was lying in an orchard under a peach tree."

"Beaten?"

"His head, anyway."

"Curious they would only hit his head. That doesn't sound like the usual sort of beating a man might get. Not to imply I'm an expert on the subject." Evelyn still doubted she could be of much help in identifying Joaquin's killer, but the particulars about how he had died were beginning to interest her. "Was the sheriff able to tell you when he died? This morning early, or last night? Possibly even yesterday?"

"I didn't ask, and he didn't say."

"When was the last time you, or anyone, saw Joaquin?" If Flora and I are going to do any real investigating, we'll need some basic facts."

"I suppose Rafael must have been the last one of us to see him. Joaquin came to the house after supper and asked to take

81

the truck, but Rafael told him no because after the Plymouth was firebombed the truck was the only vehicle the family had left. They were both at the labor office down in the barn all day yesterday, Saturday, as that was a work day. Neither of them came to the house until after supper."

Evelyn nodded, trying to put the pieces together. She was good at sniffing around, asking questions, and gathering pieces of information. Flora was better at assembling the pieces into a whole picture.

"Oh," Marisol said, "I just remembered. Rafael said Joaquin came home to put on a clean shirt before he went out."

"Hmm. That might be important," Evelyn said. "And Rafael was gone during the night, looking for Joaquin?"

"Yes, yes. Tia said she woke him at two in the morning and sent him out to search, but I was up when he came home, more like four-thirty. We were all asleep when the deputies came to arrest Rafael about seven."

Evelyn tapped her lip, thinking. "I don't mean to imply anything here, but is it impossible that Rafael may have... Well, you have no evidence to prove Rafael didn't eventually find Joaquin and...?"

"No! Those boys are so close. They always were from the time they were little. Rafael took care of his baby brother. He would never have done anything to hurt Joaquin."

Evelyn patted Marisol's hand, attempting to calm her.

"Ladies, this way please." A short, silver-haired man in wire-rimmed glasses and a white lab coat gestured at them from the door he held wide. Something even more medicinal-smelling than bleach wafted from the open doorway. Formaldehyde, Evelyn suspected, remembering her earlier experiences.

Chapter Twelve

The doctor's receptionist leaned over her counter and called to him in a sickly-sweet voice. "Oh, Doctor." She sent a scowl to Evelyn and continued her croon, "Don't take too long with those…ladies, Doctor. Remember, you have an appointment at three-thirty."

Evelyn took Marisol's elbow and they moved together through the doorway and into an inner room where a draped body lay on a porcelain-topped gurney. A small dark stain marked the grayish drape at the end where the head was presumably located.

Incongruous with the situation, the doctor gave them a wide grin. "Dr. Whitley, at your service, ladies. I'm the county coroner. Which of you ladies will be making the identification?"

Marisol made a small noise and motioned to herself. When she had his attention, she said, "He's our family, our younger cousin. I only need to see his shoulder, the left one I think, where he has a tattoo of a snake? And he has a scar on his forearm as well, the right one."

Still giving them a wide, fixed smile, the coroner swept back the drape, revealing the body of Marisol's late cousin lying face up and naked with a smaller drape below his waist.

Marisol gasped and her knees went out from under her.

Evelyn bore the weight until her friend could regain her composure. She glared angrily at Dr. Whitley, but he didn't react. He was too busy smirking at Marisol's discomfort. He reminded Evelyn of a half-grown boy teasing a younger girl with a spider.

The tattooed snake slithered over Joaquin's shoulder, clearly visible in the harsh overhead light, to the side of the young man's cruelly mangled head and face. Evelyn pointed and Marisol nodded, trying to avert her gaze from the young man's bloody features.

"Yes, that is Joaquin Pacheco, my cousin," Marisol said in a wooden tone, and buried her face in her hands, leaning on Evelyn's shoulder.

Evelyn continued to look at the body. It appeared someone had attempted to smash Joaquin's skull with several blows to the head. There were no bruises or injuries on the other visible parts of his body. She overcame her revulsion long enough to take a good look at Joaquin's face.

"You say he was killed by a blow to the head? That's your judgement as to the cause of death?"

"Yes, ma'am. You understand I have not yet examined the body. I've only just arrived. But, yes, that damage you see there does appear to be the obvious cause of death. There were several blows, including, I see here..." He pointed at a page he was reading, "at least one serious clout to the back of the head." The sheriff says he has possession of a rock that was found beside the body. He says these Mexicans got into a fight with each other and this boy got the worst of it."

Marisol snarled through clenched teeth. "We're not Mexicans. We're Californios and have been here since long before you or any of your family came here." The coroner nodded, his smile fading.

Evelyn helped Marisol stay upright with a strong arm around her waist. Her friend stared resolutely at the wall over Dr. Whitley's head.

"I can't help but wonder," Evelyn said to the coroner, "this blow here...this is to the front of his head, to his face. Are you suggesting the killer hit him from in front? I'm only wondering why Joaquin couldn't fight off his attacker if he saw the killer coming at him with a rock."

The coroner's mouth drew into a thin line and he stiffened. "There are several blows to the face, as you can see, and also it says here, a blow to the back of the head. Let's see." As he said this, he pulled Joaquin's stiff body partially over so they could see the damage inflicted on the back of Joaquin's head. Fascinated enough to have conquered her disgust, Evelyn studied the injury to the back of the young man's head. She gestured at the coroner for him to pull the body over a bit more.

"Have you examined this injury here?"

"Not as yet, as I said previously. The sheriff said the boy had been beaten to death, and that's where we've left it for now."

"I wonder, do you have a damp cloth, or something we might use to clean this injury?"

Dr. Whitley huffed, but he did dampen a lab towel. Instead of wiping the injury himself, he handed the towel to Evelyn and grinned at her hesitation.

Telling herself this task was no more upsetting than others she'd performed while a student of physiology, Evelyn wiped gingerly at the wound, coming away with dark pieces of soil and gore. She held her breath and peered into the hole that was revealed. Amongst the congealed blood, brain matter, and white cracked bone fragments at the back of the head, Evelyn caught the glint of something shiny.

"What's this here?" she said. "There's something metallic here." She pointed at what she was seeing.

The coroner didn't move, now scowling at Evelyn. Then his curiosity got the better of him and he leaned over to look. "I don't see anything," he said.

"Excuse me," Marisol mumbled. "I believe I'll go tell my aunt." She slipped out the door and was gone.

Evelyn counted, not quite to ten, but close, enough to let herself adopt a more placid tone. "I believe you may be obscuring the light by leaning this way," she said to Dr. Whitley.

"Possibly if you would turn the body over, or come to this side of the table."

The coroner raised his eyebrows at Evelyn, as though questioning her motives, then took a second look at Joaquin's head. "I do believe I see it now," he said. He reached behind himself and rummaged through a tray of tools. Even Evelyn could not watch his next movements, digging around in the gaping wound, but she heard the clink as the coroner dropped the object into a metal tray. She turned back in time to see Dr. Whitley pick up a brass-colored bullet with a pair of large pincers and give it a good looking over.

"I'll be damned," he said. "That boy had a bullet in his brain." He gazed at the bullet, turning it from side to side, then dropped it back into the tray.

Evelyn wondered how she might glean more information out of this odd little man. Possibly feeding his ego might help. "Based on your expertise as a doctor," she said, "would you say that bullet could have been present in Joaquin's brain prior to the injuries to his face?"

"Are you suggesting he might have suffered an accidental shot to the head sometime in the distant past? In my opinion, that would have been impossible. Let's see here..." He poked around at the back of Joaquin's head again, while Evelyn looked away. "No. No...look, here's a burn mark. No, I'd say this boy was shot in the back of the head at near the same time as he had his face crushed with the rock."

Evelyn glanced at the wound with a reluctant eye. She likely wouldn't know a burn mark if she saw one. "So you're saying he was shot in the head and killed, and then shortly afterward someone disfigured his face with a rock? Why would someone do that?"

"That, my dear girl, is a good question." Dr. Whitley gave Evelyn an appraising gaze.

"The intent may have been to prevent, or at least delay identification of the body, don't you think?" Evelyn said.

"Yes..."

"Which it did, I suppose, at least for a short time. Or possibly, don't you think, the individual who bashed his face was trying to disguise the actual cause of death?" Evelyn glanced up to see that Dr. Whitley's wide grin had returned.

"Yes, and look," he said. "See here where the frontal injuries didn't bleed much? According to this report, the body was found lying face up, and based on the state of rigor, this boy was killed several hours ago. Sometime overnight, I would say. These injuries would ordinarily have resulted in massive blood loss, yet there's nothing in this report about blood around the body. I suppose I would have assumed the blood soaked into the soil beneath the head, or..." He paused.

"And now, seeing this gun shot to the back of the head and not much blood on the face, you think something different?" Evelyn said.

"Maybe...may indeed be," the doctor said.

They both bent over Joaquin's body, looking for additional evidence of what might have happened to him.

Dr Whitley straightened. "Yes, well now it appears likely the blows to the face occurred long enough after death that the heart had stopped pumping and very little bleeding was associated directly with the rock attack."

Evelyn was slightly more impressed with Dr. Whitley. Despite some of his antiquated attitudes, the coroner did seem to know his business when it came to medical examination.

"What about," she said, "is it possible Joaquin was shot somewhere else altogether, and his body was later moved to the orchard?"

"Yes, yes, that would account for the lack of blood at the scene. Maybe, if I have time, I'll go out to where the body was found and look for blood soaked into the soil there. I only took the deputy's word for that."

"Do you still have the clothes he was wearing? The collar of his shirt, for example, might be informative."

"Ah, yes, it might indeed. Those things are here somewhere, unless... That sheriff's deputy may have taken them along with the rock... No, I'm sure I set them aside or... or maybe not. I think the deputy wanted to use those clothes as evidence in prosecuting the brother. His brother, as you may know, is charged with the murder."

"I have heard that," Evelyn said. "There do appear to be a number of unanswered questions, though, don't you agree?"

"Yes, yes... although nothing that would preclude the brother being the murderer."

Evelyn stared openly at the doctor. He appeared to have his mind made up, or had it made up for him by local law enforcement. Instead of discouraging her curiosity, his attitude only piqued her concern and aroused her suspicions. She took a deep breath. As long as the coroner was willing to answer every question she could come up with, she thought she should keep asking.

"It seems a necropsy has not yet been performed." She could see no evidence beyond a partial washing that anything had been done to the body. "Was one planned?"

"The modern term is autopsy," Dr. Whitley said. "When performed on a human, it's called an autopsy. And no, we didn't perform an autopsy. The deputy said everything with this case was straight-forward and I shouldn't do an autopsy. When I contacted the family by telephone, they also strongly objected."

"But such an examination is required by law, isn't it, in the case of a homicide?"

The coroner paled and tightened his lips. His grin was gone. Evelyn suspected that doing what local law enforcement directed him to do, or not do, did not extend to risking his professional position, or his medical license.

"Yes, it would be prudent," he said. "I'll return this body to the refrigerated vault and perform the autopsy first thing Monday morning."

"Good, that's best." Evelyn nodded in agreement. She was thinking about Tia Rosamaria, who was going to be distressed to hear she would not be able to give her son a proper

Christian burial for at least a few more days. Heaven only knew how she might respond when told an autopsy would be performed against her wishes. Evelyn decided she wouldn't be the one to tell the already distressed mother. She turned back to the coroner. "Can you give me some idea what else you might learn from doing an autopsy?"

Chapter Thirteen

Dr. Whitley pursed his lips and took on a thoughtful expression. "Truthfully, I suspect not much new information will be learned by conducting an autopsy on this boy. The procedure can be useful in determining the true cause of death. In this case, this recent gunshot wound to the back of the head is reasonably clear. Equally probable is that this was a healthy young man with no underlying disease or debilitating conditions. So the important question that arises here is was this a homicide or did this young man commit suicide."

"Oh." Evelyn gulped. She hadn't considered suicide. "How could that be determined? What do you think, in this case?"

"Without further examination I cannot say for certain. My inclination at this point is to say homicide. That burn mark, the presence of the bullet toward the back of the brain, and the apparent lack of an entry wound on the front of the head, those factors say to me this man was shot in the back of the head and from six to ten feet away. I'll need to look for gunpowder residue on the shirt collar to draw a more precise conclusion. Given those factors, suicide seems unlikely.

"Yes, I would guess not," Evelyn said. "I should think it would be hard to shoot oneself in the back of the head from any distance, and certainly not from six feet away."

Evelyn committed these facts to memory so she could later share them with Flora if they were needed to work out the puzzle. She also made note that the coroner was now referring to Joaquin as a "man" or at least a "young man" rather than a "boy" or only a "body," and she wondered what, precisely, had engendered this greater degree of respect.

"May I...?" She gestured at the metal tray in which the bullet they'd found rested. "May I have another look at that bullet?"

Dr. Whitley handed her the tray.

"Brass," Evelyn said. "Fairly large for a bullet, isn't it?"

"About medium-sized. That's a .38 caliber, from a .38 Special. In this case, I'd say a revolver. Bullet from a .357 is much larger. You may be thinking of a .22 caliber. Those bullets are about half the size of this one."

"A .38, huh? I wonder if Rafael owns a .38."

"Those .38s are fairly popular, but I shouldn't think he'd have much use for one. A labor supervisor might carry a rifle sometimes, or a shotgun. More to protect the workers from mountain lions or wolves. Not for shooting other workers." Almost as an afterthought, he added, "That .38 Special revolver used to be standard issue for our local law enforcement. A policeman's weapon of choice. A .38 Special revolver, made by Colt. It's true, Smith and Wesson make a .38, too, but I know the sheriff here preferred the Colt.

"And also, with the shorter barrel on a .38 revolver made by Colt, the bullet's damage can be expended inside the body, especially when the shot is to the head. I've seen those bullets shatter inside or at least ricochet around in an enclosed space like a skull, exactly like what you see here."

Evelyn had adopted a serious expression and was nodding as though evaluating the sheriff's judgement in choosing the Colt over the Smith and Wesson. In truth, of course, she hadn't the slightest idea what any of this information meant.

"What do you mean, it 'used to be standard issue?' What sort of weapon is 'standard issue' now?"

The coroner pursed his lips again. "Not one hundred percent certain. My thinking would be they'd go more for a pistol today. The pistol gives you more shots without reloading, whereas the revolver only gives you six shots before you have to stop and reload. In the case of a real shootout, your average law enforcement officer is going to want those additional shots."

Evelyn shivered. The very idea of a "shootout" made her blood run cold.

"'Course in this case," he continued, "all it took was one shot." He gave Evelyn a deliberate wink, the meaning of which left her completely in the dark. Possibly a dust mote had blown into his eye. Unlikely in this sterile environment, but any other possible explanation eluded her.

Their conversation was interrupted by loud voices in the hallway outside the door. Evelyn thought that sounded like Flora speaking and maybe the pinched-face receptionist responding.

"In here?" Flora said from just outside the door.

"You can't go in there!" came the other voice. "Heaven knows what those two have gotten up to in there for all this time."

There was a loud "shave and a haircut, two-bits" rapping. That was definitely Flora. She cracked the door and peered inside. The doctor quickly threw the stained drape over Joaquin's body.

"I'm coming now," Evelyn stepped around, blocking Flora's view into the room.

She turned back to Dr. Whitley. "I have to go. This young man's mother is waiting outside. Thank you so much. Pleasure to meet you."

"Of course," he said, tucking the drape into place. "Please do come back, any time, really, dear. Does my receptionist have your name? And a way to reach you? A telephone number, perhaps?"

Evelyn weighed whether to fib, or simply ignore his questions as she slipped through the door.

Hopping on one foot, then the other, Flora said, "Twenty-three skidoo, dear! I'm sorry, but all heck is breaking loose outside." She took Evelyn's arm and tugged her toward the exit. "Did you learn anything useful?"

"Yes, I did indeed, lots." Evelyn took a moment to marvel at how eager she had been to learn more about the crime, despite her own misgivings concerning how helpful she might prove to be in an investigation. "I'll tell you later. Thank you for encouraging me to go inside." They peered through the glass door at the Chevrolet.

"What's the problem out there?

"Well, at first Tia Rosamaria and I just sat in the automobile and visited. Then Bernice came over and asked if she could do anything to help, and Tia got mildly hysterical. She screeched at Bernice, asking her why she was with us at all, and told her to go away." Flora took another breath, glanced behind at the receptionist clearly trying to overhear their conversation, and tugged Evelyn's sleeve until they were standing on the porch with the door closed behind them.

"I have to tell you," Flora said. "On our drive over here when Tia was whispering urgently to Marisol…she was speaking Spanish, of course, but I distinctly heard the word *bruja*, then Tia pointed at Bernice." She glanced sideways for Evelyn's reaction.

"I'm sorry, you've lost me."

"Evelyn, *bruja* means a witch in Spanish. Tia was telling Marisol she thinks Bernice is a witch. I strongly suspect Tia Rosamaria believes Bernice has led her niece Marisol…well, down a garden path, if you will."

"Oh." Evelyn felt too dumbfounded to say anything else.

"Honestly. Anyway, after Tia rudely told her to go away, Bernice left, walked to the service station, over here on the other side, and got a paper cup of water. She brought that back and offered it to Tia. Bernie probably should have taken the hint and not done that. After all, she had been told to go away. Tia slapped at the paper cup and almost dashed the water on Bernice. Truly, I can't begin to know what's in Tia's mind, but there's no call for her to be so rude to poor Bernice.

"In any case, then Marisol reappeared, and I got out of the auto so they could have a quiet moment together. You know, Marisol had to tell her aunt that really was Joaquin's body in the morgue. I couldn't help but overhear. Right in the middle of that, Bernice leaned in and gave Marisol the paper cup, which again, admittedly, she should not have done. She was only trying to help but then Marisol told her to go away.

"Now Bernice is threatening to walk home." Flora leaned over and gazed to the right, down the highway. "Not so much threatening," she said. "Bernice is actually walking back along the highway. That-a-way," she pointed.

Evelyn leaned over as well and could just make out her friend Bernice disappearing along the gravel shoulder. "She can't walk all the way back to the hacienda and her Ford. It's too far."

"I know, but she's making pretty good progress. I feel so sorry for her, although she is being a drip." Flora turned a sad expression to Evelyn. "We can drive down and pick her up, can't we? We're going on to the jail next, right?"

"Yes, of course. I have to tell you though, this is one bit about accepting this job as professional investigators that has me concerned. Does chasing after Bernice go on our tab or not?"

"Not, I'd say." Flora tugged on Evelyn's arm but her friend stood fast.

"We can't really move forward with this investigation until we get a chance to ask Rafael what he knows," Evelyn said. "I'm not sure how I'll get that chance with his family wanting to visit with him today."

"Perhaps we can make arrangements to see him later, or some other day, but we did promise we'd take Marisol and her aunt out to the jail this afternoon."

"Yes. Also, sometime soon I need to pull Marisol aside. I want to tell her what I learned here. Someone's going to have to tell Tia that an autopsy will be preformed and let her know Joaquin was shot."

"What! He was shot?"

Evelyn put a finger to her lips. "Shh! I don't want to have to tell everyone right now. Give me time to tell Marisol in private, please."

They climbed back into the car, leaving the front passenger seat vacant, and caught up to Bernice, still striding along the gravel shoulder. Evelyn leaned over and pushed the door open. Quietly she said, "C'mon dear, get in. It's too far to walk." Bernice wiped her face with a sleeve. Evelyn couldn't remember ever seeing Bernice cry before this weekend. Once she was settled inside and the door slammed, Flora pulled a clean hanky from her pocketbook and offered it to Bernice. Marisol and Tia Rosamaria clung to one another and stared stonily at their laps. When they arrived at the county jail building, everyone got out except Bernice.

An unshaven Rafael was brought into a narrow room in handcuffs to sit at a small table. Marisol and Tia Rosamaria sat on the two remaining chairs, and, not being family, Evelyn and Flora stood behind. They quickly discovered it was nearly impossible to get a word in edgewise to Rafael, so mostly they kept silent and listened. Evelyn did notice that despite the disheveled state of Rafael's clothing, not a trace of blood was visible. Marisol had said the deputies arrived to arrest him early in the morning, after he'd returned from searching several hours for his brother. It seemed likely Rafael had not taken the time to clean up or change, so he probably still wore the clothes he'd been wearing during the hours of searching, and during the same time the sheriff claimed he was murdering his brother.

Evelyn was anxious to ask Rafael a question or two, especially if he had an idea why the sheriff's deputies thought he had had anything at all to do with his brother's death. What was the alleged motive for the murder? Each time Evelyn started to ask a question, Tia Rosamaria leaned in closer, clutching her pocketbook in her lap and thrusting one shoulder forward to shut Evelyn out. She chattered on about the missing Father Bertrand, and her sisters who were on their way to help.

From over Tia's head, Flora's melodious voice finally cut through the whining chatter. "Is there anything you need, Mr. Pacheco? Anything we can bring you?"

Rafael looked up, appearing for the first time to notice the woman so kindly addressing him. He gave no sign of recognizing her.

"A book?" he said. "Something to read?"

Flora smiled, revealing her delight at discovering a fellow reader. "Oh, yes," she said. "I'm glad to bring you a book. I'm afraid it won't be today, though. We're coming back tomorrow, aren't we Evelyn? I'll bring you a book tomorrow." Flora nudged Evelyn. Using facial expressions alone, Flora managed to communicate to Evelyn that bringing a book for Rafael tomorrow would be the chance she was hoping for to talk with the young man more privately.

"Yes," Evelyn agreed. "We'll come back early tomorrow afternoon." She had barely gotten the words out before Tia interrupted and commandeered the conversation again.

Evelyn smiled at Rafael and twitched her head sideways to Flora, indicating they should take their leave. They stopped at the counter in front. Evelyn asked to speak with the sheriff and was informed that he was out, being as this was late on a Sunday afternoon.

Deciding to take a chance, Evelyn asked if she might be permitted to see the rock that was being held in evidence as the potential murder weapon. This request resulted in some confusion. No one present appeared to know what might have become of that rock.

"We probably can't show you that rock anyway," one deputy informed them. "It's evidence. The sheriff would have to give his okay. You need to come back when he's here." No one present claimed to know when, precisely, that would be.

"Come back on a weekday when our girl is here," a younger deputy suggested. "She'd be the one to know where that rock is anyway."

An older deputy appeared in the door to another room, hitched his pants up, and came to the front counter. Evelyn took a step back. The deputy, Calhoun his name tag read, gave her a black look.

Oh, well, in for a penny, in for a pound, she decided. He'd probably refuse to answer, but she plowed ahead anyway. She took a quick breath and asked if he had any idea what the motive was alleged to be for Rafael to have murdered his own brother.

Chapter Fourteen

From his position behind the counter, Deputy Calhoun tightened his lips and squinted at Evelyn. "You're friends with the Pacheco family, aren't you?"

"We've only just met," Evelyn said, which was close to true. "We're private investigators, and we've been hired by the Pachecos to conduct an investigation of this murder as a professional matter."

Flora pulled one of their handsome business cards from her pocketbook and placed it in front of Calhoun, who took his time reading the three words printed on it.

"Well," he said, "you might not want to jump to any hasty conclusions on this case. Those two boys may have been brothers, but they had plenty of disagreements about labor contracting. A lot of those farmworkers thought Rafael was getting altogether too chummy with the growers and pocketing more than his share of their wages. And Joaquin had other ideas. If Rafael didn't do the deed himself, he had one of his friends do it for him. You want to be careful, ma'am. You're not getting the whole story from your new friends, is all I'm saying. And about the charges against that Mexican, you'd do better to come back on a weekday. Our girl is off today. She'll know where the paperwork is on that."

Maintaining her most polite and patient demeanor, Evelyn thanked the deputy, and promised they would be back on Monday. As they made their way to the Chevrolet, Flora slipped her arm through Evelyn's elbow and leaned in.

"That certainly gives us something new to think about, doesn't it?" she said.

"Indeed, it does, and that is exactly what I was afraid might happen if I let myself get dragged into this situation."

"You mean that you would make assumptions not supported by evidence and based on biased information?"

"Precisely."

Flora gazed across the highway for a moment, then looked at Evelyn. "Not to be contrary, but what the deputy said just now? Undoubtedly the sheriff believes those stories about conflict between Rafael and his brother, and that's likely what led him to arrest Rafael, but that doesn't make him correct."

"Ah, you're right about that. So we have a missing piece in our puzzle?"

"It would seem so, and more than one. And I don't know, of course, but I'd be willing to bet their 'girl' might be able to clear up some of these questions for us tomorrow." Flora made quote marks in the air with her fingers as she said the word girl. "Doesn't their girl have a name?" They joined Bernice in the automobile followed shortly by Marisol and her aunt, openly weeping.

Marisol patted Tia's hand. "We'll telephone Father Bertrand just as soon as we get you home. He should have returned from taking care of his affairs by now."

Tia's face scrunched into an angry scowl. "Shame on you! You know very well priests do not have affairs."

"Oh!" Marisol said. "I only meant…"

"Never mind what you meant." Tia folded both arms across her bosom and huffed. "*Dios mio*, you girls are the ones to talk."

The remainder of the trip from the county jail to the Pachecos' hacienda passed in silence. Evelyn pulled in behind Bernice's Tin Lizzie. As they drew to a stop, a large man, his skin darkened and wrinkled by a lifetime working in the sun, approached the Chevrolet and doffed his straw hat, holding it in weathered hands. Peering at Tia Rosamaria, he spoke in a kind tone in Spanish, bringing tears to her eyes. He helped her out and led her under the arbor toward the entry, holding her close with one arm around her shoulders. The others watched in silence.

Marisol slid from her seat and began thanking everyone for their help. She announced she had decided to stay over one more night with her aunt. A second aunt and a cousin were expected to arrive from Martinez before supper, but Marisol thought it best that she stay the additional night. She continued her chatter as she closed the automobile door. Her abrupt communication, and speedily delivered thank you made it clear that Evelyn and Flora could depart without any further ado. Marisol leaned against the passenger door for a moment, preventing Bernice from opening it.

"You should go on home, too," she said. "I'll make arrangements to get another shift at the hospital later this week. Tomorrow one of my cousins can take me to the ferry when I'm ready, or I can take the train from Martinez. The key for your flivver is in the ignition." Without waiting for a reply, she headed under the arbor toward the hacienda.

Startled by Marisol's hasty departure, Evelyn sprinted after her and caught her arm just before she disappeared. Flora and Bernice waited while Evelyn spoke urgently, but in quiet tones to Marisol.

"She's telling Marisol that Joaquin was killed by a gunshot," Flora told Bernice. "And that an autopsy will be preformed tomorrow."

"Oh," Bernice said. "That's going to upset everyone."

"I hope she's also reminding Marisol that, as investigators, we'll need access to as much information as the family has, or can get."

Bernice seemed not to have heard Flora. She said in a tight voice, "What a fine kettle of fish. Marisol better be careful. She can't miss even one shift at the hospital or she'll be fired. Jobs are too precious these days, even for highly skilled nurses."

Evelyn returned to the Chevrolet, smiled, she hoped in a consoling way, and began to help Bernice transfer her things from Walter's automobile to her Ford. Flora handed over her last clean hanky.

"I'm sorry you gals got dragged into this mess," Bernice said. "Didn't turn out the way I thought it would, you know?"

Evelyn patted her friend's shoulder. "Nonsense. We're always glad to be able to help, you know that."

"Yes," Flora added, leaning closer. "We're only sorry it turned out the way it did for...well, for all of you."

Bernice shook her head, anger flashing in her eyes. Keeping her voice low, she said, "Tell me, why is it our friendships always take a backseat to family? We live under the same roof. Aren't we as good as family? Evidently not, huh? Not even in our own hearts."

Evelyn continued to pat, but there didn't seem to be anything more to say, at least not at that time and place. Bernice shook her head again, and let herself into her driver's seat.

"Hold your horses!" Evelyn called, dashing back to the Chevy and digging in her pocketbook. She came up with a white envelope, waving it as she trotted to Bernice's window. "Don't forget this! And thanks again." Evelyn returned to climb in beside Flora.

"What was that?" Flora asked.

"It's a surprise."

"Ooh, I love surprises." Flora said this in a tone that indicated she was not, at the moment, enchanted with this one. "What's the surprise?"

Evelyn mimed locking her lips with a key.

"You are aware, I'm sure, it will be as much of a surprise if you tell me now, as it will be if you make me wait. And if you tell me now, you won't have to suffer me being grumpy in the meantime."

"Oh, very well. Since she'll be back in the city this week, Bernice is going to the box office to buy us tickets to see Helen Woods Jones and the women's jazz band, International Sweethearts of Rhythm, at the Majestic Hall auditorium. You've been saying how much you wanted to see them in person. It'll be a sell-out for sure, so I want to be certain we get seats."

"Oh, that is a wonderful surprise, Evie! Oh, my! See? Now I'll have weeks to be excited and look forward." Flora hugged Evelyn's arm and bounced a little on the Chevy's seat.

They made the turn onto the westbound highway and continued homeward.

"Say, who was that fellow with Tia just now?" Flora asked. "Surely he wasn't the elusive Father Bertrand."

"No. I think Marisol said his name is Luis. He's the foreman...or something like that. She said he's handling the labor contracting while Rafael is locked up."

"Humph. He's definitely handling something," Flora said with a smirk, and they both chuckled. Flora slid nearer to Evelyn and curled close.

"I feel so sad for Bernice," Flora said. "I know she gets on my last nerve sometimes, but what Tia said, calling her a witch. What's more, Marisol had no reason to treat Bernice so badly, and in front of other people, too. Did you notice, neither Marisol nor Tia so much as thanked Bernice for the use of her automobile?"

Evelyn knew that any breach of common courtesy was a serious offense in Flora's book. Flora sighed deeply, then sat up straighter. "What's that up ahead? All those cars?"

A ramshackle collection of ancient automobiles and pickup trucks lined both sides of the highway, and the orchard on the right bustled with workers dressed in tattered clothing and broad-brimmed hats. Each worker hauled a loaded sack slung over one shoulder toward a wagon with a scales mounted on it. Some of the burlap sacks were so full the workers could hardly stand up under the weight, and sweat poured down their faces as they struggled to hoist the sacks up to the scales.

"Look," Flora said. "There are women and even children working."

As soon as a worker's load was weighed, a notation made by the man on the wagon, and the peaches poured into waiting bushel baskets, each worker was handed an empty sack and they trotted away to disappear again under the trees.

"No wonder they're sweating," Evelyn said. "They have to work so fast, and in this heat, too."

"I wonder if these are the people who work for Rafael," Flora said. "They don't look like those Vigilantes."

"How much do you think they're getting paid for that back-breaking work? And on a Sunday, too."

"Not enough," Flora said. "Not nearly enough." She turned a sorrowful face to her friend. "And to think, these are the jobs they're all fighting to get."

Evelyn lowered her brow. "Almost everyone is having a hard time these days. Still, it makes me so angry to see people being abused like that for their labor. That's as bad as animals are treated. And when I think, as soon as Rafael is released, the sheriff will arrest one of these probably equally innocent souls instead." She accelerated again and went back to navigating the winding highway.

Flora shuddered and returned to snuggling. "We'll be making another trip out here to buy fruit and bring Rafael a book or two tomorrow. It wouldn't be out of our way to give Marisol a lift to the ferry landing in Alameda, right?"

"Um-hum."

They rode in silence for a short time. Then Flora said, "Do you know what I think?"

Evelyn waited a moment, then pulled away and gave her friend the fish eye "I so rarely have even the slightest idea what you think, Flora, dear. What do you think?"

"Well, what about the possibility that the good Father might really be having a romantic affair?"

Evelyn gave a bark of amusement. "If I'm not mistaken, that sort of thing is frowned on among Catholic clergy. And on a Sunday afternoon when he's supposed to be available to conduct weddings and view deceased parishioners?"

"Perhaps his lover has to work on weekdays."

Evelyn drew a long, deep breath. "That's not impossible, I suppose, but not everything is a mystery, Flora. Father Bertrand may have a perfectly reasonable explanation for his absence this afternoon."

Flora shrugged. "Well, since it's not impossible, and you know what Conan Doyle says..."

"Once you eliminate the impossible, whatever remains, no matter how improbable, must be the truth? Technically speaking I believe it was Holmes who said that, but you are correct. However improbable it might be, it's not impossible that Father Bertrand may be involved in..."

"...something he shouldn't be."

"And you're suggesting whatever he's involved in may have something to do with what happened to Joaquin?" Evelyn said.

Flora shrugged, leaving the question in the air.

"I can't say as I follow your reasoning, Flora, but I'll keep an open mind. I do have to say, for my money, Father Bertrand must have a very good excuse for disappearing on a Sunday afternoon. After all, it is his job to be available to his flock when needed."

"You know," Flora said, "this bit about the Father disappearing is like one of those puzzle pieces that's the wrong color or shape to fit into the puzzle one is working on, as though someone misplaced the piece into the wrong box. Perhaps it isn't intended to belong to our puzzle at all."

"An interesting thought, Flora. Interesting indeed."

Chapter Fifteen

Evelyn's mind wandered back to that morning on the beach when she'd lost patience with Bernice's prying into their personal lives. Could that have happened just this morning? She knew she was going to have to confess to Flora what she'd told Bernice. Evelyn glanced sideways at Flora, who was behaving in a loving manner, and even expressing some sympathy for Bernice. This might be the perfect time to confess. Still, Evelyn fervently wished she'd not let Bernice get under her skin and that she'd kept her mouth shut. She resolved to talk to Flora the minute they'd made it safely through the dark tunnel just ahead.

She got a bit of a reprieve. When they arrived at the tunnel entrance, a late model Nash was stopped in the lane, waiting for an eastbound automobile to clear the narrow passageway. They finally had their turn through and the lights of Oakland and Berkeley spread out below them, just beginning to come on with the approaching dusk. Evelyn knew the time she dreaded had come.

She interrupted Flora's drowsy humming. "I need to tell you something."

Flora stopped humming and sat up straighter. "Conversations that begin 'I need to tell you something' often end up being awkward."

Evelyn continued. "I need to tell you I said something earlier today. Something likely to turn out to have been unwise."

"How about if you stop beating around the bush so loquaciously and simply tell me what you said? Does it have something to do with Bernice?"

"Well, yes, in fact it does. I'm afraid I let Bernice get my goat, and I replied in an unwise manner."

Flora remained silent as she gazed at Evelyn.

"Do you remember on the beach this morning when Bernice was asking, as she so often does, about our lives together? And you said, 'for the love of Pete' and got up and wandered off?"

"Yes…"

"Well, after you got up, she kept pestering me, and I'm afraid…"

"Yes, I know, you said something unwise. What did you say?"

This wasn't going quite as smoothly as Evelyn had hoped it might. "Well, Bernice was implying, as she does sometimes, that perhaps we might not have quite as…well, let's say we might not be as warm as we might be."

"You and I?"

"Yes, you and I, and you must understand, I simply lost my patience—"

"As I am about to do if you don't get to the point."

"I told her not to worry and that everything was as warm as could be. In fact, I'm afraid I described you as a 'minx.'"

"A minx? What a curious thing to say."

"Yes, indeed it was curious. I'm not at all certain what came over me. In any case, that's it. That's all that was said. The minute the word was out, I joined you and that was the end of it."

Flora made no immediate reply but Evelyn was fairly certain that would not be the end of the discussion. As it turned out, she didn't need to wait long for the suspense to be over.

They arrived safely back at Walter's, fed and played with the dogs, then sat in the parlor, their feet propped on the hassock, to gather strength for the task of preparing supper.

Evelyn had hardly taken a full breath when Flora said, "Did you really describe me as a minx? What is a minx, anyway? Are you sure you didn't call me a manx?"

"No. A manx is a type of cat, if I'm not mistaken. Why would I describe you as a cat?"

"I'm sure I don't know. I don't know why you felt the need to describe me as anything at all."

Evelyn tried to think of a way to change the subject quickly, as Flora's tone was taking on that edge that meant Evelyn was on the verge of getting into trouble.

Flora went on. "What is a minx, anyway? You must know what it means if you used the word."

"Um...why don't we look it up? I'm sure Walter has a dictionary here somewhere..."

Evelyn's stalling tactics were in vain when Flora went off in search of a dictionary and returned a few moments later toting a heavy tome. "Here we go," she said. "Let's look up minx, shall we?"

Evelyn began to get a trapped feeling, but there was no going back. Together they bent over the dictionary while Flora ran one well-manicured nail down the column of tiny print.

"Oh, look. Here's a mink. Did you mean to describe me as a mink? They are kind of weasel-y," she said, gazing at the illustration. "But they do have beautiful fur. No, not a mink? Okay, here we are, minx, 'a pert girl.' Well, that's not so bad."

Evelyn almost let go of the breath she was holding. Then Flora continued reading. "It also says 'a wanton woman.' A wanton woman? Really, Evelyn?"

"That's not what I meant. I think I meant the first one. The pert girl."

Flora huffed. "What does that mean, exactly?"

"Why don't you look up the word pert?" Evelyn's voice was beginning to fade, and she looked anxiously at the door to the kitchen. "Aren't you hungry? We should whip up some supper here soon."

"Pert, it says 'saucily free and forward, flippantly cocky and assured'. Hmm. Are you sure that's what you meant, dear?"

"I may have misused the word," Evelyn said, feeling it would be better to claim to have made a mistake than to admit to a degree of honesty that would upset her friend.

Flora pretended to pull reading glasses lower on her nose and gave Evelyn a long stare. "Really? It's not like you to misuse a word. You are an educated woman, Evelyn." She went back to reading while Evelyn squirmed.

"It goes on, 'being trim and chic'. That fits, I suppose, or it did when I was younger and had more money." Flora went back to reading. "'Jaunty, like a little hat, piquantly stimulating'. What is piquantly?"

"I don't know," Evelyn said, a sinking feeling in the pit of her empty stomach. She only had a vague notion what the word meant, although she was certain she would soon learn its exact definition.

"Let's see here, piquant...ah, 'engagingly provocative'. Hmm. That does sound a bit risque, perhaps even suggestive. Not sure why you would describe me using those terms."

"Technically, I didn't describe you in that term, that is to say piquant."

"True. So much for a pert girl. Let's go back and look up this other meaning, a wanton woman."

"Why don't we quit while we're ahead?" Evelyn suggested, moving toward the kitchen and the previously mentioned supper.

"You mean while you're ahead," Flora said, still reading. "Listen to this, 'wanton, a pampered person, one given to lewd or lascivious flirtation.'" Flora's tone had taken on that edge again, although whether a tone of anger or only one of amusement, Evelyn couldn't tell. "Is that what you meant to say, Evelyn, dear?" Flora said these words to the blank side of the kitchen door as it swung shut. Discretion being the better part of valor, Evelyn had disappeared inside.

When she poked her head out a quarter of an hour later to announce she'd prepared a supper of hard-boiled eggs and buttered toast, with sliced peaches in cream, Flora was still absorbed in the dictionary.

"Gracious," Evelyn said. "What are you looking at now?"

"Oh, I got distracted. Don't you love dictionaries? One word leads you to another... Do you know what a parbuckle is?"

"No, I don't believe I do."

"See! Next time we do a crossword, I'll have such an advantage."

Evelyn was not entirely out of the woods. As Flora meandered toward the kitchen, she said, "All the same, Evie, dear...I know Bernice can sometimes be a trial, but in the future, I'll thank you not to use her provocations as an excuse to malign my character and impugn my reputation."

Evelyn smiled mischievously as she handed Flora her napkin. "Oh, I thought I was only enhancing your reputation, dear, and adding intrigue."

Flora cocked one highly skeptical eyebrow in reply.

"I do catch your drift, however," Evelyn said. "and I promise I will try to control my irritation with Bernice going forward.

Seemingly out of the blue, over supper, Flora said, "I believe I may do some shopping while we're here. Perhaps at that new Capwell's store in downtown Oakland."

Flora indulged her eye for fashion often, and shopping was one of her favorite pastimes. Evelyn wasn't surprised to hear her say she wished to visit the large department store.

"Are you looking for anything in particular?" Evelyn asked.

"Or I might wait and walk to the millinery on Lombard when we get home. I want a new hat, and perhaps Gussie can make up just the one I want using my own design. Out of felt, I should think."

"Oh, like a slouch hat? You have so many of those already."

"No, slouches are going out of style. You know, the way they make one look sort of down at the mouth. A slouch speaks to the ennui of the economic depression. What I want is a jaunty little hat. You know what I mean?"

Evelyn kept her mouth closed, sensing a trap.

"Something jaunty, like what Robin Hood might wear."

"A pert hat?"

"Yes, a pert hat. I'll wear it next time we see Bernice and Marisol."

Evelyn didn't risk a smart remark in reply, but only busied herself cleaning up the supper dishes.

Over breakfast Monday morning they reviewed their reasons for making a third trip out to Walnut Creek. Among these was the need to purchase quantities of peaches and apricots for jam-making.

"What about this for the peaches?" Flora said as she emerged from the pantry carrying a paperboard box large enough to accommodate a small child.

"Good grief! How many peaches are you planning to buy?"

"I thought we were going to make jam. If we're to make jam, Bernice says we'll need lots of peaches."

"Do you know how to make jam?" Evelyn had never known Flora to make jam before and she tried not to sound as skeptical as she felt. Flora may not have had much training in the culinary arts but in Evelyn's experience once Flora had set her mind to something, she could accomplish pretty much anything she tried.

Flora narrowed her eyes. "I watched Jaing do it once. I think one simply washes and peels the fruit, and then lets it cook it until it's…well, jammy."

"There's some sugar involved at some point," Evelyn said. "I seem to remember Mama putting in water and sugar. And it comes out to be quite a lot of jam. You have to put it in jars. Do we have any jars? And they have to be sealed in some way, so the jam doesn't spoil."

"Oh, dear, this does begin to sound more complicated than I thought."

"We're going to have to telephone Mama for instructions," Evelyn said.

"Didn't she teach you to make jam when you were a girl?"

"Mama wanted to teach me all sorts of things in the kitchen, but I told her I was going to be a career girl and wouldn't need to cook."

"I imagine that gave Mama quite a good laugh."

"An uproarious one, indeed," Evelyn said. "I wonder where we got the idea career girls wouldn't need to eat?"

"Or sew and alter clothing. I've been thinking about calling your Mama to get some instruction on how to let the seam out on that blue dress. Perhaps we both could have paid a bit more attention to how things work when we were girls. Now we have to call Mama every time we get stuck."

"That's true," Evelyn said, and laughed. "I suppose we should thank our lucky stars my mother is always at the other end of the telephone line when we can't figure something out on our own."

"Yes, we should! Your Mama is a wonderful resource for information about almost everything."

"Almost everything," Evelyn said and winked at Flora.

"We might also think about purchasing walnuts and almonds for Jaing, today," Flora said. "You know she bakes those wonderful delicate Chinese cookies with nuts."

"Don't nuts ripen in the fall?"

"Oh. Well, how was I to know? Okay, so we're making the trip to buy peaches that we're not entirely certain we know what to do with?"

"We're also going because I want to talk with Rafael and ask him some questions. And you promised you'd take him a book."

"Oh, yes, I'd almost forgotten. I should go see what we have here that he might enjoy."

"And as you suggested, we might stop on the return trip and see if we can give Marisol a ride to the ferry."

"An excellent and thoughtful idea. Shall we take a picnic, too? We may be out there a while."

"Smashing idea, if you want to pack the picnic. If we're going to sit in the automobile all day, let's take the dogs for a good long walk before we go. That way, they'll stay out of trouble until we return."

Chapter Sixteen

They leashed up both rambunctious terriers and headed toward the Alameda shoreline at a brisk pace. Walter's dog Spike appeared not to have had the benefit of the rigorous leash-training Spritz had enjoyed at Flora's able hand. Spike dashed, first right, then left, then spun the leash in a circle, effectively hog-tying Evelyn. They made better progress when Flora shortened Spike's leash and periodically corrected him as they went along.

"Where are we going, anyway?" Flora said, gazing at the industrial area. Abandoned warehouses loomed over the pot-holed street to their right, while granite rocks and gravely beaches spotted with piles of drying seaweed lined the shoreline to their left, the air scented with rotting matter.

"As far as we can, I suppose," Evelyn said. "This may be part of what Walter says used to be the town called Encinal."

Flora looked around. "It's hard to believe there were ever coastal oak trees here isn't it? That's what the word *encinal* means in Spanish, coastal oaks. Our school janitor taught me that. He lives on Encinal Street in San Francisco."

"Señor Alvarez has taught you quite a few words in Spanish, hasn't he?"

"I ask a lot of questions. I think one should be able to speak a few words at least, of every language one might encounter. Please, and thank you, and the like."

A loud blowing sound to their right distracted them. A moment later, the rounded top of a hot air balloon rose into sight from behind a brick warehouse. The whoosh of its ignitor heating more air filled the morning sky. "Oh, that must be coming from the airdrome," Flora said. "That balloon must be war surplus." They watched in silence as the giant gray balloon lifted halfway above a roofline, where it stopped, tethered by long ropes.

"Walter told me there's a big airdrome just a few blocks over that way," Flora said. "He didn't mention hot air balloons, but he said it might be possible to catch a ride on a dirigible. Just for a quick pleasure trip, you understand, if we were to go over there."

"Did he now?"

"Yes. He said there's even a commercial airship terminal there. And something called The Air Ferry is going to begin commuter flights from Alameda to San Francisco soon. If we want to try it, there's already air service from Oakland to San Francisco, although the fare is a dollar fifty each way."

"Hmm." Evelyn didn't share Flora's excitement.

"Just imagine, Evie, flying on an airship all the way back to Philadelphia in a matter of hours, instead of taking that interminable train trip." Flora glanced at the skeptical expression on her friend's face. "I'm guessing you don't find the idea of a ride on an airship appealing?"

Evelyn didn't want to be a spoil sport. Still, even a short ride on a vehicle where she couldn't see, or even imagine, its means of support was more than she could stomach. "How about if we wait a few months...or years...until the mechanics can fully test dirigibles and airships, and work out all the potential flaws first?"

"Phooey," Flora muttered in a soft voice.

They stayed back from the rocky shoreline, reeking as it did of rotting seaweed and dead fish. The detritus posed a disaster waiting to happen for two curious terriers, excited about the opportunity to roll in anything smelly.

As they approached the edge of the island of Alameda, San Francisco's skyline came into view, shimmering through the morning mist that hung over the bay waters. From this distance, the gleaming-white city seemed island-like, cut off from the other cities scattered in a wide circle around the edges of the bay.

Despite their surroundings, neither could let their thoughts wander far from the crimes they'd been hired to investigate.

"Have you had any new thoughts, Evelyn, about who might have killed Joaquin, or why? When it was only vandalism we said we'd take it one step at a time, but I wonder about that approach since the situation appears to be getting us slowly into hotter and hotter water."

"That's a good question. It's a bit like quicksand, isn't it?" Evelyn stroked her chin with a thumb as she considered her answer. "We agreed to collect evidence leading to the release of Rafael, and with the evidence that Joaquin was killed by a gunshot, and from a gun Rafael likely does not possess, the sheriff might no longer have any reason to hold Rafael."

"You were the one responsible for finding that bullet. I knew you'd be able to help. If the sheriff does release Rafael, does that mean our job is done?"

"That's a big 'if' though. So far, evidence of the gunshot has not been enough to give Rafael his freedom. It's possible the best way to get Rafael out of jail and not have some other innocent person charged might be for us to find the real murderer. As you can tell, I have become intrigued with the circumstances surrounding the crime."

"That is a curious puzzle." Flora nodded thoughtfully. "A shot to the back of the head, execution-style, and delivered from a short distance away. That was no accident, right? Someone did that intentionally."

"Yes, I expect you're correct about that. Someone either forced Joaquin to turn around and stand still, however that was done, or surprised him from behind."

Flora stopped walking, one hand over her mouth. "Oh, that just makes me sick to think about."

"Me, too."

Flora was quiet for a moment. "It seems to me that someone would have heard a gunshot fired in the orchard. Farmworkers, or the people living in the Pachecos' barn, or even Rafael out searching for his brother. I shouldn't think gunfire is a common enough occurrence that the sound wouldn't attract someone's attention."

"Good point. He may have been shot indoors and his body moved later to the orchard."

"What are the odds, do you think, we could get someone to direct us to the place where Joaquin's body was found?"

"Do you mean so we could judge for ourselves the likelihood Joaquin had been killed there or somewhere else entirely?"

"That's what I was thinking. Or even see how much blood was shed there. Do we know anyone who could tell us where they found him?"

"Good question, dear. Let's think about that. Here's another clue," Evelyn said, appreciating her friend's insights. "The shot came from a specific kind of gun, one that's not common and not that many people own. It was a .38 Special, a revolver, made by Colt."

"You're saying, if we could find a person who owns that model of gun...?"

"Or has access to that gun."

"Yes. First we should confirm that Rafael does not have a gun like that, or anyone in his family either, or any of his pals."

"Good thought," Evelyn said. "Let's add that to the list of questions we want to ask Rafael. And we also want to ask if any of these so-called Vigilantes carry a weapon matching that description."

"First we'd have to find one of those Vigilantes who'll talk to us. And couldn't any one of those people simply lie about owning or having access to such a revolver? How could we know for sure, short of finding the actual weapon involved?"

"More good questions, my dear. There are getting to be so many guns in the world, mere possession of that type of weapon would not be incriminating beyond any doubt."

"It would also be helpful to find someone with a motive."

"Yes, someone with both that gun, and a plausible reason to want Joaquin dead. That would be a more convincing suspect than someone with either of those alone."

"And when thinking about a motive," Flora said, "don't you think an execution like that...don't you think that could indicate some kind of personal vengeance?"

"Inflicted by someone who had something specific against Joaquin?"

"Yes, or wanted to punish him. Something like that?"

They walked on in silence for a few moments, contemplating.

Flora stopped again and turned to Evelyn. "In your considered opinion, was Joaquin's death intentional?"

"That much seems clear. However hot-blooded, spur-of-the-moment the shooting might have been, it was an intentional act, followed by an effort to hide the crime. Whoever did this decided not to try to hide the body, always a risky business, but instead to disguise the cause and place of death, and thus, presumably, at the very least, delay the identification of the killer."

"Perhaps giving the killer time to get away or go into hiding. Do you think there might be more than one person involved?"

"Hmm," Evelyn gazed into the misty distance. "You may very well be correct, my dear. I hadn't thought about that."

"Obviously only one person shot Joaquin, but there could have been any number of people involved in carrying the body to the orchard and staging the scene. And you know what? If we ask to be directed to where the body was found, anyone who can give us the correct answer would then be suspect in the placing of the body...at least in my mind."

"That's true. Or what if one person shot Joaquin and then later calmed down and took his body to the orchard," Evelyn suggested.

"Not two people, but one person in two moods?" Flora nodded. "This theory also requires a place, not the orchard, but another place where the shooting happened. If we could find that place..."

"Although it has been well over twenty-four hours now, so a good deal of cleaning up could have been done," Evelyn reminded her friend. "The place where Joaquin was shot may remain forever unknown."

Both dogs were pulling at their leads, and the ladies resumed their stroll.

"Well, Sherlock Holmes, we need to find someone with the means, that is possession of a .38 Special revolver, a motive, or reason to murder Joaquin, and the opportunity, meaning a private place in which to strike the fatal blow. And also they'd need a way to get the body out to the orchard without being seen."

"Yes," Evelyn agreed. "As I said, the most effective way to exonerate Rafael may be to find who really did kill Joaquin. What with the politics of the labor situation and the sheriff department's apparent bias, we might be the only ones willing to search for the real murderer."

"Very well," Flora said. "The hunt is on. We should begin with a list of possible suspects." She stopped and scanned the shoreline ahead. "Do you see that shack up there? And look, there's another one just beyond? It's hazy, but you can see more of them down closer to the water. Do you see those?" She pointed.

"Oh, dear."

"What?"

"I think that must be one of those Hoovervilles that are

springing up everywhere. We should probably turn back."

"That's so sad," Flora said. "Such a dismal place for those poor people who've lost their homes. And what do they do for clean water and sanitation? Do you think President Hoover will be re-elected this year? I can't think of anyone except my father who supports him or his policies."

"It looks like the Democrats are going to nominate Governor Franklin Roosevelt at their convention in Chicago next week. He says all the right things about creating jobs and helping people. Still, I'm not sure anyone could pull us out of this terrible economic slowdown."

They turned toward home, still chatting.

Flora said, "I'm certain my father would take issue, but at least Roosevelt wants to try something new, and he wants to get the whole federal government involved in helping the country recover. I think we should trust him."

They'd reached the place where Evelyn wanted to cross the broad empty avenue. She stopped Flora with a hand, a usual but unnecessary gesture since the wide street with its abandoned warehouses and closed store fronts carried no traffic.

"I'm inclined to agree," Evelyn said. "Roosevelt seems to understand the working class, but he comes from money, you know."

"Doesn't every politician, especially the ones who want to be president? I simply don't see Hoover doing anything to help anyone except bankers and people who already have more than their share."

Flora packed a hearty lunch and Evelyn stowed their picnic basket on the rear seat next to the empty paperboard box intended for peaches. They climbed aboard, ready for another trip to the sweet valley on the other side of the tunnel. This time, both wore light-weight cotton day dresses to accommodate the afternoon heat, and brimmed hats to protect from the brilliant sun. Evelyn backed out of the garage and they were off.

Chapter Seventeen

As they waited at the signal for their turn to enter the Posey Tube, Evelyn pointed in the distance to her right. "You know, over there on the estuary there's a huge Del Monte fruit processing plant. We could pick up canned peaches by the crate there, if we should so desire."

Flora rolled her eyes and shook her head. "What would your Mama think, hearing you suggest we buy tinned fruit instead of canning our own, nice and fresh."

"Oh, I couldn't agree more. It's only, I'm still concerned we really don't have any idea how to do this, not to mention if we even have everything we'll need. Canning food can be dangerous if you don't know what you're doing."

"Don't worry so. We'll call Mama tomorrow morning, and she'll set us right."

Evelyn tried to dismiss her misgivings. The drive to Walnut Creek was a peaceful one, the two-lane highway winding through oak woodlands, then acres of walnut orchards, peaches, and pears. The almond orchards were still sporting white puffs of blossoms, and even in mid-June, a bit of water remained burbling in the creek alongside the highway.

They passed the fruit stand at Acalanes Road and Evelyn slowed for a good look. In the late morning, the board front was propped open, and a few of the wooden boxes displayed fruit. A small dark man slouched alone in the shadows at the rear. He'd pulled his *sombrero* low and appeared to be sleeping.

"That doesn't look very inviting," Flora said. "It looks almost sinister."

"We'll stop on the way back," Evelyn said. "Possibly there'll be more produce here by then, and more customers. We don't want our fruit sitting on the back seat in the sun all day anyway. We'll run our errands and have our picnic before we buy fruit."

Evelyn was half-hoping Rafael would already have been released by the time they arrived at the county jail. Instead, they were asked to sit and wait while one of the deputies brought Rafael to the small interview room.

"What's that you've brought Rafael to read?"

Flora showed Evelyn the garish cover of *Tarzan the Terrible* by Edgar Rice Burroughs. "I found it in Wally's room. This one is already well-read and worn a bit. I've been wanting to start buying the boys the whole set. We could get them several for Christmas and then another one or two every year for their birthdays or Christmas gifts."

"Gracious, how many are there?"

"Around fourteen, I think. And he keeps writing them. Shows no sign of slowing down. If my scheme works, we could be set for gifts for the boys until they go off to college."

"You know," Evelyn said, "if I were you I'd be careful about how much poking around in that eleven-year-old boy's bedroom I'd do."

Flora turned a wide-eyed stare to Evelyn. "Whatever do you mean?" Flora did have one brother, but he was seven years older, and they had never been close. Evelyn had Walter, four years older, and three stair-step younger brothers, all of whom had gotten into one kind of mischief or another. Evelyn knew a good deal more about growing boys than she really cared to know.

She smiled, considering which of her experiences she could share with her friend. Flora was certainly no longer the innocent girl she had been when they first met, but Evelyn would still not describe her friend as worldly-wise.

Flora broke into Evelyn's musings. "On the topic of secrets boys might keep, I've been thinking about how little we've really learned about Rafael. We've seen now, for example, how his workers are treated. A bit more inquiry into his life, at least his business life might be in order, in my opinion—"

"Ladies?" the deputy called, interrupting the question Flora had been formulating. Evelyn was left to wonder what they might find, should they decide to conduct future explorations into Rafael's possible motives.

The deputy ushered them into the windowless interview room where Rafael sat, his hands cuffed together in his lap. Marisol's cousin looked somewhat the worse for wear, appearing exhausted, unshaven, and attired in a rumpled blue work shirt and baggy war surplus trousers. Dark circles underlined his eyes. Even in his mid-twenties, he looked to have aged a decade since they'd seen him the day before.

"We're sorry to see you're still here," Evelyn said. "I was given to understand you would be released as soon as the coroner completed his...paperwork. Has anyone told you when you might be able to go home?"

Rafael gazed earnestly at Evelyn. "No," he said, and shook his head. "They told me Miss Winslow found the bullet. That's you, yes? Joaquin was shot, but I didn't do it. *Además*, besides, I have a good alibi. I will be home by tonight, God willing." He forced a thin smile.

Under the watchful eye of the deputy propped against the back wall, Flora leaned closer. "We're shocked at what has happened to you, being arrested like this, and we're so sorry about the death of your brother."

"Yes, we are," Evelyn said, gazing at him in sorrow.

A worn-out expression returned to Rafael's face. He tried to rub his forehead with one hand shackled to the other, then gave up.

"Gracious," Evelyn said. "Can't they at least take those horrible medieval things off?"

"They only put them on me while I have visitors," he said. To Evelyn's ear, his tone was laden with sarcasm and disgust. "It's to prevent me from overpowering you helpless ladies, or making a daring escape."

Evelyn raised her eyebrows, but had no idea how to respond to such nonsense. "Oh. Well, I would like to ask you a question or two, if you don't mind? We'll make it snappy, in order to get you out of those things as quickly as possible."

"*Bueno.*" Rafael nodded.

"We're hoping to learn something that might help us find the person who really killed your brother."

Evelyn realized that, after expressing initial reluctance she had come to feel more inclined to pursue the murder investigation. She glanced at Flora who shared her smile, doubtless also noting the change.

"I don't know much," Rafael said. "I was home most of that night. I visited with Marisol in the evening. We all went to bed at almost midnight. Mama came to wake me at two in the morning, crying about Joaquin still not home. He gets into trouble sometimes, but always he comes home by that time, no later. I woke up *mis amigos* from the barn. Two guys, Luis and Martín. I was with those two guys the whole time we searched, but we didn't find Joaquin. We knocked on doors, woke up many people asking after my brother. It was four thirty or so when I got home. Marisol was up to meet me. I went to sleep until it would be a decent hour to start searching again. The deputies came around seven to arrest me. They would not say why, or hardly even what were the charges against me. That's really all I knew." He made eye contact with Evelyn and shrugged. "What else can I tell you?"

"When was the last time you saw your brother?"

Rafael scrunched his nose, making Evelyn wonder if he was staving off tears. "The last time I saw Joaquin," he said, his voice cracking. "That was Saturday after supper. He didn't come home for supper. He came after, about six? He didn't stay. He washed up and changed his shirt. You understand? *Comprendes?*"

Flora piped up. "And then he left and he didn't say where he was going? Or did you know where he was going?"

"No, not at all," Rafael said, shifting in his chair. "Joaquin always has friends, a life outside the family." Rafael shifted uncomfortably again. Evelyn could feel Flora staring at her. She didn't need to make eye contact with her friend to know what Flora was thinking. Whatever Joaquin had gone out to do, it was something he probably shouldn't have been doing.

"Joaquin certainly was a most attractive young man," Flora said. "We met him at your father's funeral."

Rafael had assumed an expression of misery, his eyes pinched almost closed, his mouth forming a grimace. It was hard to say whether his expression reflected his reaction to the topic of Joaquin's behavior, thoughts about his brother's death, or something else entirely.

"Joaquin wanted to take the truck, but I said no. Some criminal set fire to the Plymouth, you know. I told Joaquin to leave the truck at home. He must've asked someone in the barn for a ride. Later, no one would say."

Evelyn gazed at her hands, folded on the table in front of her. She thought about what other pieces of information she needed to have in order for them to assemble this puzzle. "What about that Plymouth?" she said. "Do you know, or have any idea who set that fire? Who would have a reason to do that?"

"No." Rafael shook his head again. "We all heard the explosion in the middle of the night, Friday night, but when I got out there whoever did it was gone. The guys in the barn did not see anyone either."

"Is it possible someone from the barn could have set the auto on fire…for whatever reason?"

Rafael leveled his gaze at Evelyn. "No one in the barn would do that. Those guys are *mis amigos*."

Evelyn nodded. "Is the sheriff investigating that crime?"

"Mama Rosamaria did not report that to the sheriff. You must understand, if Mama reports that, it is most likely the sheriff will arrest someone who lives in the barn, someone—"

"A friend of yours," Flora said, "or one of your employees?"

"Yeah, yeah. He would arrest one of our people instead of who really did it." Rafael bowed his head for a moment. "I will keep asking and listening. Sooner or later someone will boast, and someone else will hear and come and tell me. That's how we take care of problems like that. It's better not to even tell the sheriff."

"Let me ask you this," Evelyn continued. "More in the interest of keeping you and your family out of any additional trouble. Do you or anyone in your family own or have access to a .38 Special revolver, one made by Colt? Or do you know anyone who owns or has access to a gun like that?"

Rafael's brow furrowed. "My father owned a rifle. He passed that down to me. He used it to scare off critters. I haven't had any use for it. It's a Winchester. It's hanging over the kitchen fireplace at home if you want to see it. I don't think it's been fired, or even cleaned, since my father used it last. We have a shotgun. Mama uses that to scare the crows away from the vegetable garden and the fruit trees in our yard."

"No handguns?"

"No. What use would I have for a handgun? Those are for people who want to shoot other people, or for *policías*. No, in ordinary times, we have no use for handguns."

"And Joaquin? He also wouldn't have access to any handguns?"

"Not that I know. Joaquin can be secretive, sometimes.

Still, I think I would know if he had a gun."

Evelyn nodded slowly. She had no way of judging the accuracy of Rafael's statement.

"All right. Thank you." Evelyn glanced at Flora to see if she had any questions.

Flora looked pensive. "We've heard a rumor that you and Joaquin may have been at odds over some labor contracting practices. Is there any truth to that rumor?"

A scowl flashed across the young man's face. "No. Joaquin and I, sometimes we argue, but not over the business. He has little interest in the business anyway, and not much thought about it."

"How do you suppose that rumor got started, if there's no truth to it?"

"Yes," Evelyn said. "Who would benefit from having that rumor spread?"

Rafael gave a quick glance over his shoulder toward the deputy behind him, and leaned as close as he dared. "The sheriff and his deputies, of course. They want to arrest a farmworker, any farmworker, and I would also say...possibly protect one of their own."

The deputy's beefy hand landed hard on Rafael's shoulder.

"That's enough!" he said. "Time's up."

"Another question," Evelyn said, sending a pleading glance to the deputy, then looking back at Rafael. "The sheriff said Joaquin was found early in the morning in an orchard. A farmworker saw his body when he was on his way to work. There seems to be some question about whether Joaquin was killed right there in the orchard, or killed somewhere else and later brought there. If he didn't die in the orchard, can you think where else he might have been when he was killed?"

Chapter Eighteen

Rafael shook his head slowly, but didn't answer Evelyn's question about where Joaquin might have been when he was killed. It had not escaped Evelyn's attention that the young man consistently referred to his brother in the present tense, as though unaccepting of the fact that Joaquin had died. She hoped her question would not upset him more.

"I didn't know about Joaquin not being killed in the orchard. I thought… I thought that's where he…you understand. No, I don't know where he might have been. Any idea I had where I thought Joaquin might have gone, that's where we searched and didn't find him. Anywhere else he might have been, I don't know." Rafael's head slumped. "I don't know."

Flora reached a comforting hand toward Rafael, but the deputy shifted his weight and glared at her. She withdrew her hand, glaring right back.

Evelyn sighed. She couldn't believe she was pestering this poor suffering man, and for what, really? "One last question," she said, "and then we'll leave you in peace." The irony of her comment only struck her when she glanced again at the block walls surrounding them. She cleared her throat and started again. "Do you have any thoughts about who else we might talk to about Joaquin's whereabouts the night he died? And I do have another question, which is, do you even want our help? Or would you prefer we simply go home and let you take up the search when they release you?"

Considering Rafael had no real idea who they were, or why they were involved in this investigation at all, he might easily prefer they stop sticking their noses into what might be considered none of their business. On the other hand, Evelyn felt outrage at the injustice of first arresting a man for whom law enforcement had no incriminating evidence, and now the threat of releasing Rafael only to have them go after another equally innocent man. Her sense of injustice had drawn her into this investigation, and her tenacity compelled her to pursue it to its rightful conclusion. No matter Rafael's response to her question, she was not prepared to simply find a pretty place for a picnic, purchase the fruit they wanted, and let the Pachecos and the sheriff take over any investigating.

"You are kind," Rafael said. "If you did not ask questions, I would be on my way to state prison by now. And you ladies are so nice. People might answer your questions who would not talk to me. If you could find out whatever you can until I get out of this place, I would be thankful."

"You do know," Evelyn said, "I mean Marisol has told you, hasn't she, Miss Fitzgerald and I have been hired by your family as investigators?"

"Yes, my mother told me. We're most grateful for your help. It is too late to save Joaquin," his voice cracked again, "but any amount, whatever it costs to get me out of here."

"Of course," Flora said. "We're planning to visit the fruit stand near your hacienda today. We'd like to get some peaches for jam. Is there anyone there, or near there, we might talk to, perhaps a friend of Joaquin's who might know something?"

"Oh!" he said. "Don't go to that fruit stand. The one on the highway at Acalanes Road? Is that the one you mean?"

"Why shouldn't we go there?" Evelyn asked.

"That stand is a front for the Vigilantes, a place they

meet. The fruit there is no good anyway. Stopping there would be dangerous for you. There's another stand, a much larger one, at the edge of town here, on the other side of the road."

"You mean the one just across the highway from the coroner's office?" Evelyn said, but Rafael gave her a blank look. "Never mind," she said. "I know the place you mean."

Evelyn considered asking Rafael for a suggestion about a place to have their picnic lunch, but the contrast between their planned lovely afternoon and his present circumstances stopped her. She settled for smiling at him with sympathy and encouragement.

"We're so sorry you're still stuck here, dear," Evelyn said. "You'll be released soon, I'm sure." She turned to Flora. "Perhaps we should try to talk to the sheriff ourselves, as long as we're here?"

"Yes, that's an excellent idea," Flora said. She slid the book she'd brought with her across the table, where Rafael stared for a moment at the lurid cover.

"Thank you so much, ma'am. I never read this one. Tarzan is one of my favorites."

"Yes, apeman of the jungle," Flora said. "I'm a fan, too. I wasn't sure what you liked to read, but everyone loves Tarzan. Do you know a new movie has just been released? This one stars Johnny Weissmuller as Tarzan. You know, that Olympic swimmer?"

"Really?" A cloud crossed the young man's face. "I hope I get out in time to see it. Thank you. I have counted the cracks in the ceiling of my cell too many times."

When they asked at the front counter they were informed the sheriff was off on some official business in Martinez that Monday noon, leaving the balding Deputy Calhoun in charge again. He greeted the Misses Winslow and Fitzgerald with distrustful and narrowed eyes, then ushered them into his tiny office. The space was barely larger than the interview room in which they'd met with Rafael, although at least this room had a window. A desk took center stage, with a well broken-in rolling chair behind, and one straight-backed chair for a single visitor. Evelyn could hardly get herself squeezed in to sit down. Once she had taken the chair in the tight space, wearing a brimmed hat seemed like too much, so she lifted off her summer straw and held it in her lap.

Calhoun took his place behind the desk, his rounded belly spilling over the top, the buttons on his uniform shirt strained nearly to bursting. A second chair was brought and wedged to the side of the desk, half in the doorway. Being more inclined to want an easy escape available, Flora took the chair by the door and left her brimmed slouch firmly planted over her coiffure.

Deputy Calhoun explained that he had posed their previous day's questions to the sheriff and received permission to discuss the details of the case with them. Not knowing how long he might make himself available to answer questions raised by someone he knew only as a mere interested citizen, Evelyn decided to begin with issues Calhoun might be most able to answer. She waited only until introductions were complete, then launched right into her concerns.

"I saw the bullet that was lodged in Joaquin Pacheco's brain," she began. "The coroner informed me that bullet was fired from a .38 Special revolver. I've heard from various sources, officers employed in your department carry that type of a weapon. Is that true?" Evelyn watched as Deputy Calhoun's lips grew tighter and he pulled his head back just enough to indicate some annoyance with the topic. Her brusque tone was not winning his cooperation. She glanced at Flora, hoping her friend would catch her meaning.

"That is to say," Flora said in her most ladylike tone, "we're not for one minute suggesting that any of the sheriff's deputies might have been involved in this incident. Only trying to understand something about the weapon used. The coroner was the one who mentioned the law enforcement angle. Obviously, anyone could own the gun in question. We're only asking if your officers are issued a similar weapon." She smiled at Deputy Calhoun.

To Evelyn's astonishment, the change in tone was enough to earn a more cooperative response.

"First," he said, nodding to Flora, "we require our deputies purchase their own firearms. The meager budgets supplied by the taxpayers of this county are not sufficient to provide us with the sidearms needed to perform our duties." Evelyn made note of his grievance. One never knew when a piece of information like that might come in handy.

The deputy shifted in his creaking chair and continued. "Second, yes, we do have deputies carry .38 Specials. We like 'em to have those made by Colt, but beginning, oh, a couple years ago, we all went to the Colt pistol, not the revolver."

He then embarked on a monologue, laced with technical jargon, detailing the advantages of the Colt model .38 Special over that of a Smith & Wesson, and particularly the differences and virtues of a pistol versus a revolver. These latter virtues seemed to consist primarily of an ability to shoot more bullets in a shorter time with the pistol. The revolver had to be cocked each time a shot was fired to enable the loading of another bullet into the firing chamber.

Evelyn and Flora nodded along as he spoke, but neither gleaned much more from the deputy's tutorial than that the pistol was the preferred weapon and thus what this county's deputies carried. The revolver model that had fired the bullet into Joaquin's brain was not the weapon currently used by a deputy in his professional capacity.

Calhoun stopped talking and Flora gave him a thin smile and murmured, "Thank you."

"Yes, thank you," Evelyn said. "Also according to the coroner, Joaquin's head was bludgeoned with a large rock found later at the scene beside the body. Do you have that rock in your possession? The coroner thought the rock was being held here as possible evidence."

Deputy Calhoun held Evelyn's gaze for a long moment. "Yes, you asked about that yesterday. The sheriff told me it was okay to let you have a look at the rock. Let me ask, see if someone knows where that rock's gotten to." He made a move as though to rise from behind his desk. Seeing the impossibility of that, what with Flora and her chair blocking the doorway, he instead called out to someone in the outer office.

"Hey, kid!" he yelled. A moment later a second deputy, who looked to be about sixteen years old, poked his head in the open doorway. "We still got that rock?" Calhoun asked. "You know, the one was beside that body yesterday?"

The young deputy bobbed his head enthusiastically. "Oh, yeah, we got that right here...uh, somewhere," he said, not moving.

"Well?" Calhoun waited, then added, "You want to bring that rock in here, please?"

"Oh! Oh, yeah. Well, to be perfectly honest, sir, I don't know exactly where that rock got put...sir."

Calhoun's already red face grew even redder and his brow lowered. "Ask the girl. She'll know."

"Oh, yes, sir. Right on it, sir." The young deputy scurried away on his errand.

While they waited, Evelyn asked when Rafael might be released. Deputy Calhoun confirmed they were only waiting for the coroner's report on the autopsy.

"Yes," he said. "As I explained to you earlier, the sheriff has left me in charge. Since Mr. Pacheco has an alibi, I'll most likely be releasing him once that report gets here, as long as nothing else comes up. You can't get around the fact someone shot that boy, though, and it's up to me to find out who. With all the ruckus out there, we'll find one of those other farmworkers with the gun. I have no doubt. I told you before, they fight with each other all the time over who knows what all. It was a labor dispute, you mark my words."

Evelyn tried to erase her confused expression. "Do you

know any farmworkers who have that type of weapon? The one solid piece of evidence we have at this point is that Joaquin was shot with a weapon of that type."

"Do you know if any of those Vigilantes own such a revolver?" Flora added, in an agreeable tone.

"Yes," Evelyn said. "If it was a labor dispute as you suggest, wouldn't it be more likely that one of those Vigilantes or…someone other than another farmworker, would have been the one to have had a disagreement with Joaquin? What's the sheriff's thinking on that possibility?"

Calhoun lowered his brow again at Evelyn's barely disguised implication that a deputy might have been directly involved in the shooting. Evelyn eased back almost imperceptibly, turning one shoulder slightly in Flora's direction.

"I believe what my friend is suggesting…" Flora said, again in a sweet voice, while at the same time giving her bull-in-the-china-shop friend a reproving glance. "If Joaquin Pacheco was shot with the same type of weapon that used to be carried by the deputies, how likely is it the gun was stolen from a deputy? Or acquired by some other means? There were deputies at the riots, to keep order, correct? Perhaps in the confusion, one of those Vigilantes grabbed a gun?"

Calhoun shook his head angrily and said, "You'll pardon my saying so, but that's a ridiculous idea. I've just this moment told you our deputies carry pistols, not revolvers. In any case, you'd have to ask the sheriff himself what he's thinking. I'm not in his head. He knows about the bullet. He knows it was fired from what used to be the standard law enforcement revolver. He also knows none of his deputies are to blame, if for no other reason than the revolver is no longer the weapon carried by his deputies."

Flora nodded. "I can imagine though, for example, a few deputies may have sold their previous revolvers when the pistol became the preferred weapon in the department. If that happened, suspicion could fall on almost anyone."

"Yes, exactly." Calhoun agreed with this pretty visitor

with the sweet smile.

Evelyn listened, but with a small scowl on her face. "Or, equally likely, suspicion might fall on a retired deputy, a family member, or even on a current employee who held onto his revolver, for whatever reason."

Chapter Nineteen

The young deputy dispatched to collect the rock had returned from his errand and was leaning through the doorway. He nodded energetically. "Your dad, Calhoun! Your dad retired last year. He probably still has his revolver, doncha' think?"

Deputy Calhoun raised his eyes slowly to meet those of his young colleague. In a flat tone he said, "Is that the rock?" He reached for a box the deputy held in one hand. Evelyn and Flora's eyes met, both storing that bit of information in memory, should it turn out to be significant later.

Calhoun opened the box and the young deputy leaned over to join him in looking inside. Unable to contain themselves, both Flora and Evelyn rose slightly to peer into the box. A single hunk of granite about the size of a large fist lay in the box, encrusted with dirt and streaks of red-brown on one side.

"I see there's not much blood on this rock," Evelyn said. "Is there more on…on the other side?" She gestured her request to have the rock turned over. The young deputy obliged. Evelyn noted he was not wearing gloves, or using any other means to prevent the deposit of trace evidence of his own.

"I gather there are no fingerprints on the rock?"

"Fingerprints on a rock?" Calhoun said, sneering at

Evelyn. "I hardly think so."

"Wait," said Flora, "Look, I see a smear." An awkward moment ensued as all four tried to get their heads over the box at once. Eventually, all had taken a good look at the smear of blood on the flatter side of the rock. It would take a careful examination with a magnifying glass but the definite edge of a fingerprint was left there in blood.

"Well," Evelyn said. "That's something isn't it? That rock and the print left on it may not be connected with the gunshot or the real murderer, but a proper examination might at least reveal who tried to disguise Mr. Pacheco's death as a beating rather than a gunshot."

"Or perhaps all the injuries were inflicted by the same person," Flora said.

"Yes." Evelyn agreed. "That might indeed be the case." She turned to Calhoun. "May we rest assured, sir, that this rock and the blood smear on it will be examined for possible evidence leading to the identification of the rock wielder?"

"Of course," Calhoun said. "That's why we have it here. I'm still of a mind though, that another of the farmworkers, if not Rafael, then one of his buddies, killed Joaquin. Maybe one of those Vigilantes did the deed, but to my mind it was more likely another farmworker. We're looking for another suspect and an arrest is pending."

"I don't understand," Evelyn said. "How can an arrest be imminent if no one has any idea who killed Mr. Pacheco? You don't mean to say you have already identified a specific suspect, do you?"

Deputy Calhoun's scowl was back. "I'm not at liberty to say. Now if you'll excuse me, I need to get back to work." He stood, leaving them no alternative but to edge their way out of the narrow office.

As they continued through the larger room where all the other deputies sat at desks spilling over with file folders and loose papers, Flora dipped her head, drawing Evelyn's attention to the only other woman in the room.

"Must be 'the girl,'" Flora said in a whisper as they watched the woman standing at a filing cabinet with an armload of pages to be filed.

"Wish we could talk to her," Evelyn whispered back. "I'll bet she knows more than all of these guys combined."

Flora took Evelyn's elbow as they made their way back to the Chevrolet. "Rafael left one item off his list of why we should continue to pursue this case," Flora said.

"Yes? What's that?"

"He forgot to mention the two of us together are extraordinarily clever when it comes to working out the intricacies of a puzzle like this one."

"We are, indeed," Evelyn agreed and she enjoyed a chuckle at Flora's wisdom. "And along those lines, I wonder if you noted…" Evelyn stopped and stared at her friend. "With all our talk about the killer needing to have access to that particular type of weapon, and in front of the deputy too, the sheriff could easily plant such a revolver on an innocent farmworker for an easy frame-up."

Flora scowled. "Good to keep in mind."

They drove slowly into the town of Walnut Creek and toward Civic Park surrounding the Carnegie Library there. A short walk from the library, they found a wide oak to spread their picnic blanket under and enjoyed a filling lunch of bread, cheese, homemade pickles, and hard-boiled eggs.

They lay back for a short rest. As she gazed at the clouds sailing above the branches overhead, Evelyn realized that much of the self-doubt she'd felt about becoming involved in the search for Joaquin's assailant had been relieved. She and Flora together had gleaned valuable information and insights which had previously been ignored by those whose prejudices had blinded them to the evidence. Added to that was Evelyn's increasingly intense motivation to see that an innocent person was not arrested in the place of the true killer.

"You know," Flora said as she hitched herself onto one elbow. "If it's motive we're after, there is a fairly obvious one."

"Have you put the whole picture together already, dear? What's your idea?"

"Just this: if someone really wants to take over the Pacheco's labor contracting business, killing Joaquin and framing Rafael for the murder would get the job done neatly."

Evelyn sat up. "You are one hundred percent right about that, dear. Brilliant deduction. If that's what happened, who's your primary suspect?"

Flora squinted into the sunlight for half a second. "Why I suppose the foreman Luis would be the primary suspect, in that case. He's already been given responsibility for the job."

"And he has apparently ingratiated himself to Tia Rosamaria," Evelyn added. "That's one strong theory for what happened. Now what we need is evidence to prove that theory."

"Without—"

"Yes, of course, without allowing our theory to drive what evidence we seek."

They gathered their things, returned everything to the Chevrolet, and continued their journey. Evelyn spotted the recommended fruit stand ahead on the left and pulled the automobile into a graveled area set aside for parking vehicles. "Did you ever decide how many peaches you intend to purchase, Flora?"

"Lots. If we get too many to eat, we'll make jam, and if we get too many to make jam, we'll simply give some away. They are so juicy right now, I could eat one at every meal and for snacks too. Do you suppose Spritz would like peaches as well?"

Evelyn had not considered this possibility. "I'd be afraid feeding peaches to the dogs would give them the trots."

"Oh. I shouldn't like to have to clean up Pearl's house

after sick dogs. Perhaps I won't offer any peaches to Spritz. It would be fun to see if she'd even try them though, wouldn't it?"

"Up to you, dear. Strictly up to you." They collected their shopping bags, then Evelyn stopped. "I recently read that Scott Paper, you know the toilet tissue company in Philadelphia? They're now making paper kitchen towels. That would be an ideal product to use to clean up dog messes. You know, in situations where one doesn't really want to have to launder the towel used for clean up."

"Now that does sound like a good idea. Perhaps we should look for that product next time we visit the dry goods store. Or have Walter bring us back some when he returns from Philadelphia."

Rafael had been correct about the quality of the fruit offered at the stand in town. Flora selected bright orange apricots, fragrant strawberries, and more peaches than Evelyn could even imagine would be needed for jam. The stand also offered late-season peas in the pod and string beans in a variety of colors. Those would make delicious additions to meals in the days ahead. Flora rinsed a few of the string beans in the spigot at the side of the stand and placed those on a shopping bag between them for snacks on the way home.

"I'm going to get some potatoes and carrots, and an onion, too," Evelyn said. "I want to make a stew tomorrow. We can stop at the butcher shop on Webster St. and see if they have a bit of meat to flavor the stew."

"They won't likely have anything left today. Perhaps we can go early tomorrow. It's still a puzzle to me why, even if one has the money to spend, one often cannot find any meat to buy."

Evelyn selected her onion and said, "The business section had an article about how ranchers have had to cull their herds because so few people can afford to buy meat these days. And ranchers don't have any more money than the rest of us, so they can't afford to feed herds of cattle or pigs. We'll have to take what we can get but even a small bit of brisket should be enough to flavor my stew, especially with all these delicious fresh vegetables."

"As long as we're so near," Flora said, gazing at the coroner's office on the other side of the highway, "should we stop? Do you have more questions for Dr. Whitley?"

Evelyn gave it some thought. "At this point, my only question for the coroner would be when he expects to get that autopsy report to the sheriff so Rafael can be released. I wouldn't want to slow him down." She picked through the carrots until she had a handful of juicy young ones, handed those to Flora and stepped away.

Evelyn scrutinized the low block building across the road. "Truth is, I would like to ask about the blood on Joaquin's clothing, or possibly even see his shirt. I'm beginning to wonder if we'll ever find the location where Joaquin was shot, especially if local law enforcement is going to be so uncooperative. Still, I'd rather we finish our other errands and get back. We've been leaving the poor dogs alone too much as it is, and I don't want to take the chance they'll get themselves into mischief if they're left any longer. Let's plan to make another trip soon. We won't find any more about Joaquin's death we if don't keep looking."

The produce man helped them carry their box of peaches and several bags of other purchases to the automobile and tuck everything onto the floor in the rear where it wouldn't roll around during the trip along the winding highway. Flora placed a packet wrapped in brown paper atop the bags of fruit, and turned to the man.

"*Gracias, gracias.*" she said multiple times, bowing her head each time, then hopped onto her seat. "How embarrassing," she said.

"What's that?"

"I got into that habit when I'm talking to Jaing of bobbing my head whenever I say something in Chinese. She does it when she's talking to us, right? So I guess I learned it from her. That man must think I suffer from some nervous disorder."

Distracted with getting the automobile engine to catch, Evelyn only laughed.

"Speaking of nuts," Flora continued, "that *hombre* told me *los bolbones* would not ripen until about September."

"Los bolbones?

"Yes, that's walnuts. I learned a new word today."

"Attagirl. Soon we'll have to take you to Mexico so you can practice."

Flora huffed. "Plenty of people here in California are descendants of Spaniards. I can learn from them." She slammed her door closed. *"Allons-y!"*

"Oh, French, too, is it? Evelyn said, and laughed again. "What's in that paper packet on top of the fruit?"

"That's something called pectin. They told me I'd need it to make the fruit turn into jam."

"Really? Pectin, huh? I hope Mama knows what that is and how one uses it because I certainly don't."

"Nope, me either. They said I'd need it though, so I bought it." Evelyn headed the automobile toward downtown Walnut Creek and their next destination.

"As I think about it," she said, "we really should stop at the hacienda when we get close. I told Marisol yesterday we'd stop to see if she needed a ride to the ferry. Also, if we see him around, I'd like to have a word with the foreman, Luis."

"Good idea," Flora said. "We should also ask about the arrangements being made for a service for Joaquin. We'll want to attend that."

"Yes, that's right. Good thinking, Flora."

"What pieces of the puzzle are we likely to learn from Luis?" Flora asked. "Rafael told us Luis went with him to look for Joaquin that night. If Luis had something to do with killing Joaquin, could he have made it back to the barn in time? Remember, Rafael said he rounded up Luis and Martín in the barn at shortly after two in the morning to go look for Joaquin."

"Did Luis have time to find Joaquin, kill him, and get the body moved to the orchard, you mean?"

"Yes," Flora said. "Luis might have managed to squeeze all that into the time allowed, but—"

"Unlikely," Evelyn finished, as she navigated a curve in the highway.

"Perhaps we should stop at that other fruit stand, too, as long as we're here," Flora said. "Just to see what we can see. Rafael said the Vigilantes sometimes gather there. We might learn something."

"You've just no end of good ideas today, dear, although remember Rafael also told us to steer clear, as that place could be dangerous."

Flora was quiet for a few moments. "One has to wonder why those deputies are in such a hurry to arrest a Californio for Joaquin's murder."

"I do indeed wonder. Why do you suppose that's true?"

"Here's another theory of the murder. I hate to be a cynic, but perhaps the deputies suspect one of their own and want to keep that idea off the table."

Evelyn nodded slowly. "Well, it might be. What motive would a deputy have for killing Joaquin? Surely none of them want to take over the labor contracting business."

Chapter Twenty

Flora gazed pensively out the window as they drove. "You know," she said, "Calhoun told us they were all set to arrest another farmworker."

"That's the way I heard it," Evelyn said. "I didn't hear anything about any additional investigation, any search for evidence, or any attempt to identify someone with a motive to kill Joaquin. My concern is just that. Even if the sheriff does release Rafael, he'll only arrest some other innocent person. A person maybe without the resources Rafael has use of to get himself released. Or a person without an alibi."

"Or a person who doesn't have concerned friends like us."

"Yes, that too." Evelyn slowed the automobile and pointed ahead. "Here's that other fruit stand, the one Rafael said had been taken over by the Vigilantes. Did you want to stop?"

They both gazed at the ramshackle structure. Three battered pickup trucks parked at haphazard angles stood out front, along with a couple of dirty and older model sedans. Tall shadowy figures could be seen holding a bull session behind the fruit boxes. The dark man with the *sombrero* they'd noticed earlier was nowhere to be seen.

"Remember," Evelyn said, "Rafael warned us away from this place. He said it might be dangerous."

"Perhaps we should go up to the hacienda first."

Evelyn steered to the right, heading up the road to the Pachecos' hacienda. She wheeled around the driveway in front of the adobe and stopped the car. They glanced at one another, and let a few seconds elapse.

Flora turned to look under the shadowed arbor leading to the front door. "Are you waiting for me to go to the door?"

"No...not necessarily. In some cultures, you know, a visitor is expected to wait until someone in the house opens the door." They both looked under the arbor again, but no movement was visible.

Evelyn said, "They have to know we're out here. They would have heard our automobile arrive."

"And someone's here, because there's another automobile parked on the side there, next to the burned Plymouth."

"That's a good point. Possibly they already have visitors. I suppose we should at least go knock, however culturally inappropriate that might be."

"I'll go," Flora said, levering open the passenger door and stepping out.

"I'll come with you." Evelyn scurried to catch up.

Flora stopped and smiled at her friend. "Very well, but be sure to have the ignition key ready..."

"In case we need to make a fast get-away?"

"Precisely."

Two minutes after Flora's sharp rap, the heavy wooden door creaked open, and an unfamiliar older woman in a white apron and cap peered out.

"*Buenos días,*" Flora said. "I am Miss Fitzgerald. I am a friend, *una amiga,* of *Tia Rosamaria.* Is she at home? Or *Senorita Marisol?*"

"*Sí, sí,*" the woman said, her face lighting up in a wide smile. She opened the door more fully, gesturing them inside.

"*En el salón,*" she said, pointing, then she disappeared behind the kitchen door.

Seated elegantly on the wide sofa, Marisol's aunt and

another woman looked at them briefly in surprise. Rosamaria said hello in English, but did not invite them to sit. The other woman was about Rosamaria's age. Their long, brightly-colored skirts draped around them and graying hair was piled atop their heads.

"*Permitame a presentar mi hermana, Señora Hidalgo Sanchez del Martinez,*" Tia Rosamaria said without rising. She presented her sister to them with an out-stretched hand.

A look of bewilderment flashed across Evelyn's face at the sudden flood of Spanish.

Flora nodded graciously. "*Buenos días,*" she said. And with that, she had very nearly exhausted her Spanish vocabulary.

Evelyn stayed behind Flora, making friendly-sounding murmurs.

It was clear that Tia remembered Flora when the older woman recounted the sad tale of Flora's husband buried under a poppy-strewn field in Flanders, all delivered in Spanish. After appropriate-sounding condolences were offered, and accepted, Flora explained, in English, that they had just come from seeing Rafael, that he seemed none the worse for wear, an idiom that had to be reworded, and that all were hopeful he would be released from the county jail soon.

"*Sí,* tonight for dinner for sure, they told me." Tia nodded vigorously.

Flora then asked about Marisol, who had not appeared in the sitting room.

'Oh, but Marisol has gone already," Tia said. "Her cousin Ysabel drove her to the hospital in Oakland."

"Oh?" Flora said in an uncertain tone. "The hospital? Is Marisol—?"

"She's fine. She's fine," Tia Rosamaria shook her head. "Marisol only went to the hospital to inquire about employment. Marisol is a well-respected nurse in an emergency room. She's hoping to find a job closer to here, so she can live with me in this *hacienda grande.*" Rosamaria's last words were spoken with a flourish, indicating the vastness of the *hacienda*.

"I see," Flora said. "And you have your sister here now to help you?"

Tia Rosamaria and her sister both nodded and murmured in pleasant tones.

"Very well, *muy bien*," Flora said, not bobbing her head. "We should be on our way, then." There was a brief awkward pause, then Flora said, "We'll see ourselves out." As they found their way Flora called, *"Adios."*

Once the door was firmly closed behind them, Flora turned to Evelyn. "Humph!" she said. "They weren't very courteous, were they? And what was all that balderdash about Marisol moving in with her?"

"We'd better talk about that later," Evelyn said, taking Flora's elbow.

They climbed into the Chevrolet, looked at one another, and sighed, glad to have that awkward errand finished. In no time, they were back at the intersection, and gazing again at the run-down fruit shed. The older model vehicles parked in front had been joined by a county sheriff's sedan. Several figures could be seen in the shadows at the back of the shed.

"What are you thinking?" Flora said.

"I know we want to get home, but it does look like there's some activity going on over there. Possibly a chance to learn something important. Those fellows look like they might know about guns, for example. Especially the deputy there. He might have some ideas. And how dangerous could it be with him here? This is my chance to ask a deputy some questions without the spying eyes of Calhoun."

"We could pull in and pretend we're interested in those sad-looking watermelons," Flora suggested.

Evelyn gave Flora a quick glance, shrugged her shoulders and said, "What, me worry?" She looked both ways and pulled the automobile into an empty space in front of the fruit stand.

"Here goes nothing," Flora said, climbing out behind Evelyn so as to avoid stepping onto the highway. They pasted smiles on their faces and walked toward the large wooden box containing watermelons. Three men standing under the roof of the shed regarded the women in silence.

"Oh, look, Evie," Flora said, "watermelons." Flora sounded for all the world as though she was not the least bit frightened. She called out to the men, "Are these watermelons ripe already? Isn't it a bit early in the season for them?"

The men shifted, and one stepped forward. Now that they were closer to the shed, Evelyn could more clearly see the uniformed deputy. A moment too late, she recognized him as one of the deputies she'd seen at the county jail earlier in the day. He was sure to be suspicious about why she was still poking around so close to the Pachecos' family home. In fact, all three men glowered at them with angry faces. The odds appeared to be against getting any useful information out of those fellows.

"Oh, hello," she said in a tone that indicated she was pleased to see the deputy. "Nice to see you again." She gave him a little wave.

Before he had time to reply, a clamor of shouting and cheering voices rang out from behind the shed. A canvas drape blocked the view, but it sounded as though quite a crowd of people had gathered back there and were engaged in some sort of a game. A winner had clearly just been announced. Sounds of congratulatory laughter and back-slapping followed the clamor.

"Didn't you two go up to the Pachecos' place just now?" the deputy said, narrowing his eyes at the new arrivals.

Evelyn let go of Flora's elbow and confronted the man, prepared to answer his question while at the same time thinking fast about what information she might be able to get from him before making her escape.

"Ooh," Flora said brightly, "what's going on back here?" She moved between empty wooden bins and lifted the canvas curtain that formed the backdrop to the fruit stand. "Sounds like fun!"

Evelyn yelped in dismay, but it was too late, Flora was already out of sight, leaving a narrow gap in the canvas where she'd disappeared. Evelyn took one step in the direction of the gap, but a couple of men came through just then, one eagerly counting dollar bills. Maybe, Evelyn thought, the game was about to break up and Flora would return quickly. Gambling games were illegal…and a sheriff's deputy was right there. Was Flora about to be arrested and tossed in the county hoosegow along with Rafael? She looked with alarm at the deputy. He didn't appear to be about to arrest anyone. In fact, the fellow counting his winnings had joined the men confronting Evelyn. He showed no signs of dashing away to avoid arrest.

"Miss Fitzgerald!" Evelyn called sharply, to no response. A minute later the loud clamoring began again. Evelyn could also hear a woman's laughter. Not Flora's, but at least, she thought with relief, Flora wasn't the only woman back there with the gamblers.

Raising his voice to be heard over the raucous crowd, the frowning deputy said, "What are you doing here, ma'am? What do you want?"

Evelyn made note of the expressions on the other men's faces. Not all of them shared the deputy's scowling countenance, so she decided to continue her friendly tone. If the deputy wasn't willing, maybe one of these others would be open to being helpful. She did sincerely hope to gain some useful information from this encounter, although the way this group was closing in around her did not feel at all friendly.

Trying to control her voice, which threatened to tremble, Evelyn said, "Yes, we were just up at the Pacheco place. Marisol Pacheco is a friend of ours. You probably know her cousin, Rafael? He's about to be released by the sheriff, I suppose you know?" Evelyn felt as though she was talking to a wall of life-sized stone statues. No one even moved, let alone answered her questions.

Oh, well, in for a penny, in for a pound, she thought, and she ventured another question. "As long as we've run into you, I wonder if anyone here knows anybody who owns a .38 Special revolver manufactured by Colt? We've recently learned that

Joaquin Pacheco was shot with that make and model of weapon. We're only trying to help the Pachecos learn what happened to Joaquin, if we can." There, she thought, that should stir some sort of trouble up, and possibly even something useful.

The reaction she got was mostly hostile. Two of the men turned and headed back behind the canvas. The remaining men crowded closer to her and the angry looks intensified.

At last, through tightened lips, one of the stoutest men spoke. "Nobody here's gonna talk to any friend of those Mexicans," the heavy-set man said.

Evelyn thought about, then discarded the idea of offering a quick history lesson about how the Pachecos and nearly all of the other Spanish-speaking families in this area were not Mexicans but Californios, and had mostly all been born right here. These men did not look as though they would appreciate her efforts in that regard. Instead, she was beginning to realize this was an unlikely circumstance from which to gain any useful information. She considered how best to safely extract both herself and Flora from this dicey engagement.

"I see," she said. "Well, in as much as these watermelons do not appear to be fully ripened, I suppose my friend and I will be on our way." She took one step in the direction of Walter's Chevrolet, and bumped into the dirty shirt front and intimidating chest of a man who had failed to step aside. She looked up at his face leering down at her. "Excuse me," she said, and took another step, attempting to slide between him and the equally menacing man to his right. That man also closed ranks, trapping her.

Another bark of excitement rang out from the crowd behind the canvas, interrupting the difficult predicament in which Evelyn found herself. A couple of men turned to see what the excitement was about as three or four more men came through the canvas flap. Evelyn took a chance and slipped through as the men in front moved about. Instead of taking advantage of the opportunity to escape, she headed for that gap in the canvas wall, thinking of Flora. The threatening men seemed for a moment to have forgotten her. Taking a deep breath, she went to peer through the opening. What she saw shocked her.

The game was being played in the dirt, with several players squatting over a rough square scrapped in the dust. Flora appeared to be having the time of her life, laughing and slapping the back of the man counting out his winnings.

"Here now!" Evelyn exclaimed in dismay. "Miss Fitzgerald! We really must leave. Now! Let's go!"

Evelyn was relieved and thankful to see the game might be breaking up, as several people were moving in the direction of the exit, including, finally, Flora.

Chapter Twenty-One

Evelyn wended her way between fruit bins toward their automobile, waving urgently for Flora to follow. As she drew even with a rusty red pickup, she caught a narrow-eyed glare from the driver's seat, and hurried her pace. She climbed aboard Walter's Chevrolet and started the engine. Even after several seconds, Flora had still not taken her seat.

Evelyn swiveled to find out what the hold-up was just in time to see Flora squirm out from one man's unappreciated embrace. Catching sight of Evelyn's urgent expression, Flora's laughter dampened and she dashed toward the passenger side of the Chevrolet, one hand clutching her hat, still on but askew.

Flora leapt on the running board and stuck her grinning face through the open window. "C'mon, Evie! Let's get out of here!"

"Step down and get in the automobile, Flora."

"Well, phooey. At the very least I could climb in through the window."

"This is a hardtop, Flora dear. You'd knock yourself silly trying to climb in the window." Evelyn lowered her voice, she hoped below the audible range, and muttered, "As if you don't sometimes behave as though you've already been knocked silly." She raised her voice, "Please open the door and get in, Flora."

Two of the pickup trucks pulled out at the same time and Evelyn nearly wrecked Walter's automobile by narrowly missing a green one as it made a u-turn directly in front of her. She resisted the urge to try out the horn in favor of avoiding any potential altercation. By veering slightly left across the lane, they were off, headed west on the winding highway toward the tunnel.

Evelyn wanted dreadfully to ask what Flora had been doing behind the canvas flap, and what, if anything, her friend might have learned. Instead, she waited to catch her breath and let her heart rate slow. Also, the red pickup she'd noted earlier appeared to have followed them onto the highway. It was holding back, almost but not quite out of sight. Despite the fact that any vehicle on this narrow highway would necessarily appear to be following the one in front of it, she still felt as though they were being tailed. Probably just a mad thought. Evelyn sped up to a less than cautious velocity and began to enjoy the sensation of steering, expertly taking the automobile through the curves of the highway.

"Slow down, Evelyn. You're going to drive us into a ditch."

"Nonsense. I'm in full control."

"Please. If I can't ride on the running board, you can't drive like a woman gone wild."

Evelyn scowled and took her foot off the accelerator to let the vehicle slow, checking in the rearview mirror anxiously for any sight of the pickup. She didn't see anything but that didn't mean he wasn't back there somewhere. Her anxiety, compounded through the day, spilled over into anger. "What in blazes were you doing in back of that shed with those ruffians anyway? Gambling like some common trollop, looked like."

Flora reacted as though oblivious to Evelyn's anxiety. "Oh, that was fun!" she said, straightening her hat. "They were playing a game called Shooter with dice and placing bets. Good thing I didn't even have a whole dollar with me. Bets were a quarter. I placed two bets and lost both of them. I am afraid I lost our change from when we bought the produce, I think a total of sixty cents. Bodie loaned me the fifteen cents to make up the difference for the third bet, but I lost that on the first roll, then he said he'd take what I owed him out 'on trade' which turned out to be—"

Flora glanced at her friend and stopped talking when Evelyn sent her a tense expression. Then Flora took a breath and started in again as gaily as before. "Anyway, it was all in good fun, and I might have gained a few pieces of information, perhaps something useful to our investigation. I wasn't really too scared. Bodie said I was his 'lucky charm' and asked me to roll the dice once, but there was another woman there and she got a little testy about that, so I said I didn't know how and gave her the dice. And, oh, did you notice the actual trollop back there with us? Francie? Her face was covered in heavy pancake makeup. Way too much kohl and ooh, that lipstick! She was the nicest person, though, honestly. When Bodie started getting fresh with me Francie told him, she said, 'that one's not for sale, Bodie.' Can you even imagine?"

Flora slid a side-eyed glance to her friend. Evelyn couldn't decide if Flora's chatter was helping her calm down or only making her mood darker. She searched the rearview mirror. Flora turned and looked behind where the red pickup was not only in sight but beginning to gain on them.

"Are we being pursued?" Flora asked.

"I don't know, but he keeps getting closer. He's one of the guys from the fruit stand." Evelyn pressed harder on the accelerator and the Chevy shot forward, taking the next curve at a dangerous rate of speed. Frightened, Evelyn focused on keeping to the middle of the highway, risking a collision with possible on-coming traffic.

The Chevy's wheels squealed through the next curve and Flora yelped. "You have to slow down, Evelyn! You don't want to wreck Walter's auto or get us hurt." She glanced behind again. "Not to mention you'll damage our beautiful fresh fruit." Turning to face forward, she added, "Or splatter it all over the brand-new upholstery."

Evelyn glanced in the mirror again. "When did you become so sensible, dear? Anyway, he'll catch up to us if we slow. Then we might really get hurt. Who knows what he has in mind." One tire left the pavement on the next curve, making the automobile shiver. Evelyn pulled back onto the asphalt.

"All right," Flora said. "That's it. He's only one man. What's he going to do?"

"Shoot us?" Evelyn chanced a quick glance and caught the fear in Flora's angry scowl. "Okay, okay, you're right, I'll slow down. Clearly we're not going to be able to out-run his truck. I would stop and see what he wants, but I don't want to strand us out here in the middle of nowhere. He looks disreputable."

"Oh, horsefeathers, Evelyn. Just because he's driving a battered pickup truck does not mean he isn't a perfect gentleman. When did you turn into such a snob? I met most of those men at the fruit stand and I didn't think they were dangerous. Anyway, there are no towns or even cross streets until we get to the other side of the tunnel. You simply cannot keep speeding." Flora glanced behind them again. "Look, he's waving."

"What?" Sure enough, Evelyn could see the man waving and pointing ahead at an upcoming wide spot on the shoulder.

"Pull over here, Evie. I'll go back and see what he wants."

Evelyn rolled the Chevy onto the gravel and stopped.

"No, Flora you stay put. I'll go."

"What if he shoots you? I don't know how to drive this contraption. We'll both be stuck. Anyway, look. He's sort of waving again. We should both stay put. Here he comes."

Evelyn watched in the side mirror as the tall man in worn dungarees and a flannel shirt ambled toward her side of the automobile. He removed a home-rolled cigarette from his lip, pinched the lit end, and tucked what remained above his ear, tipping his hat back as he did so. From all appearances, he carried no firearm, and held his hand up in a friendly manner when he drew even with her window.

"How-do," he said, and both women murmured polite

replies. Flora gave Evelyn a glance and shrugged, indicating she didn't recognize him.

Evelyn did. He'd been one of the threatening men standing too near her at the fruit stand.

"You scared us," Flora said. "Did you want something?"

He leaned down toward the window and gave Flora a good looking-over, then straightened and addressed Evelyn.

"Heard you askin' back at the fruit shed about a Colt .38 revolver, and askin' questions about who mighta killed Joaquin Pacheco." The man rolled his head to the side and hawked up a wad of spit.

Evelyn cringed and shifted a tad farther from her window. In spite of his ill-mannered behavior, something about his demeanor and the way he referenced the murder put Evelyn a bit more at ease. He sounded almost as though he might have been friendly with Joaquin. "That's right," Evelyn said. "Really more just trying to help out where we can. Did you have something to tell us?"

In a slow and gravelly voice, he replied, "Well now, what I got is more a word of advice." He checked the road behind them for traffic, and continued. "That deputy you was talkin' to, he's not gonna take kindly to you suggestin' a deputy had anything to do with what happened to Joaquin. You'd best back-off before you get yourself into some serious trouble. That's all I'm suggestin' here."

"Thank you, we appreciate your concern," Evelyn said. "If I may be permitted to say so however, it does sound as though you might have more information about what happened to Joaquin than you're telling us."

The pickup driver pushed his hands deeper into the pockets of his dungarees and chewed his lip. "Well…let me just say this. The official story is Joaquin died as a result of the labor disputes going on in these orchards. That's what you're askin' around about, yeah?"

Evelyn simply nodded. The man was speaking so slowly, she didn't want to delay him any further by adding her two cents.

"Well...all I'm sayin' is, Joaquin Pacheco did not die because of some labor dispute. That boy was someplace he shouldn'ta been, as usual, and that was what got him killed. His death didn't have nothin' to do with any labor dispute." Gently, he slapped the roof of the Chevrolet. "You two ladies had best go on home and forget about this whole ugly thing. That's my advice, just go on home."

As he turned to head back to his truck, Flora hopped out and came around to the highway side. "Hold your horses a minute, sir," she said. "We're not going home, as you suggest, until we make sure Rafael isn't blamed for his brother's death. So how do you know Joaquin was killed because he was some-place he should not have been? You must know something more than that?"

The man scuffed a worn work boot in the gravel, sighed and looked off across the highway. "It's a personal matter, ma'am. Those questions your friend is askin'...those ques-tions about the Colt revolver...those questions are gonna to get the sheriff and his deputies all in a lather. They don't carry those revolvers any more, but they know who does, and they'll protect their brothers, even the ones who aren't in uniform any longer. They know who had a reason to kill Joaquin and they know it was a good reason, a personal matter." He pulled the last half of his cigarette from above his ear and rolled it between his fingers, then went on quietly. "I suppose that's true about Rafael, though. That's not right, the sheriff holding him for the murder. If the sheriff doesn't let him go, and soon, there's gonna be some confusion in that jail and Rafael will get hisself killed somehow." The man turned away, and got serious about returning to his pickup.

"Wait!" Flora called. "What's your name?"

"Jus' say a lil bird told you!" he called back. "An I mean it about goin' on home. We'd all just as soon not see your faces out here again. You get my drift?"

Evelyn and Flora watched as the pickup made a u-turn

and rolled off back toward town.

"Huh!" Evelyn said as she cranked the ignition and pulled the Chevy onto the highway. "That seems like a big piece of the puzzle right there."

"The part about why Joaquin was killed, yes," Flora said, watching behind them. She turned to face forward. "But I still think that 'lil bird' didn't tell us everything he knows. He's keeping secrets. At least he didn't shoot us."

Evelyn sent Flora an incredulous stare before realizing her friend was making an attempt at humor. They both laughed in relief.

"And at least this wasn't a trip for biscuits," Evelyn said. "We did learn some new and valuable pieces of information. Now we have to put these new pieces together into a whole picture. And maybe we can do that without any more poking at that hornet's nest."

Shaken by their encounter with the anonymous "Lil Bird" they were quiet for most of the return trip. As they reached what felt like the relative safety of Oakland, Flora began chattering about what they might have learned.

"For example," Flora said at one point, "when we were visiting at the jail, did it seem to you like Rafael was uncomfortable with your questions about where Joaquin might have gone? It was almost as though Rafael knew more than he was saying."

"Yes, as though he thought he knew where Joaquin had gone, but didn't want to tell us."

"So, do you think he did know?"

Evelyn gave that idea some thought while she navigated the busy late afternoon downtown traffic. "I do suppose that's possible," she finally said, "but if Rafael knew where Joaquin had gone, why didn't he simply go there that night, find Joaquin, and drag him home?"

"Oh, good point," Flora said. Looking ahead, she caught her breath and held it as they entered the Posey Tube.

Halfway through the Tube, Evelyn said, "You know dear,

one of these days we're going to get stuck in traffic inside this Tube and you're going to run out of air."

Flora's cheeks were already puffed out and her face was turning a deep red. Nevertheless, she nodded gamely and held on until they emerged into the fresh air and sunshine.

"There now," Flora said as she placed Spritz and Spike's dishes on the floor, both heaped with something the dogs deemed quite tasty. "I'm perishing! What do we have for supper? And I'm in the mood for a hearty meal tonight. All of this investigating gives me a healthy appetite."

"Pearl left us that quart of mulligatawny she canned. We can throw together some biscuits and honey, and we've got all of these vegetables." Evelyn gestured at the boxes and bags piled on kitchen counters around them. "Would that do?"

"Oh, nicely. Let's get busy so we can eat before I fall over in a dead faint."

Chapter Twenty-Two

After supper they collapsed in the parlor, the evening news broadcast just beginning to air on the wireless. The program was filled with reports from Chicago and the Republican National Convention due to open there the following day. Not being much interested in the topic, Evelyn changed the station before the news ended, and tuned into the upcoming broadcast of *Amos 'n Andy*.

"What do you think? Will this do? *Myrt and Myrtle* is on afterwards."

"I suppose." Flora scrunched up her face in distaste. "They are both kind of silly. *Voice of Firestone* is on NBC Monday nights. We could listen to classical music and chat or play some cards."

Evelyn fussed with the radio again until she had the requested programming dialed in, while Flora fetched the playing cards and began to shuffle them.

"Is it your impression, as it is mine," Flora said, "that it was likely a man connected in some way with the sheriff's department who shot Joaquin? At least that's what I got from what Lil Bird said."

"Oh? Is that what you heard? Seems like a bit of a leap from what he said, although I will be the first to admit you can often be startlingly insightful. Isn't it equally likely someone could have purchased that weapon when the deputies were asked to upgrade to the pistol? Otherwise you're suggesting a current deputy simply held onto his revolver when the department switched."

"Yes, it could have gone that way. I'm only saying, it sounded to me as though Lil Bird was trying to tell us the culprit was connected, either a retired or a current deputy. What about Deputy Calhoun's father? The younger deputy said Calhoun's father might still have his revolver, right? Or anyone in his family could have had access to his revolver."

Evelyn tapped her lip. "Before we become overwhelmed with all the possibilities and get confused, let's take a moment to appreciate what we learned today. Lil Bird said Joaquin was killed because he was in a place where he had no business being, and because of a personal matter. What does that suggest to you?"

Flora gave the question two seconds' thought. "Well, the first thing that pops into my head is that Lil Bird was trying to steer us away from our favorite theory."

"That someone killed Joaquin and framed Rafael to gain control of the business?"

"Yes. And in my view we shouldn't let ourselves stray too far from that theory unless and until we uncover evidence to the contrary. Especially because if it begins to look as though our inquiries will lead to Rafael being released, our villain may need to arrange to have Rafael killed while in custody instead. That may not have been the original plan, but would serve just as well."

Evelyn lowered her brow in an angry frown, furious at the possibility.

"But if we must give up our favorite theory," Flora continued, "it begins to seem that a romantic liaison gone wrong might be equally likely to have led to Joaquin's death. One could interpret Lil Bird's words to mean that Joaquin was carrying on with someone he had no business being with."

"That's more or less what I am thinking also," Evelyn agreed. "A romantic liaison. Or possibly Joaquin knew about a forbidden or unexpected romantic liaison between other people and was silenced for fear he would reveal that secret. Remember, what Lil Bird actually said was that Joaquin was killed because he was someplace he shouldn't have been, and it was a personal matter."

Flora turned wide eyes to Evelyn. "A forbidden...?"

"Or unforeseen."

"You're talking about what Father Bertrand might have been up to last Sunday afternoon, aren't you? Except Joaquin was already dead by then. Or are you suggesting Joaquin might have been the one having the forbidden affair and the priest killed Joaquin Saturday night? And he preached and served communion at the Sunday morning service and disappeared after that? I'm confused."

"When you put it like that the whole thing sounds absurdly implausible, doesn't it?"

"Indeed, it does. Do we have any other likely suspects?" Flora asked.

"What about the possibility that foreman Luis and Tia Rosamaria might be up to something? I mean, we chuckled when we saw them together, but that's not an impossibility."

Flora nodded. "True, they might be up to something, but while it might be unexpected, that's hardly a forbidden liaison. Tia is a widow. She's free to see whomever she likes. All the same, when you add in the political ramifications of the labor business and Luis's at least temporary taking over of that, anything might be possible."

"Yes. We don't know, you know, whether Marisol's uncle left that business to his sons, or to his wife."

"True, and now we're back to the solution where Luis formed a romantic liaison with the true owner, Tia, and killed Joaquin and framed Rafael so he could gain control of the business."

"That hardly seems possible, Flora. Tia has her own son killed and the other framed? Luis might have a strong motive for the crime but didn't Rafael tell us Luis was at the barn when he set out to look for Joaquin Saturday night? And Luis even came with him to search. How could Luis have killed Joaquin and been back at the barn in time to meet Rafael?"

Flora squinted. "But if he managed that, he could have led Rafael astray in the search to be sure they didn't find Joaquin that night."

Evelyn put her cards down and stared into space for a few moments. "That's true, Flora. It might have happened that way. We need to find out if Luis has a better alibi. Add that to the list of pieces of this puzzle we still need. Still, I don't know about you but for my money the very idea that Rosamaria would allow any harm to come to either of her sons is ludicrous."

"I agree," Flora said. "Not even worth considering."

They both sighed deeply.

"We just have to start over," Flora said. "A romantic liaison…Wasn't Rafael saying as much this morning when he told us Joaquin came home and put on a clean shirt? Doesn't that imply Joaquin had a assignation?"

"Yes," Evelyn said. "Rafael was being a bit ambivalent, but that seemed to be what he was implying."

"And that's closer to what Lil Bird was suggesting, that it was Joaquin himself who was having the romantic liaison."

"Hold the phone," Evelyn said. "We're the ones who came up with the romantic liaison angle. All Lil Bird said was that Joaquin was someplace he shouldn't have been—"

"And he said that was not unusual for Joaquin," Flora said.

"Yes. Also, Lil Bird said Joaquin's murder had nothing at all to do with a labor dispute—"

"Unless Lil Bird was trying to steer us away from someone he's trying to protect," Flora interrupted again. "But beyond a romantic angle, how many options are there for 'something he shouldn't have been doing?' Gambling? No, apparently gambling is not a crime, or at least doesn't come to the notice of law enforcement. Drinking? No. Producing and selling alcohol is illegal but sitting around drinking isn't going to get Joaquin killed. Being inappropriate with another man's wife is about the only taboo left for Joaquin."

"Or someone's daughter."

Flora gave Evelyn a wide-eyed look. "Interesting possibility," she said. "We'd need to know more about the players to know anything about that. In fact, we need more clues in general before we can put this puzzle together. Go out and find me more clues, Evie."

"Not very likely any time soon, dear. Remember, the other thing Lil Bird told us was to stay away from the fruit orchards for our own safety. I think for the time being we should stay right here in Alameda and work this puzzle with the pieces we already have."

Standing to fuss with the dials on Walter's new console, Flora said, "How do you tune this expensive-looking gizmo? I'm in the mood for a drama and it's almost time for *Mysteries in Paris* on CBS." Flora finally got the correct station tuned in, adjusted the volume, and stepped in front of Evelyn. "Scoot over," she said. "I can hear better from here." They squirmed to fit into Walter's big chair and settled.

When the program ended, they discussed going up to bed, but neither could summon the energy to move.

"We didn't talk about it, Evie. What do you think is going to happen with Bernice and Marisol? It sounds to me like Marisol is looking for a way out."

"It does, indeed, if Tia's got the story right."

"You think perhaps she doesn't?"

"She may be just blowing smoke, or at least basing what she said on wishful thinking. Without talking to Marisol herself, we can't know what's really in Marisol's mind."

"True," Flora said. "Still, she certainly treated Bernice

badly this weekend, I thought. Heaven knows, Bernice can get on a person's nerves, but I thought Marisol was unnecessarily rude."

"Marisol's under a lot of pressure from her aunt," Evelyn said. "Tia Rosamaria seems to expect Marisol to step in and take care of her. I did sense that Tia doesn't have much respect for Marisol and Bernice's friendship."

Flora sighed. "No, she doesn't seem to. I hope you're right about Tia talking through her hat. Marisol leaving would break Bernice's heart. She can be annoying, but she's still a dear."

Evelyn put an arm around Flora's shoulder and gave her a quick squeeze.

"And you're a dear for caring, Flora. All we can do is wait to see what happens, and be there to pick up the pieces, if need be. Here's the jingle for the next program coming on. If we don't get upstairs now, we'll be here all night, and I believe my foot has already fallen asleep ahead of the rest of me."

Tuesday, Evelyn kept to her usual early wakening. She spent the hour until Flora arose searching the basement shelves for empty jam jars and other supplies they would need for their day of canning fruit. She also made a list of questions to ask her mother about jam-making and peach-preserving. Long distance telephone calls could be expensive, so it was best to write all the questions down before placing the call. She even had a few questions for Pearl, assuming she and her family had safely arrived in Philadelphia last night, as scheduled.

The air was hazy but the sun well up by the time Flora appeared in the kitchen, her dark hair still tousled from sleep. She was ravenous for breakfast, and excited to get the day underway. Before she even finished her steaming bowl of Malt-O-Meal, she proposed they take the dogs on another morning walk. They decided to head south this time, avoiding the growing shantytown they'd encountered the day before.

At first, Spike walked nicely with Flora. The low skylines of towns south of San Francisco appeared along the horizon in front of them, shimmering from across the bay.

"Oh,dear," Flora said, peering into the haze ahead and close to the ground. "What is that over there near the water? Is that a cat?"

Evelyn didn't even have time to look up before Spritz heard the magic word, jerked, slipped her lead, and headed straight for a tabby cat peacefully enjoying a breakfast of dead sea life. Spike saw his littermate take off and the cat sprinting away. He ran in a circle around Flora's ankles, pulling her off her feet as he did so. This was accompanied by a good deal of excited barking and a yelp as Flora went down.

Letting the terriers go, Evelyn helped Flora to her feet. "Are you hurt?"

"Spritz! Come here!" Flora rubbed her wrist and balanced gingerly on one foot. She was more focused on regaining control of her dog than she was on any injury suffered. She hobbled toward the dogs, who had the cat "treed" on a wooden pier post above the reach of their snapping teeth.

"Here now!" Evelyn called, following her friend. "Eew! What is this gunk?" She lifted one shoe out of a rotting mess.

Stymied in their efforts to reach the tabby, both dogs caught an enticing whiff of whatever Evelyn had stepped into and raced back. Spritz threw herself into the skin, bones and decaying body parts, and rolled enthusiastically. Spike jumped in right behind her.

Flora squealed with disgust as she fished the dog's leads out and pulled them away. "No wonder no one comes to this part of the shoreline."

Progress toward home was hindered by both women hobbling, one on an injured ankle and the other with one shoe so covered in the unpleasant mess that her foot squished every time she took a step. The smelly terriers were as happy as they could be, stopping now and then to lick at Evelyn's shoe.

Working quickly together, they got the dogs into a steel laundry tub in the backyard with plenty of soap and water. Even after Spritz and Spike were scrubbed clean, the stench seemed to permeate everything. The dogs were left to their own company in the backyard.

Evelyn and Flora stripped shoes and stockings in the basement and took the stairs into the kitchen in their bare feet.

"Well, one thing's for sure," Evelyn said. "We won't be doing much investigating with both of us limping on our injuries this morning."

They went upstairs to wash and change in preparation for the day of jam-making ahead. Then they sat at the dining table and perused Evelyn's list of questions. "I searched last night," Flora said, "and Pearl has a half a bag of sugar, but we should ask if she has more. We may need to make a run to the dry goods store if she doesn't have more on hand."

"Good point," Evelyn said, adding that question to her list."Let's get Mama on the horn."

Mama Winslow was happy to hear from them, of course, and even more pleased to hear they were embarking on a jam-making adventure. She listed for them various pots, measuring devices, and a sugar thermometer they would need, and described some necessary procedures. And she knew exactly what to do with the packet of pectin. Flora took frantic notes.

Pearl proved even more helpful when she took over the telephone. She directed them first to her much-stained and well-thumbed 1925 edition of *Good Housekeeping Book of Menus, Recipes, and Household Discoveries* on the shelf over the stove. Flora took it down, flipped a few of the sticky pages and muttered that she knew exactly what they would be giving Pearl for her birthday this year.

Chapter Twenty-Three

After listening to a few of Evelyn's questions, Pearl told them she would call Lolly, the woman who came in to "do for" her. Lolly knew everything there was to know about canning and related arts. If Lolly was available, Pearl assured them, she'd be able to get them "out of any sort of a jam" they might find themselves in. Everyone enjoyed a hearty and relieved laugh over Pearl's probably unintended pun.

Evelyn had significantly more confidence when she dis-connected the call, but by the time all the necessary equipment and supplies were piled on every flat surface in the kitchen, both women felt a bit overwhelmed.

"Well," Flora said, "I can tell you one thing already. Next time I have a simple meal like a taste of jam on toast, I'll have a whole new appreciation."

"Let's get started with one batch and see how that goes. Possibly Lolly will be here by the time we need to do anything too complicated."

"Yes, the bit about dropping a blob of the hot mixture into a bowl of cold water to see if it jams-up has me flummoxed. I hope we can figure out this thermometer thing." Flora held the glass bulb upside down and toyed with its metal clamp.

"You can get started peeling and slicing peaches while I wash jars. And what do you think about having the radio on? The Republican convention is being broadcast today."

"Ugh!" Flora said. "If I want to hear the rantings of raving Republicans I'll listen to my father. They're only going to nominate Hoover again, and this country will continue to spin toward disaster. Rich businessmen might be able to control elections but they know nothing about what ordinary people need. How about some lively music instead?"

They had a pot of peaches and sugar bubbling with Flora keeping a close eye on the thermometer by the time Lolly rolled up the rear stairs bearing an extra bag of sugar and a wide grin. Her round body, almost wider than it was tall, filled the doorway, and her booming voice rang through the kitchen as she introduced herself. She pulled an apron out of her tote and somehow got it tied behind herself while she tut-tutted over their progress and announced they'd done exactly as they should have.

For most of the remainder of the day, the three women danced a coordinated ballet in the kitchen, preparing peaches, apricots, and strawberries, watching the fruit bubble and boil, and melting and pouring thin layers of paraffin carefully over the top of each cooled jam-filled jar.

Evelyn did sneak into the parlor at one point to listen in on the radio broadcast of the convention in Chicago, finding that Flora had been correct. Those Republicans seemed only to be concerned with the profits of big business and she didn't hear a word about the plight of the unemployed. One had to wonder how long the businessmen thought they could continue to stay in business with so many would-be consumers out of work and not buying anything. When she returned to the kitchen, Flora was inquiring about Lolly's husband.

Unlike so many, Lolly explained, her husband was gainfully employed in a secure position.

"He's a shift supervisor," she said, "at the Giant Powder Company north of Richmond, jus' a streetcar ride from the house. Been there going on ten years."

"That sounds like a good job," Flora said. "Why don't some of these unemployed factory workers get themselves hired there, instead of trying to steal farmworkers' jobs?"

"Oh," Lolly laughed. "Don't nobody but us Negro folks want to work for Giant Powder. They make dynamite, don't you know? Whole plant there in Richmond blows up ever' so often. Kills everyone in sight. We figure all of us are living on borrowed time. In the meanwhile, it's steady work, and it pays good.

"Now you take our boy Steven, he recently graduated from secondary school. We're hoping he'll get himself a nice safe job with the military, now the war is over."

A short while later, Evelyn emerged from the basement stairwell bearing the last small box of pint jars with rings. She also carried her walking shoes, now scrubbed clean of any trace of whatever she'd stepped in. "I washed and washed these," she said, "only to find when they were finally clean this one's falling apart. See?" She showed Lolly and Flora where the sole of one of her well-worn shoes was peeling loose from the leather upper. "Guess I'll have to wear my Sunday shoes until I can afford to buy new walking shoes."

"Nonsense!" Lolly said. "That's nothing a little mucilage and a bit of twine can't fix. Gotta 'make-do' these days. You can't go running out buying new shoes every time one shows a little wear."

She sent Flora up to Pearl's bedroom closet to fetch the sewing basket and Evelyn into the pantry to find the small bottle of mucilage with its orange rubber applicator. The young women watched, fascinated, while Lolly squeezed a healthy layer of the sticky substance between the pieces and then sewed the sole back to the upper with a heavy needle and thick thread.

"This isn't the thread I'd use to fix shoes, but it's all Mrs. Winslow's got. She probably uses this to mend up the boys' Levis. This'll do for now. If you'll take it easy on that shoe, I'll bring the right thread next time I come. There you go!" she said after about twenty minutes of work. "Now set that one out where the mucilage can dry, and you got yourself a like-new pair of walking shoes." Evelyn marveled as she carried her "like-new" shoe to the back porch to dry, well out of the reach of the curious dogs.

By mid-afternoon the counters in Pearl's kitchen were laden with colorful jars of jam and canned fruit. Lolly had been loaded up with enough jam to last a season and gone her way with a promise that she'd return on Thursday to do the laundry and Hoovering.

Both Evelyn and Flora collapsed in heaps into chairs in the parlor.

"I think I should never want one more spoonful of jam as long as I live," Flora said.

"That is unfortunate, as we now possess enough jars of jam to sustain us for the remainder of our days."

"And beyond. This isn't exactly the vacation of adventure I had envisioned."

Evelyn smiled in reply. "No, but you know what?"

"What?"

"Now we know how to make jam in case we ever do have to do it again."

"True," Flora agreed. "Do you want to walk out to buy a newspaper? There might be an article about Joaquin's death, or about the labor situation in the fruit orchards."

"For once," Evelyn said, "I think I've had enough of the news. Let's listen to some absorbing radio drama and call it a day."

When she arrived downstairs Wednesday morning, Flora found Evelyn at the dining table poring over the brochures they'd collected during the past spring, each extolling the virtues of one attraction or another within a short drive of Walter's Alameda home. Placed on the kitchen table, Flora found a cereal bowl, spoon, the Cheerios box, and a small dish of sliced peaches waiting for her.

"There's coffee in the pot," Evelyn said. "And plenty of fresh milk in the Frigidaire."

Flora gathered up her breakfast and carried everything in to sit beside Evelyn and her brochures. "What exciting misadventure do you have planned for us today? Are we going to let Rafael stew in jail while we have a day of fun?"

Evelyn watched Flora spoon up her cereal. "We haven't heard one way or the other about Rafael," she said. "I can't think what else we might do, at least not this morning. And the truth is, what I'd really like to do this afternoon is take a nice long swim. This investigation has got me tied up in knots. I need time to relax before I can figure anything out, and I think a swim would be just the ticket."

"Um-hum." Flora said.

Evelyn knew her friend accepted the diversion she found in open water swimming even though she didn't understand it. "To that end, I was looking for a small adventure for this morning that you might find enjoyable and a good distraction as well."

"And what have you come up with?"

"How about this?" Evelyn slid a folder with a photograph of a tall bell tower to Flora. "How about we go to the University of California campus in Berkeley? We can stroll the beautiful grounds. A couple of small museums on campus are open to the public. We could also climb to the top of the campanile and enjoy the view from there. It's eight stories up. And if we're still there at noon, the bell ringers play a carillon. See? It says Sather Tower has thirteen bells, twelve to play the carillon and one to ring out the hours. It's the third highest clock tower in the world, built in 1915."

Flora perused the brochure in silence, not evidencing any degree of wild enthusiasm about Evelyn's idea.

Evelyn realized she'd have to sweeten the pot. "There's a large bookstore south of campus. Here." She pointed at a map.

"At the end of Telegraph Ave. Sather Gate Books."

Flora's eyebrows had risen into the "now I might be willing" range. "Could we go out someplace nice for a meal after?"

"Certainly," Evelyn agreed, and the deal was struck. "We'd best get a wiggle on though, if we hope to get through all of that and back here by, say three?"

Flora tipped up her cereal bowl to drink the last of the sweet milk and headed upstairs to dress for their outing. Evelyn had already decided to leave her walking shoes on the back porch for another day. The outing they had planned called for a nicer day dress and her Sunday shoes anyway.

They hadn't been on their way for more than a few minutes when Evelyn sniffed and turned to her friend.

"Good gracious, Flora! You smell like a French chippie."

"Over did it on the perfume, did I? I didn't want even a whiff of dead fish in Walter's car. I found this French perfume on Pearl's dresser. I didn't think there'd be any harm in making Walter's car smell like his wife's perfume."

"That fragrance must be a gift she never uses. I don't believe I've ever smelled it on Pearl. Never mind. Walter will only think I've been chauffeuring high-class call girls in his automobile."

"That does beg the question, though..." Flora said, cocking an eyebrow at Evelyn.

"Yes, what's that?"

"How is it exactly you have any idea what a 'French chippie' smells like? You guessed the perfume right off, before I told you. Had some experience with French chippies, have you?"

Evelyn stifled a chuckle and gave Flora an enigmatic wink.

The morning fog had receded far out to sea, making the view from the top of the campanile indeed spectacular. Flora enjoyed a good long browse through the stacks at the bookstore, and was persuaded to come away with only as many new books as they could comfortably carry back to the Chevrolet, including a new cookbook for Pearl and a couple of Tarzan stories for the nephews.

They enjoyed a tour of the recently completed Berkeley Women's City Club, a short walk away, followed by bowls of cold cucumber soup and crab salads in the sumptuously appointed dining room.

Chapter Twenty-Four

Even after they'd been served lunch, Evelyn felt herself distracted by thoughts of what might be going on in the fruit orchards to the east. Had Rafael been released? Was Marisol still with her aunt today?

Flora waved the brochure they'd been given. "Did you know," she said, pointing at a photograph on the cover, "this building and complex was designed by the architect Julia Morgan? She's the same architect who's designing that huge spread in San Simeon."

Evelyn leaned to the side and read from the brochure. "William Randolph Hearst's La Cuesta Encantada."

"That's the one," Flora said, as she savored another chunk of delicately flavored crab.

Evelyn's only reply was a preoccupied "Hmm."

"Something on your mind?"

"Sorry. I don't mean to change the subject," Evelyn said, "but the other day you hinted you might have learned useful information when you slipped behind the fruit shed to join the gamblers. Did you mean you'd learned something about Joaquin's murder?"

"Perhaps."

"Well, what did you learn?"

"What did I learn? Let me think…" Flora continued to chew for another minute. "Here's one thing I overheard, although I don't see how it could be helpful. It caught my attention is all."

"Yes?"

"A fellow came back, I guess from being up front? He must have been in the conversation when you were asking if they knew anyone who owned one of those revolvers."

"Yes?"

"I overheard him ask that other woman, you know, the one who was so snippy to me? He asked her something like, 'Didn't Hank hang onto his .38 revolver?'"

"Who's Hank?"

Flora widened her eyes and shrugged. "How would I know?"

"Fair enough. What was the snippy woman's reply?"

"I couldn't hear, exactly. Everyone was yelling and laughing, and really, I'm afraid I wasn't paying much attention. I did try to tune in when I heard the part about the gun, but I only heard her say something about how 'Hank is such a dewdropper,' and then someone else yelled, "Yeah, where is that old nellie?' At least that's what I think he said."

"Hmm. You're right, it doesn't make much sense. Do you know what's meant by calling someone a nellie?"

"No, I do not. Nor a dewdropper either." Must be an entirely different linguistic world out there that we know nothing about.

"I think a dewdropper is a fellow who sleeps all day and won't get a job."

"It's an insult?"

Evelyn nodded, thinking again. "You know, Flora, we might be barking up the wrong tree by searching for this revolver. It's possible there are so many of those out there, we'll never find the right one."

"Needle in a haystack," Flora said, putting down her fork and dabbing at her mouth with the linen napkin.

"True," Evelyn said. "Possibly we'd be better off searching for a location providing an opportunity to commit the murder. A place where a gunshot would not be heard or noticed, and where no one would witness the crime."

"Or we could spend our time searching for someone with a motive," Flora said. "I mean other than those we've already put on our list."

"Indeed. Did you by any chance happen to catch the snippy woman's name?"

"The guys called her Olive. I didn't get a last name, and I didn't catch on to why the fellas thought she would know about the whereabouts of this Hank character."

"And what about the other woman you mentioned, Francie?"

Flora dropped her chin into one hand, her elbow politely tucked into her lap. "Hmm..." She paused. "To my way of thinking, while Francie might be a valuable source of information about the characters and motives in this drama, I can't really picture her as a potential villain. She seemed an easy-going type."

Evelyn huffed in frustration. "Well, one thing we know for sure is that someone shot Joaquin. Convoluted means, motives, and opportunities aside for the moment, if we can figure out who Joaquin was with, we'll have found our murderer. If we find ourselves a jealous husband, for example, that'll be a step in the direction of finding Joaquin's killer."

Flora shook her head. "Having a romantic entanglement with someone else's wife should not result in a death sentence."

"It does though, you know, too often. And then there's this other piece..."

"What's that?" Flora asked.

"Well, remember, as curious as we might be, we have been warned off any future investigating, and in a serious way more than once. Possibly we should stick to persuading the sheriff to release Rafael and end our involvement with that."

A dissatisfied frown crossed Flora's brow. "Are you suggesting we may never know who killed Joaquin?"

"Possibly. I could live with that. I'm afraid, however, I would really blow a fuse if the sheriff chose someone other than the actual murderer to blame. If the sheriff is going to arrest anyone for Joaquin's murder, it should be the real killer or no one."

"Remember, Lil Bird said the person who killed Joaquin had a good reason."

"True. You know what galls me about that? From what Lil Bird said, it's obvious someone knows exactly who killed Joaquin."

"And also, no one is going to tell us who that someone is."

"Yes!" Evelyn said with an angry huff. "And since the sheriff shows no particular inclination to prosecute the actual guilty party, I fear you and I may have to be the ones to figure out who that is in what amounts to a guessing game."

"Even after being warned to stop looking." Flora said.

They gazed at one another, considering. "Well," Evelyn said, "maybe like we decided at the beginning. We'll take it one step at a time and see where that gets us. What do you think?"

"What else can we do? We're not the type of people to turn a blind eye to injustice, are we? And in any case, the Pachecos will pay us. Count me in."

They decided Evelyn would make her afternoon swim at the Neptune Beach amusement park. That way, as Evelyn swam, Flora would be free to stroll around the midway, enjoy the sights, and perhaps sample the offerings at the salt-water taffy booth.

As a general rule, once Evelyn entered the water and gained her rhythm, all worries and concerns faded from consciousness. Swimming was a release and more so the longer her swim went on. On this day, she found it difficult to let go of her anxiety. She felt frustrated at not being able to put the puzzle pieces of Joaquin's murder into a whole picture. Eventually, she realized the reason the picture refused to form was because too many pieces were still missing, and nothing more could be learned while she was swimming and worrying. She relaxed into her usual methodical, meditative tempo and was finally able to let her problems go.

After more than an hour, Evelyn emerged from the water, fingers as wrinkled as tiny prunes, her exhausted limbs rubbery. She met up with Flora on the beach, and changed into her street clothes in one of the small bath houses provided. They left the park, stopping on the way out to treat themselves to an icy delight.

"You ladies should try our new double treats," the salesman said, grinning broadly. "We invented 'em right here. See? For one nickel you get two ice treats frozen together. You break them apart..." He demonstrated. "And there you go, one treat for each of you for only one nickel. Nifty, huh?" Since he'd already broken the red ice in half, and it was starting to melt, Flora handed him a nickel.

"What do you call these?" she asked.

"My boss invented these himself. He called them 'icysicles' but his kids wanted him to call them 'popsicles' 'cause he's their Pop."

"Cute," Flora said as she tasted her dripping treat on a wooden stick.

Reaching the intersection where they usually turned left, Evelyn noticed a newsie selling papers on the corner up ahead.

"I'd like to get a newspaper," she said. "Let's go as far as that corner." They purchased the Oakland daily paper and made their left turn. They were couple of blocks farther along when they ran into a small crowd on the sidewalk where two police sedans were parked in front of a small, neat house.

"What's happening?" Flora asked a frizzy-haired woman in a flowered housedress.

"It's the Werners," she said. "Greta and her kids are gettin' evicted."

A heavy-set man stood fuming next to her. "Damn banks!" he said in a loud voice. "Damn landlord, damn bankers!"

The small crowd parted at his angry words and Evelyn and Flora could see a pathetic pile of household furnishings and clothes on the sidewalk ahead. Police officers emerged from the house carrying paperboard boxes filled with the sound of breaking china. A couple of small children toddled excitedly from the porch across the yard and back, while an older child pulled a broken doll from the pile, gazing glumly at the ruined toy.

On the porch steps, a woman sat. Greta Werner, Evelyn had to assume, her head in her hands.

"I'm telling you!" the man yelled, louder this time. "Those damn bankers are taking this property just like they took those other two. They're gonna take every house on this block, tear 'em down, and build big places for the rich."

Flora could see the two sad little houses he pointed to, boarded up and empty.

"Yeah!" Someone else joined in. "Everybody knows Gus Werner is looking for work. When he gets a job, he'll catch up on those house payments."

"Darn right," a tall thin man said. "He's not a shiftless no-good. He's a welder. See that gate back there?" He pointed at the scrollwork of a handsome wrought iron gate along the side of the house. "Gus made that himself. Why, he's even got himself listed to be hired if they ever get started on that darn bridge across the Golden Gate."

Another woman said, "The Werners, they been here since before the kids were born. Just like the rest of us on this block, hard-working, God-fearing homeowners."

"Darn right!" the tall man said. "And Gus is a veteran, too. What now? Gus's gonna come back, find his whole family gone, his home torn down."

The frizzy-haired woman turned to Flora and put her hand over her mouth, speaking so as not to be overheard. "That Gus's been gone pert near four months now. Went out one night sayin' he was gonna get some milk for the kiddies, then never came home. Same as Bobby Tiller over there, across the street."

"They never came home?" Flora said, in a shocked tone.

A third woman answered, equally quietly. "What else are they gonna do?" she said. "Can't find work. Can't support the wife and babies. Come home empty-handed day after day. After a while, they just up and leave. Nothing else they can do."

The frizzy-haired woman answered. "I heard Gus went back east to join up with those Bonus Army fellers in Washington, DC. Veteran's trying to get the government to turn loose of that bonus all those war veterans was promised."

"Damn bankers!" the first man yelled again. "And damn you coppers for doing their bidding. Shame on you!"

"Hush, Howard," the frizzy-haired woman said, slapping at his arm. "You're not gonna do anyone any good if you get yourself arrested."

Loud slams rang out as a police officer pulled the front door shut and drove nails into the jamb to keep it closed. Greta Werner stood, picked up the smallest toddler, his gray-tinged diaper sagging, and called the other two children to her.

"What's she going to do now?" Flora said, quietly.

The other women stared at her for a moment, then the frizzy-haired one said, "What do you think? She's gonna do the same thing you'd do if you had three little ones to feed and no money."

Evelyn felt horrified at the whole scene. She wrapped an arm around Flora's waist and pushed through the group to hurry them homeward. Flora's face had reddened and tears threatened to spill as they walked.

"Isn't there something we could do to help that poor family?" Flora said.

"I wish we could do something, but thousands of foreclosures are happening all over the country, and millions are out of work. I don't know what we could do that would make any real difference." They walked on in silence, neither able to find words for their feelings.

Chapter Twenty-Five

Later, tucked into the cozy chairs in Walter and Pearl's parlor, Evelyn interrupted Flora's reading to point out an article she'd found in the newspaper. "Look," she said. "It says here upwards of twenty thousand veterans are setting up a tent city on Capitol Hill in Washington, DC. They're vowing to stay until they get their war bonuses, and Congress is behind them, even most of the Republicans."

"Good," Flora said. "They earned it, although I imagine Hoover's not going to be on their side."

The telephone rang a bit later, but neither Flora nor Evelyn wanted to rally themselves to answer it. Evelyn, who had, after all, spent more than an hour open-water swimming that afternoon, won the staring contest, and Flora went to pick up the jangling device. She was back in a flash, announcing the call was from Marisol, who was at home in San Francisco and wished to speak with Evelyn.

Marisol's unwelcome news was that her cousin Rafael had suffered a beating while in custody. Instead of being sent home, he had been transferred to a nearby hospital. Marisol reported that Tia Rosamaria was in hysterics again.

Weeping, she pleaded with Evelyn for help. She argued that Evelyn had established a good connection with the coroner and had a much better chance of persuading him to send that autopsy report to the sheriff. That seemed to be the only thing holding up Rafael's release. She also argued strongly that Evelyn would hold more sway with the sheriff or his deputies and asked her to visit there again also.

What Evelyn told Marisol was that she would need to discuss the situation with Flora. What she didn't say was she really felt she had no choice. She'd already inserted herself into the middle of the situation and Marisol was correct. She and Flora might be the only ones with enough rapport both with the coroner and the sheriff to have any hope of intervening successfully. However much Evelyn might wish to extract herself, it was too late to refuse to be involved. She ended the telephone call with an assurance to Marisol that she would do whatever she could and would keep her friend up-to-date on her progress.

For her part, Marisol planned to take the ferry from San Francisco as soon as her shift ended on Friday so she could be with her aunt for the weekend.

Evelyn disconnected and rejoined Flora, who had been eavesdropping anyway. Flora gave Evelyn a questioning look.

"Here we go again,"Evelyn said, having gained Flora's agreement to another trip the following day. "Gallivanting off to the countryside in search of a murderer."

"Wouldn't it be a good idea to get the coroner on the telephone in the morning and let him know you're coming? That way he'll be sure to be there. Dr. Whitley wouldn't want to miss a visit from his favorite spinster," Flora teased.

"Excellent plan," Evelyn answered, refusing to take the bait. "And I want to look into this retired or ex-deputy angle with regard to the revolver. I am also most curious to know what Lil Bird meant by Joaquin's murderer having a 'good reason' for killing him. He seemed to be referring to something very specific. Oh, and don't you think it would be a good idea if you could track down your heavily made-up friend Francie?"

Flora pretended to pull reading glasses lower on her nose. "My 'friend,' you say? I shouldn't like it to get back to Mother that I have become jolly friends with a painted trollop. That sort of rumor could have unhappy consequences, as I'm certain you are aware."

Evelyn laughed. "Very well, dear. I shall try to keep that under my hat. Nevertheless, I do suspect you are correct in surmising that the lady in question might be an excellent source of information. Who would know more about the personalities in a community than the town trollop?"

"You may be right," Flora said. "Is there someone specific you're wanting to know more about?"

"Well, for example, I'd like to more fully identify this Olive person you mentioned who evidently knows that Hank fellow who someone thought might own a gun of the type we're looking to find. Surely she hadn't gone to the gambling game by herself. Who was with her?"

Flora pursed her lips. "I really didn't notice," she said. "Bodie, perhaps? The fella who was rolling the dice?"

"And what about that Hank who may be, to some degree or another, a 'nellie.' At the very least, Francie might be able to enlighten us as to what on earth is meant by calling someone a nellie."

"You know, as you use that term repeatedly in context, I have begun to develop some suspicion as to what it means," Flora said.

"As have I, but let's not jump to unwarranted conclusions. The use of that term may have been meant only as a hateful insult."

Flora nodded slowly. "You know, in our vast experience at crime solving, I suspect we're at the stage where we continue to gather every bit of information we can find, from every source, and sort it out later."

"Like a jigsaw puzzle." Evelyn nodded.

"And how!" Flora said. "Let's find more pieces and then figure out how they fit together. And where, may I ask, in all of this is Marisol? Is she able to assist in any way with this investigation? Or are her energies more needed in caring for her aunt?"

"Apparently Marisol's cousin and the aunt from Martinez need to return to their own homes and their husbands and children, so until Rafael can be rescued the weight of care-taking the aunt falls on Marisol's shoulders."

Evelyn was up before dawn. After her Quaker oatmeal, toast, and coffee, she sat down to make a list of the people she hoped to visit on this next trip and the additional questions she had.

Flora appeared later. "I know," she said, "you have in mind to visit Dr. Whitley to try to light a fire under him with regard to finishing up that autopsy report, but what else might we do today?"

"Another visit to see Rafael is in order," Evelyn said as she gave a final swipe of the dishtowel to the pan in which she'd cooked their morning oatmeal. "Since he's now in the hospital it might be easier to get more information out of him. And you might consider pilfering another of Wally's Tarzan books to take along."

"Anything else? Should we pack another picnic or buy something there?"

"I don't believe we need any more fruit, if that's what you're asking about."

Flora laughed. "Not for a few more days, anyway. No, I was mostly asking so I'd have some idea what to wear."

"Oh, good point. I did have an idea that we might drive as far as that town called Alamo. We can park alongside the road there and then hike up to the summit of the mountain, Mount Diablo. There's a new state park there."

"If there's a state park up there, why can't we simply drive to the top?"

"Where's the fun in that?" It was Evelyn's turn to laugh. "It's only about two miles. Anyway, I have no idea as to the condition of the road, and don't want to get into a pickle with Walter's new automobile."

"When you say, 'fun,' you mean walking two miles straight up a mountain, right?"

"Yes, and then two more miles down. Did you pack walking togs? Or something more comfortable to hike in than a day dress?"

"It'll be hot in the valley, Evie. What could be more comfortable than a light-weight day dress? Your walking togs are heavy wool. I shouldn't think those would be comfortable in the heat."

"Hmm. I expect you're right about that. I should wear a dress. That would be more appropriate for our other business, in any case. Comfortable shoes are a must, though, and a hat with a broad brim to keep the sun off. Now where did my newly repaired walking shoes get to?"

"And did you pack your nifty rucksack? We need something so we can carry our snacks. Also, remember Lolly is coming today to do the laundry and whatnot. I'm running upstairs to strip the beds and bring the sheets down."

"Yes, good idea. Marisol may stay here Friday night and I'd like to offer her clean sheets if she does."

Flora's timing was perfect, as she got the sheets and the rest of the laundry heaped in baskets on the wide back porch just as Lolly bustled in, ready to go to work. She was happy to have the company of both dogs, and waved Evelyn and Flora off on their adventures for the day.

When they cruised past the fruit shed that had housed the gambling game earlier in the week it was shuttered and boarded up and no vehicles were parked out front. In any case, they didn't have time to stop as Evelyn had a ten o'clock appointment with the coroner.

When they pulled up, Dr Whitley stood peering through the glass door eagerly awaiting Evelyn's arrival. His receptionist sat glowering behind her counter, even more sour-faced than she had been days before.

The doctor smiled broadly and took Evelyn's hands in his. He barely acknowledged Flora when she was introduced. This was a somewhat unusual experience for Flora, who raised her eyebrows but otherwise gave no outward sign of surprise.

"Please," the doctor said, tugging Evelyn's hand. "Come back to my office where we can speak privately. I suppose your friend may come also, if you like."

Evelyn cast Flora a desperate and earnestly pleading look. With an enigmatic smile, Flora followed the pair down the narrow hallway. The room the doctor led them into was filled with several filing cabinets and a small but sturdy table for a desk. It did not look like a space where the doctor spent much time. Still, Evelyn thought, it was probably better than chatting over a cadaver in the morgue.

"So nice to see you again, Miss Winslow," he said. "And Miss...ah..." He'd already forgotten Flora's name.

"Fitzgerald," Evelyn supplied, while Flora drew a business card from her pocketbook and slid it across the table.

"Yes, of course, my apologies," he said, turning his eyes to Evelyn. "And how may I help you this morning?"

Evelyn bit her tongue. Was the good doctor laboring under the impression this was a social call?

"May I remind you," she said, "at our last encounter you gave me to understand your autopsy of Mr. Joaquin Pacheco would reveal the true cause of the man's death, and you would be forwarding those results immediately to the sheriff's department. Is that the case, or did I misunderstand?"

Flora widened her eyes just slightly and Evelyn took a breath, trying to modulate her tone, which was tending toward snappish. Really, something about this man's attitude was trying her patience.

"Ah, yes," he said as he began to sort through a stack of papers on one corner of the table. "I believe that report is here…somewhere…" He turned to another stack. "Or here?"

Utilizing her skills at reading upside-down, honed by scanning the contents of student notes being passed from desk to desk, Flora said, "If I'm not mistaken, sir, the report you're seeking is under your elbow there." She pointed. "Just there, under your right elbow."

"Ah, yes, here it is," he said, pulling out the two-page report and smoothing it carefully.

"Just so I'm clear," Evelyn said, taking a terse tone. "You have not transmitted those results to the sheriff? Because, as I'm sure you know, Rafael Pacheco is still being held in custody. In fact, yesterday Mr. Pacheco suffered a beating at the jail and has now been transferred to the county hospital with his injuries. If the results of your autopsy prove he could not have killed his brother, your delay in forwarding that report may have caused Mr. Pacheco a good deal of unnecessary suffering."

"Um-hm." Dr. Whitley stared at the page before him.

Evelyn was nearly on her last nerve. "Can you at least tell me why you've not sent the report to the sheriff?"

The man gave Evelyn an insipid smile. "Well, my dear, the primary reason the sheriff does not already have my report is that he asked me to hold onto it. He said he'd stop by and pick it up. I believe he said Friday. That would be tomorrow."

The news that the sheriff had asked the coroner to withhold his report about Joaquin's death, leaving Rafael stewing in a jail cell, infuriated and confused Evelyn.

Chapter Twenty-Six

"You know," Dr. Whitley said as he shifted uncomfortably in his chair. "You may be expecting too much from this autopsy report. For example," he tapped the top page, "while I discussed my findings that Joaquin died of a gunshot from a .38 Special revolver, those findings in no way prove Rafael's innocence. Nobody has yet found the weapon, and there's no way to know who fired the shot that killed this young man. If I'm not mistaken, that's why the sheriff continues to hold Rafael."

Both Evelyn and Flora sat rigid, listening. Evelyn tried to formulate a question that might throw light on who had really killed Joaquin. Or at least reveal some other fact on which to hang her hat about Rafael's probable innocence.

Whitley also sat in silence, watching Evelyn's perplexed face.

"What about the time of death?" Flora asked.

"Oh, yes! Good thinking, dear," Evelyn said, patting Flora's hand gratefully. She turned back to Dr, Whitley. "Did your examination reveal anything about the time of Joaquin's death?"

Dr. Whitley pulled his head back and his already thin lips tightened until they all but disappeared. He gave Evelyn an intense stare, and she gazed back, at a loss as to the cause of his sudden and obvious upset. He looked down at his report and began to read. "Yes," he said. "As you know, the body was found early, at about six-thirty in the morning. By the time anyone examined it, the body was in a mid-stage of rigor and body temperature was reduced noticeably. Based on the state of rigor and calculation of the Glaister equation..." The doctor raised his eyes and met Evelyn's, as though she would know exactly to what he was referring. "Based on the evidence to hand, Mr. Pacheco experienced physiological death at approximately one o'clock, give or take an hour. Between midnight and two, Saturday night to Sunday morning. As I've also noted here, he was killed elsewhere and his body was later moved to the orchard."

Evelyn sat back abruptly. "Well."

Having suddenly decided to reveal all, Dr. Whitley was not finished. "I can also report with certainty the cause of death was a gunshot wound to the back of the head, and death was not due to blunt force trauma as previously surmised. The rock was used on his head well after physiological death. While the young man bled heavily around the site of the gunshot wound as evidenced from the blood found on his clothing, there is little evidence of blood having been shed from the facial wounds.

"While we're on the subject of clothing, attached here to the back of my report is the list of Joaquin Pacheco's personal effects." He flipped the page and showed them a list of clothing that included Joaquin's western boots. "You'll want to note I found a wallet containing four dollars in cash. In the front pocket of his pants I also found a single house key on a leather fob and a second smaller unattached and unidentified key."

"Hmm," Evelyn said. "And you've no idea what that second key might unlock, then, do you?"

"How could I possibly know that?" Whitley said, his voice still tense.

Evelyn tried a tight smile. "Well, thank you very much." The doctor's suddenly icy tone made her nervous. At least he'd been more forthcoming with information. In any case, he appeared to have told them everything he was going to tell.

"We'll let you get back to work, then," she said. Both women rose and shuffled to the door.

"We do sincerely hope—" Flora started. Evelyn shared Flora's sentiment and interrupted her friend.

"Yes, we do hope that report will get to the sheriff quickly. As a matter of fact, our next stop will be at the county jail. Would it be possible we could take the report to the sheriff ourselves?"

"Or perhaps a copy?" Flora said.

Dr. Whitley stood and pulled his precious report closer, avoiding eye contact. "This is an NCR form and the only copy is my file copy. Obviously, I cannot let civilians take the original to the sheriff. Good day."

They hurried to their automobile, climbed inside, and slammed the doors. "My word," Evelyn said. "He certainly got huffy all of a sudden."

"Yes, a change of heart, I daresay."

"What do you mean? Did I miss something?"

Flora caught Evelyn's gaze. "Yes, I'd say you did miss something."

"Well, what?"

"Let me ask you first, and I'm not teasing you here, but you did notice that upon our arrival the doctor took something of a, shall we say, a personal interest in you?"

"Oh, phooey!"

"Are you saying you hadn't noticed?"

"Well, possibly, but that's neither here nor there. We came on a purely business visit."

"Oh, Evelyn, you are such a dear girl." Flora pulled Evelyn's head close and placed a chaste kiss on her cheek before releasing her.

"Do you think Dr. Whitley got snappish after I called you 'dear?'" Evelyn said, one eyebrow cocked.

"As a trained investigator I strongly suspect that was indeed the source of his displeasure."

"Oh, I can't believe that. My opinion is he was vexed that you thought of that time of death angle. He likes to think he's the one in charge, and your question showed he wasn't telling us everything."

"Perhaps you're right." Flora said.

Evelyn smiled and shook her head. "Heaven knows what he's thinking now," she said, laughing. "Oh, well, the important thing, and I am so grateful you brought it up, is that Rafael has an unshakeable alibi for the estimated time of his brother's death. Rafael was at home with Marisol and his mother until about two in the morning when his mother woke him to tell him Joaquin had not come home."

"Exactly what I had in mind, and that's why that report will exonerate Rafael. Also, and I don't like to be a cynic about this, but it is likely the sheriff already knows this to be true. If that's the case, why do you suppose he's continuing to keep Rafael in custody?"

"Good question. Possibly we'll get lucky and run into the sheriff when we stop at the jail."

"*Allons-y!*"

Evelyn engaged the ignition, and they were off on the next leg of their journey.

Despite this being Thursday and thus a weekday, the sheriff was again unavailable. Evelyn and Flora were shunted to Deputy Calhoun to ask their questions, this time standing at the reception counter in the front of the room with all the deputies watching. Evelyn noticed "the girl" was hard at work again filing papers. In Evelyn's estimation she looked to be roughly the same age as Evelyn herself, early to mid-thirties, and thus hardly a girl at all.

They first learned Rafael was still at the county hospital in Martinez even though, according to Calhoun, his injuries were minor. Their principal question at that point was why Rafael was still being held by the sheriff.

Calhoun's answer did not do much more than illuminate how and why Rafael had come to be detained for the crime of his brother's murder in the first place.

"Sure," Calhoun said, "Rafael has an alibi for the time the murder, but the sheriff's not going to release him until we've got another suspect in jail. You know how untrustworthy those Mexicans are, and the way those families stick together. If we release Rafael before we've got someone else in jail his amigos will hide him and he'll disappear."

Evelyn had gone from calm to fuming in almost less time than it took for Calhoun to utter the word "Mexican." "They are not Mexicans," she said through gritted teeth. "They are from right here in California. Look around you. San Francisco? Alamo? Martinez? Even the town of Pacheco? You're surrounded by Spanish names because you live in California. Does it never once dawn on you that most Spanish-speaking people here are not moving up from Mexico, but were here long before you and the other English-speaking people, the Germans, the French, and the others who invaded this state?"

Flora gently tapped Evelyn's arm. Once she had her attention, Flora glanced at her friend, rubbed her right eyebrow, and cut a look to the door. It was a long-standing and well understood signal.

Evelyn scowled and tightened her lips. She said, "Excuse me," and walked stiffly out of the office.

Flora turned back to Deputy Calhoun. "Please excuse my friend. We've had a trying day. We do have a few more questions, and we're hoping you might help us find some answers."

"Shoot."

"To begin with, last time we were here you told us you would be looking into that bloody fingerprint smear on the rock. Were you able to identify that fingerprint?"

"Nope, except it isn't Rafael's.

"And has there been any progress made on finding the revolver used in the shooting?"

"What are you, now? A newspaper reporter?"

Flora gave him a level stare, brooking no side-tracking or humor. She could be as serious and as businesslike as Evelyn, when the situation called for such behavior.

Calhoun cleared his throat and looked around at the deputies working at desks behind him. No one made eye contact. "No," he said to Flora. "We have the bullet, but not the gun. Our investigating detective said he can't find any evidence Rafael owns or borrowed a revolver like that one."

"And has your detective been able to identify any credible motive, or reason why Rafael might kill his brother?"

"No, but that doesn't mean there isn't one."

"Indeed. What you're telling me is that Rafael had no means or motive for the murder, and now knowing the time of death, he also had no opportunity to commit it, is that correct?"

Deputy Calhoun unclenched his jaw long enough to say, "Yep."

"And no evidence tying him to the scene where the body was found?"

"Nope."

Flora took a step back and gazed at the countertop for a moment, then looked up. "Surely you can see, it becomes increasingly obvious to anyone with a half a wit, the only reason you're holding Rafael is that, according to you, he's Mexican? Perhaps I should call a newspaper reporter."

It was Calhoun's turn to fume. He puffed out his cheeks and his face turned a disturbing shade of red.

"I told you before," he said, "the sheriff thinks the killer is gonna to turn out to be either another farmworker, or maybe one of these Vigilantes trying to find work in the orchards. Those Vigilante guys are the ones who really hate the Mexicans…the farmworkers…whatever you wanna call 'em."

Flora nodded, listening. "The sheriff's idea is that one of the Vigilantes shot Joaquin out of prejudice and race hatred?"

"Or it was a farmworker."

"You know, if prejudice and race hatred against people with Spanish names was the motive for this murder, there's almost no end of potential suspects. You may never find the real murderer."

Deputy Calhoun nodded in agreement, although still glaring at Flora with narrowed eyes.

"Not to mention," Flora said, "that begs the question as to why Rafael continues to be detained, or why he was arrested in the first place. As a matter of fact, you should be aware the Pacheco family has engaged the services of a top-notch attorney. That gentleman promises to not only secure Rafael's release, but also to sue the county for unlawfully arresting and detaining Mr. Pacheco." She tapped the countertop repeatedly with one bright red fingernail. The deputy narrowed his glare even more but had apparently said all he was going to say on the subject.

Flora took a breath and visibly shifted gears. She rested one hand on the countertop and tipped her head in a more friendly manner. "Let me ask you another question on a different topic."

Calhoun's shoulders dropped slightly, giving Flora a signal he might be open to a change of subject. "The other day," she said, "I saw one of your deputies out at the fruit stand. Do you know, or would he know or remember some of the other folks who were there? I'm thinking in particular about a fellow I met out there by the name of Bodie." With a coquettish dip of her chin and a smile, Flora gave Deputy Calhoun to understand that she had a special interest in finding this Bodie fellow.

"Oh, sure, I know Bodie. Only thing is…"

Flora waited, then repeated her question with raised eyebrows and a shrug.

Calhoun looked at the deputies behind him again nervously, then lowered his voice to almost a whisper. "Thing is, Bodie's a married man, ma'am. And if I were you, I wouldn't mess with his Jeanine. Bodie's no angel, you understand, but Jeanine can be real mean if she catches you or any other woman sniffing around her Bodie. You understand?"

Flora managed to work up a convincing-looking pout. "Yes, I understand. Well, how about, do you know Francie? She was there too. Do you know how I might locate her?"

Deputy Calhoun's lips curled into a nasty smirk. He looked around at the other deputies in the room, most of whom studiously pretended not to be listening to their conversation. "Lady here wants to get in touch with Francie," he called. "Anybody here doesn't know how to reach Francie?" This earned a chorus of snickers.

One deputy called out from the back of the room, "If you're that desperate, ma'am, our girl here might be open to earnin' an odd buck or two."

"Nah," an older deputy said. "From what I hear, our girl's already got herself a man friend."

"Oh yeah?" came the answer. "Who's the lucky guy?"

The older deputy replied with a locking-his-lips gesture and a wink. The "girl" reddened but kept right on filing papers as though she'd not heard a word.

Deputy Calhoun turned to Flora, reached into a back pocket, and pulled out his worn leather wallet. A brief search of its contents resulted in a much-folded slip of paper. He copied the faint number inscribed there onto a notepad, tore that page off, and handed it to Flora. "You girls have a good time now, won't you?"

Chapter Twenty-Seven

Flora held Deputy Calhoun's leering gaze for a full second before she muttered, "Thank you," and exited the station.

Evelyn watched as Flora walked toward the Chevrolet, her face turning an uncharacteristic and more embarrassed shade of red with every step she took.

Once seated, Flora gave Evelyn a full report of everything she'd learned. "I know we wanted to ask with whom Joaquin might have had a romantic entanglement, but it didn't seem appropriate to bring that topic up with the deputies listening in. I did ask Calhoun how we might reach Bodie. According to him, Bodie has a jealous wife who wouldn't take kindly to good-looking young women asking after her husband. He suggested she might over-react. In any case, as I think more about it, that Bodie character didn't seem too bright anyway, and might not be a reliable source of information of a sensitive nature."

She paused as though undecided about sharing the next bit with Evelyn. "Calhoun did give me a telephone number for Francie." She waved the notepad page. "He seemed to think we, or at least I, was interested in telephoning Francie 'for a good time,' as they say."

"What! Why I've a mind to march right back in there and punch that smarmy man."

"I know, right in the kisser, huh?" Flora gave a shaky laugh.

They both gazed for a moment at the front door to the county jail.

"I'm guessing I shouldn't do that," Evelyn said. "Those fellows in there are armed, and I don't want you to have to be driving out here tomorrow to bail me out of jail. Let's go off on our hike and keep our eyes open for a public telephone."

They found the access road toward the summit of Mount Diablo without mishap and pulled over where the asphalt ended. As Evelyn had predicted, this left a hike of approximately two miles ahead of them, and at a steady uphill grade. Shortly after they began, they ran across a trailside sign reading "Rock City" which pointed to an interesting-looking side trail. Still full of pent-up energy, and being on the young side, they decided to chance it, and shortly found themselves in the midst of fascinating rock formations and caves carved into the sandstone escarpments by the wind.

After a brief tour of Rock City, they returned to the main trail and continued their trek. About halfway along, Flora remembered to tell Evelyn about her spur-of-the-moment fib to Calhoun that the Pacheco family had hired an attorney.

"I wouldn't be a bit surprised if they have, in fact, done so," Evelyn said. "I'll add that to our list of issues to speak with Marisol about."

They reached the flattish viewing area at the summit just as their appetites for the snacks packed in their rucksack peaked. Settling in the shade of a large boulder, they ate cold meat sandwiches and cheese. When they'd had their fill, they stood and walked slowly around the flattened area, marveling at the views from every direction. They ended with a long stare out to the west.

"Oh, this is indeed a lovely view," Flora said. "California just seems to go on forever from up here."

Evelyn was focused more closely on the valley below them. "You know, it strikes me that somewhere down there but not too far away, are all the answers to the riddles about who killed Joaquin and why. The answers are spread out before us if we could only see them."

"For example," Flora mused, "what about the Alisal family who live down there in Danville? Marisol suggested they might want to take over the labor contracting business. Should we look into that possibility?"

"At least they have a motive to want the Pachecos out of the picture," Evelyn agreed. "Like any other investigation, though, we'd need a place to start. Add that to our list."

"Unless you take Lil Bird at his word...you know, that Joaquin's murder was down to a personal matter," Flora said.

The return trip went faster than the way up, if a bit more treacherous, with sliding gravel underfoot and little to grab onto to stay upright. Evelyn's damaged walking shoe began to show signs of disintegrating about halfway down, but Lolly's repair held long enough to get her back to the automobile.

"Well," Flora said. "That was lovely, and I'm so glad we did it, because—"

"Because now we don't have to do it again," Evelyn said, finishing a favorite joke.

As they cruised through the hamlet of Walnut Creek, they spotted a sign indicating the presence of a public telephone inside Markley Bros. Soda Fountain. They carefully assembled coins from their pocketbooks and marched in together to telephone Francie. Flora dialed and held the earpiece to her head while Evelyn dropped coins into the device at Flora's direction. They hoped to convince Francie to meet them somewhere private enough to have a conversation. Noticing two women seated at the soda fountain eyeing Flora as she dialed, Evelyn used her body to block the device. Flora put one hand over her mouth. Even so, the other customers could easily overhear, especially since Flora had to ask for Francie several times once the connection had been made. The number was the correct one, but Francie was not available to speak with them. Flora left Walter's telephone number and thanked the voice on the other end of the line just before the telephone operator joined the conversation to request more coins be deposited. The machine set up a cheerful jingling as Evelyn watched their money disappear into the slot.

"Oh, well, never mind," Evelyn said as they climbed back into the Chevrolet. "If Marisol stays with us tomorrow night, we'll have to come out here again to bring her to her aunt's. It's a long distance telephone call but we can call Francie from Walter's and set up a place to meet on Saturday."

"You don't want to ask Francie about Joaquin's love life over the telephone?"

"No, you know, I like to look a person in the eye with a delicate conversation like that. Very well, we're off to home now."

"*Allons-y*! Except I'm famished."

"Would you like me to stop for more peaches?"

"No, thank you. I'll manage. You know what, though?"

"What's that?"

"I certainly hope Francie doesn't telephone Walter's number after your family has returned from Philadelphia. Can you imagine Pearl answering the telephone and finding a trollop on the other end?"

The last of the thick mulligatawny was satisfying for a late-afternoon supper, and especially when followed up with generous helpings of the peach cobbler Lolly had left for them on the counter.

Pushing back from the table, Flora said, "That was delicious, but I still miss Jaing. Can't we send for her to join us here? We're not managing all that well cooking for ourselves, and it seems like we're on an endless cycle of deciding what to eat, shopping, cooking, and cleaning up, only to find it's time to start over again."

"You'll get no argument from me about that endless cycle," Evelyn said, "but even though we're doing better than a lot of other people, our money doesn't grow on trees. Let's think of doing without Jaing's help for these three weeks as a lesson in what Lolly called 'making do,' shall we?"

"Humph! I'd hardly consider living off Pearl's amply supplied larder as 'making do,' but I suppose I understand your point." Flora began clearing the table.

Aware that she'd eaten a tad too much of the delicious cobbler, Evelyn went for a lie down on the sofa, one hand blocking the light of the setting sun from her eyes.

Flora emerged from the kitchen, savoring a bit of something on a spoon, and saw Evelyn lying down.

"Are you all right?"

"Yes, of course, I just felt like a little nap."

Flora licked the spoon again, still gazing at Evelyn. "Wouldn't you be more comfortable upstairs? I could do with a lie down myself."

Evelyn moved her hand just enough to look at Flora with one eye. "It's not that sort of a nap, dear."

Flora looked at Evelyn a moment longer, then sashayed toward Walter's chair. "Suit yourself," she said, and curled up with her latest novel. A few moments later, a gentle snoring could be heard from Evelyn's end of the sofa.

Just before the broadcast of the national evening news was due to come on, the telephone rang.

"I'm never sure if we should answer Walter's telephone," Flora said from her nest deep in the chair.

Evelyn sat up, blinking, and started for the telephone. "Walter did ask us to answer and to take messages. And we did leave that message for Francie to call." She hurried to reach the device before the caller gave up trying. "Winslow residence, Evelyn Winslow speaking." The party on the other end of the line continued to breathe audibly, but said nothing for a moment, then smacked chewing gum, or at least that's what it sounded like to Evelyn, an experienced schoolteacher. "Hello?"

The gum smacked once more, and a woman's voice cleared her throat.

"Uh, hello?" the woman on the other end said. "I was told to call this number for a Flora Fitzgerald?"

"Oh, of course, certainly, I'll just ask her to come to the telephone. May I say who's calling?"

"Uh…I'd rather not."

"Oh. All right then. Please hold the line for Miss Fitzgerald."

Evelyn placed the handset gently on the entry table and stepped into Flora's line of sight. "It's for you, dear. She'd rather not give her name."

"Oh! That must be…" Flora scurried to the telephone and picked up the handset. "Hello? This is Miss Flora Fitzgerald." She turned to look back at Evelyn. "Oh, Francie, hello. Thank you so much for returning my call. We met, do you remember? We met at the gambling game behind the fruit shed on, when was that? Monday? Do you remember?" Flora paused while she listened. "Yes, oh, good. With Bodie, yes." Flora listened again. "Oh, no, that's perfectly fine. No, no…yes, I follow you. Yes, of course. Perfectly understandable.

"Listen, the reason we called you is this. We'd like to meet with you. It seems like you know so many people, and we'd, well, we have some questions we thought you could help us answer. Questions about, well, about who might have known Joaquin Pacheco." Flora stopped talking for a short time, throwing in an occasional, "uh-huh."

"I see," she finally said, her shoulders drooping in a deflated manner.

"Tell her we'd like to take her out for a nice meal," Evelyn urged. Flora nodded. Really, Evelyn thought, if we can't get Francie to fill in some of these blanks, we'll be hard pressed to solve this mystery.

When an opening presented itself in the other end of the conversation, Flora made the offer, following up with, "We have an automobile, so we could choose a place to meet in another town, if you'd prefer?"

Flora smiled and nodded at Evelyn. "Good. Yes, that would be lovely. We can pick you up on Saturday, say eleven-thirty?" Evelyn nodded back. "Yes, so this coming Saturday…yes, eleven-thirty in the morning. We'll meet you, well, how about at Markley's Soda Fountain? We know where that's located." A few seconds later Flora gestured frantically for a pencil and paper and scribbled a note. "Yes…yes…yes, that will be fine." She finished the telephone call with expressions of gratitude and a big smile for Evelyn.

"Success!" Flora exclaimed. "She didn't want to meet us at the soda fountain, although it wasn't clear to me whether she was trying to protect our reputations or hers." This gave both of them a fit of nervous giggles.

"Where will we take her?" Evelyn said. "We can't very well take her to the Claremont Hotel or the Berkeley Women's Club."

"No, no, she knows a place if we'll drive."

"Good, then that's all set. Thank you."

"This will be fun," Flora said. "I have so many questions… you know, as research."

Evelyn laughed again. "Oh," she said, "I almost forgot. There's a letter for you from your sister. It's there by the telephone. Flora slit open her envelope, and settled in to read. Mitzi's letters were always newsy, filled with tales about the antics of Flora's nieces and nephew and updates about the rest of the family.

"Ooh," she said aloud. "Rolf bought Mitzi a brand new Chrysler for her very own. A Series CH roadster, whatever that is, dark green with white-wall tires."

"Hmm. Rolf must be faring well through this economic situation if he can afford to buy his wife her own automobile."

"Yes, well…he does work for my father, remember."

"I had no idea shipbuilding had remained so lucrative in this market."

"Oh, Father's shipyards are always busy. He made bundles building fleets for the Navy during the war."

"Who's he building ships for now?"

Flora tapped her lip, considering the question. "Perhaps the Navy lost so many ships during The Great War, it has need of new ones?"

"Possibly. The war ended almost fifteen years ago, and as far as I know, we're not anticipating another one. I'm not sure why we'd need a larger naval fleet."

"The Navy may know more than they're saying about the world situation," Flora said. "As you've often pointed out, there are ominous rumblings from Germany. I know von Hindenburg was re-elected president, but the power of those Nazis only seems to grow stronger."

"Surely you're not suggesting your father may be profiteering by building ships for a newly revived German military? The Treaty of Versailles, to which Germany is a signatory, prohibits Germany from rebuilding its navy and rearming."

"I don't know. I could ask Mitzi for a few more details. Do you suppose I might have a future as a spy?" Flora said. They both laughed, then grew serious. In their experience, the world situation always had the potential to turn grim without much warning.

"Perhaps Father's up to his old shenanigans again," Flora said "building parts for Germany's U-boats."

"The Germans claim to have only peaceful purposes in mind for their newly designed U-boats," Evelyn pointed out.

"Hard to fathom what peaceful purposes there might be for underwater boats, isn't it?"

"Was that a pun, Miss Fitzgerald?"

"Ah, well, sometimes one must find the humor in order to avoid the anxiety. Ugh. Let's change the subject."

"We could summarize our investigation at this point, so we know where to start with Francie, and what else we need to know. Who are our current suspects, for example, and what are their motives?"

Flora narrowed her eyes. "It seems to me that's exactly why we're stuck. We have these vague ideas about perhaps Joaquin saw something he shouldn't have seen, or did something he shouldn't have done, or was with someone he shouldn't have been with, but beyond those ideas we really don't have a useful clue."

Evelyn agreed. "We need to know more specifically about Joaquin. Rafael claims he doesn't know who his brother might have been seeing. Considering they are family, Marisol also doesn't seem to know much about Joaquin's...ah...affairs. We'll need to ask Francie if she knows the names of Joaquin's friends or girlfriends."

"Say," Flora perked up. "What about that foreman, Luis? He might know a little something about Joaquin's life. And you do remember, we thought for a moment that Luis himself might be a suspect? And, well, not to divert our energies, but I shouldn't like us to lose sight of the fact that we were originally hired to investigate those acts of vandalism against the Pachecos. What about those?"

"Brilliant, Flora. As Joaquin's coworker, Luis may be the closest Joaquin had to a friend, and he also might be just the person to know or suspect who the vandals might be. Add that to the list of our next questions. I think we might finally be at the place where we can see the holes in the puzzle where pieces are missing."

Chapter Twenty-Eight

The sun rose Friday morning enveloped in a thick layer of bay fog. Evelyn could barely make out the house across the street through the dismal mist, and it only seemed to grow thicker as the morning progressed. By the time Flora was up, dressed, and fed, even an outing in the automobile seemed risky. It was Friday, though, and Evelyn had promised Walter she would go to his store, reconcile the accounts for the week, and make the bank deposit. For her part, Flora was looking forward to a shopping trip at the Capwell's department store that had opened in August of 1929. It was located only two blocks from Winslow's Office Supplies in downtown Oakland.

Evelyn parked the Chevrolet halfway between their two destinations, and they arranged to meet at the luncheonette in the basement of Capwell's at noon.

Their tasks completed, they waited for a booth. Flora brought up the subject of buying new walking shoes for Evelyn. She had gone through the shoe department and had an idea of the price that would have to be paid for new leather walking shoes.

"One dollar and eighty-nine cents," she reported.

"Gracious, that's dear," Evelyn said. "I have another plan. I picked up this adhesive at Walter's store. It's not soluble in water like mucilage. I'm going to use that, and the needle and thread the way Lolly showed us. I'm going to make those shoes last forever."

Evelyn knew Flora admired ingenuity and industriousness, but hoped she wouldn't be expected to live up to the same ideal. As Flora had argued on many occasions, shoes and apparel did eventually go out of style.

They were seated and perused the menu.

"This is not exactly the Berkeley Women's Club is it?" Flora said, and gave a sniff, which made Evelyn laugh.

"As if we have the sort of money and are the sort of women to belong to the Berkeley Women's Club," she said. "No crab salad for us today. We'll have to 'make do' with grilled cheese on sliced bread and tomato soup with Premium saltines in cellophane packets."

"Actually, that sounds like exactly what I want on this dreary day," Flora told her. "Oh, say, I've just remembered something Deputy Calhoun mentioned yesterday, that might help us out."

"Oh? What's that?"

"Calhoun told me the sheriff had assigned an investigating detective to the case of Joaquin's murder. We should probably try to talk to that detective, right? We could at least give him whatever information we've uncovered."

"I suppose. Are you assuming this man is trustworthy, and will conduct a fair investigation? Or will he only try to find evidence that will implicate Rafael or another innocent farmworker?"

"Hmm, good point. We could at least find out who this detective is, and perhaps meet him. Try to judge his character and trustworthiness."

"Agreed. Add that to the list of what we'd like to accomplish tomorrow. When Marisol comes tonight, she can update us on Rafael's current condition and whereabouts, and possibly we can talk to him again, too."

They arrived back at Walter's in the early afternoon and decided to take both dogs on a long walk through the neighborhood. Evelyn tied on her damaged walking shoes, hoping they wouldn't give out on her. Flora tossed her a sweater against the only slightly thinner shroud of fog. By striding briskly, they made it the mile and a half to the former site of an Ohlone Indian burial mound on the eastern end of the island of Alameda. They followed the directions posted on a small sign and walked the entire circumference of the former mound but found no evidence of the sacred burials once conducted there. Streetcar lines had been cut directly through the gravesite, obliterating any remains. The lands where the Ohlone dead had once been laid respectfully to rest were occupied by homes, streets, and businesses.

It was later than they expected by the time they returned home. They hurried through supper to arrive at the ferry landing in time to collect Marisol. Burdened with two large carpetbags and her pocketbook, Marisol was one of the last to appear on the landing. Evelyn hurried forward to assist with carrying her baggage and they loaded up the automobile.

Marisol insisted she wasn't hungry, but when they got to the house Flora fixed a plate for her anyway. When confronted with a steaming bowl of vegetable stew, flavored with brisket, and a dessert plate of peach cobbler, Marisol found enough of an appetite to clean both plates.

"Mercy!" Marisol said, pushing back her chair. "I had no idea you could cook, Flora."

Evelyn smiled broadly. "Flora is getting quite handy in the kitchen for a girl who'd never so much as boiled water when I first met her. Why do you know, just the other day she made us a lovely cheese soufflé with garden vegetables for supper?"

"Jaing did the vegetables," Flora said. "They always come out limp when I do them. And, by the way, I cannot take credit for the peach cobbler. Lolly, the woman who does the house for Pearl, made the cobbler."

"Nevertheless," Evelyn said. "Any day now you'll be able to take over all the cooking and we can let Jaing's cooking responsibilities go."

"Perish the thought! Two weeks of my cooking and you'll be ready to let me go! Besides, who do you think taught me to cook?"

They waited until they'd settled in the parlor before Flora brought up the subject of Marisol's friendship with Bernice, one of those irksome problems no one seemed to want to talk about.

"Oh, dear, dear, Bernice," Marisol said. "She's convinced I'm going to leave her. That's one reason I didn't want her to come with me this weekend. She's taken to her bed, weeping. I simply could not deal with both Bernice and Tia Rosamaria demanding my consolation and reassurance at the same time. And if I give attention to one, the other one gets even more demanding. I'm telling you, it's enough to drive a woman berserk."

"Well, then..." Evelyn said. "Does this mean you're not leaving Bernice?"

"Yes," Flora said, "because your aunt gave us to understand you were trying to find a nursing position in Oakland and would be moving in with her."

"That's wishful thinking on her part," Marisol said. "Or rather, I may have given her that impression simply to placate her."

"I'm sorry to have been eavesdropping," Flora said, "but in the automobile the other day I heard Tia call Bernice—in Spanish—she called Bernice a witch. That was so unkind. Did she truly say that or did I misunderstand?"

Marisol sighed and gazed at her hands, clasped in her lap. She picked a piece of lint from her skirt and sighed again.

"You have to understand…Tia is an uneducated and ignorant woman. She believes in evil spirits and the like. For years she's told me Bernice is a witch and has cursed me with a spell. She knows we live together in San Francisco, but she believes I only stay because Bernice has bewitched me."

"Incredible," Evelyn said, sending a horrified expression to Flora.

"And now," Marisol continued, "with this business of Joaquin being killed and Rafael arrested, she believes even more strongly that I should break free of Bernice's curse and return to the family. I'm hoping with the passage of time Tia will calm down. She needs me right now, and she needs to grieve Joaquin's death. Bernice has to understand that and calm herself."

Evelyn tried again. "Are you saying you're not going to leave Bernice? Because right now I know her heart is breaking from the fear you will."

"I have no plans to leave her, if Bernice can be patient through this hard time. In any case, you know, it's not as though Bernice and I are family."

That gave both Evelyn and Flora a start. They exchanged a surreptitious disapproving glance.

"You don't think of yourself as family to Bernice?" Flora asked, "Even after all these years together?"

Marisol's brow had furrowed in confusion. "But we're not," she said. "It's not as though we're married…or could ever be." Flora huffed. Marisol was still gazing into her lap, so Flora sent Evelyn her angry scowl instead.

Marisol waved dismissively and abruptly changed the subject, asking how their investigation into Joaquin's death was proceeding.

"Yes, well," Flora said. "Back on the topic of his death, is it possible, in your opinion, that Joaquin may have been attacked by, for example say, a jealous husband? We've heard Joaquin might have been a bit of a rascal. Can you tell us anything about that possibility? To your knowledge, was he—"

Evelyn gestured with a hand slice across her throat and Flora returned her look with a glare. "I'm only suggesting," Evelyn said in a murmur, "you let the woman answer." Flora shook off her small fit of pique and both she and Evelyn turned to Marisol to hear how she would answer Flora's questions.

"You two," Marisol said with a smile, and shook her head. "To your point, I'm not sure I would be the one to know anything about Joaquin's romantic life. As you may know, Joaquin was not even twenty years old. And I hadn't seen him since my uncle died, almost a year ago. It's true, Joaquin was very cute. I would describe him as more of a flirt than a rascal. He was hardly old enough to have gotten into the kind of trouble you're suggesting, but there's no question he was flirtatious, perhaps overly so."

"Oh, I do remember that, and at his own father's funeral, too." Flora looked down and batted her eyes as though she had been offended by the boy Joaquin's attentions.

Marisol gave Flora a bemused expression. "Why are you asking about a jealous husband? I thought Joaquin had been killed as a result of the labor unrest between the farmworkers and the Vigilantes. Are you saying you don't think that's true? Has your investigation revealed it wasn't those Vigilantes who killed my cousin?"

Evelyn fielded that one. She leaned forward, her eyes softening in compassion. "We've done a bit of looking into the matter and have come to believe it may be possible Joaquin was not killed as part of the labor unrest."

"Although..." Flora said, then paused until both of the others had turned in her direction.

"Yes?" Evelyn said.

"Well, we did have that theory he might have been killed and Rafael framed—"

"Ah, yes, that's not completely off the table yet is it?" Evelyn turned back to Marisol. "Of course we don't believe Rafael had anything to do with Joaquin's death, but what about the possibility someone else might have killed Joaquin and tried to frame Rafael in order to leave a vacuum of leadership at the top where this killer could take advantage?"

"Yes," Flora said. "What do you know about the foreman Luis, for example?"

"Oh," Marisol said, clearly shocked at the very notion. "I don't think...I don't know, of course, but Luis is very close to the family. I don't see how...or why..."

"Yes," Flora said, "we did notice he seemed to be close to Tia."

Marisol flashed Flora a suspicious glance.

In an attempt to diffuse the increasingly awkward conversation, Evelyn shifted direction. "Or do you know anyone else who might want to take over the business? Luis was only our first thought. Earlier you mentioned the Alisal family."

"Or possibly Joaquin's murder was committed for more personal reasons. For one thing, the coroner is saying the murderer was someone Joaquin trusted enough to be physically close to at the time the shot was fired. Do you know any of Joaquin's friends?" Evelyn gave Marisol several moments to think that through.

"No, I'm not that close to either of those cousins. Why would the sheriff have held onto Rafael for so long if he knew the murder was committed by someone else?"

Evelyn shook her head. "The answer to that question probably doesn't bear too much scrutiny. What's the situation now? Has Rafael finally been released?"

"Oh, yes, I should have said. My other aunt, the one from Martinez, she took Tia Rosamaria to see an attorney, a Californio who has helped the family in the past. The attorney went straight to the sheriff and got Rafael released from custody. He was in the hospital, you know? Anyway, Rafael is hurt, but he's home now."

"Thank goodness for that," Flora murmured under her breath.

"*Pues*," Marisol continued, "Rafael is released, but the lawyer says the sheriff still thinks it was a farmworker who killed Joaquin. He said the sheriff is searching now for someone else to blame."

Flora shook her head, dismay reflected on her brow. "I think it's really terrible what's happening to Rafael and the Californios. After all, they were here first. Those harvesting jobs should be theirs."

Marisol gave Flora a bleak smile. "You know, it's not as though my ancestors, the Spaniards, treated the Ohlone any better when they arrived in the sixteen hundreds. The Ohlone were here long before the Spaniards, and yet the Spaniards exploited the Ohlone terribly. In fact, in many cases Californios are direct descendants of Ohlone women and the Spaniards who...who fathered their children."

"There's nothing simple about any of this, is there?" Evelyn said, with a sad expression. "In any case, Flora and I have a few more avenues of inquiry we'd like to pursue. We'll keep you informed.

"And on that cheery note, I'd like to listen to the radio program *The March of Time* just coming on. The newspaper said tonight's program is about the Bonus Army marching into Washington and setting up camp. We heard a little about that earlier this week."

That night as they prepared for bed, Flora said to Evelyn, "I feel like we're at the stage where we have collected important pieces of the puzzle and now we're having to turn the pieces around and about to try to figure out just how they fit."

Marisol was up Saturday morning and impatiently waiting for her ride to her aunt's house at least a half an hour before Flora made her leisurely appearance downstairs. The ride was quiet, each of the young women lost in their own thoughts.

Reaching the driveway to the hacienda, Evelyn started to turn the wheel and was stopped by four men blocking the entrance. Fortunately, Marisol recognized at least two of them. She rolled her window open and waved.

"*Hola, Martín*, it's only me! Please let us through."

"Hmm," Flora said. "It looks as though the Pachecos took your suggestion, Evelyn, and hired farmworkers to stand guard."

They encountered two other men patrolling in front of the barn and another man, this one armed with a rifle, standing near the entry to the hacienda. Marisol hopped out quickly once there and gave no sign she had any intention of inviting them inside.

"Oh, no she doesn't," Evelyn said, grabbing her pocketbook and following. Flora scrambled to catch up. Surprised to find them close behind, Marisol did allow them entry.

By way of explanation, Evelyn said, "We need to have a word with Rafael."

The recently released, clean-shaven, and showered Rafael was installed in a wide chair in the sitting room. He sported a swollen black eye and a pair of crutches leaned against the arm of the chair. He accepted their condolences and asked about the progress of their inquiries. Evelyn offered again to let him take over, since he had finally been allowed to return home, free of all charges, but he was insistent.

"I have more than enough to take care of," he said. "And I will be making certain the fellows who did this to me get their just rewards. You ladies should continue your investigation." He inquired if they needed anything more from him and Flora remembered to ask if he knew who Joaquin's friends might have been.

Rafael's brow furrowed and he shook his head. "Joaquin had his own friends. If his death was down to something other than this labor unrest, I wouldn't know. That's what I'm hoping you can uncover." He sighed deeply.

"Time for you to go," Marisol said, "Rafael needs his rest." She ushered them abruptly out. Under the arbor, Evelyn said, "Her manners leave something to be desired, don't they? Anyway, Rafael is home, and the family has engaged the services of an able attorney."

"He said we're not off the case, though. Joaquin is still dead, and we still don't know who did it."

"Yes, and according to everything we've been able to learn, some other farmworker will now be charged with Joaquin's murder. That makes my blood boil."

Flora nodded in agreement. "We're not there yet, but I do I feel like we've made some progress toward understanding what really happened to Joaquin. You want to keep asking questions, right?"

Evelyn gave one emphatic nod. "Yes, I do. We started this because Marisol pulled us in, but now I feel like we have to find the true answer, and Rafael was clear, we're still on the clock."

"We can't let an innocent person be charged."

"I feel certain we can ferret out the answers we need. What do you say we stop at the barn and ask for Luis? You can be sweet and ask him about friends Joaquin might have had, and I'll watch to see if he acts in any way that might indicate guilt."

Flora gazed in the direction of the barn, hidden just beyond the trees. "Yes, all right, but remember we have this lunch appointment with Francie today, so let's don't take too long with Luis."

Chapter Twenty-Nine

Evelyn let the Chevrolet roll to a stop in front of the barn and they climbed out. It being mid-morning on a workday, the Pachecos' labor office/barn appeared to be deserted except for the two guards, who directed them inside when they asked for Luis. They tiptoed into the dusty and darkened interior. Toward the rear of the building, they heard the sounds of hammering and chatter in Spanish.

In the far corner a single individual sat on a straw bale, his presence revealed by the glowing red tip of a cigarette growing brighter, then fading.

"*Por favor?*" Flora's voice quavered. "*Luis? Donde esta Luis?*" They moved closer to more clearly see the smoker.

The man lifted his chin toward a lighted doorway to their right. Inside, Luis sat with his elbows propped on a desk, hatless, his head in his hands. He looked up, then stood when Evelyn and Flora came to the doorway. He nodded as Evelyn introduced themselves as friends of Marisol's, gestured at several chairs lined up against the wall, and took his seat again.

Evelyn had decided the most profitable approach would be a straight forward one, even though Luis was a possible suspect. She managed to explain their theory about the business take-over without accusing Luis himself.

Luis's response was a bark of mocking laughter. "Ha!" he said. "If anyone wants this headache of a business, he's welcome to it."

"What on earth do you mean," Evelyn said. "We thought this was a successful and lucrative going concern. Are you saying it's not?"

Once Luis got started venting his frustrations, it seemed he would never stop. "Not at the present," he said. "Not with all of this violence and uncertainty. Rafael's had to cut his profits to almost nothing now the growers know they can pay so little and still get workers. Rafael can't cut wages to his crews, so he has to cut his own income.

"All these Vigilantes and others are fighting now, but they won't want the work once they try it, and at one third the pay of their previous jobs. We only have a couple weeks left of peaches and apricots, then the workers need to move out to the valley for melons and corn for the summer. Then back here for pears, apples, and nuts. Then down to Salinas for the winter crops. Those Vigilantes are used to good factory jobs and going home to their families at the end of the day. None of them want to take over this business, I can promise you that."

Evelyn and Flora could only nod encouragingly as Luis continued.

"Of course none of that means one of those fools didn't kill Joaquin for some other reason. I suppose you know they're not having much luck framing Rafael, but that won't stop the sheriff from trying to pin the murder on someone else.

"No, you might be on to something with your theory, but I don't think so." Luis shook his head as though in despair. "That poor boy. He was looking for trouble, but for his mother's sake I'm sorry he found it."

Evelyn made sympathetic sounds and glanced at Flora.

Since Luis seemed quite proficient in English, Flora didn't bother with her stumbling Spanish. "We were hoping you might be able to tell us, who were Joaquin's friends? Do you know?"

Luis gave a quick huff, glanced at Flora, then rolled his eyes and looked away. "Other than his work friends, I don't, and I don't think you would want to either," he said.

Evelyn found this enigmatic answer quite unsatisfactory. If Luis thought she would not want to know certain of Joaquin's friends he must at least have some idea who those friends were.

"Who are you talking about?" she said somewhat abruptly. The change in tone did not go over well, or possibly it was the topic that put Luis off. He lowered his brow, shook his head, and stood.

"Pleased to meet you," he said as he gestured them toward the door. "I got to get back to work. I've got men patrolling all this property, the hacienda, the barn, everywhere. And Rafael is having some of these farmworkers repair the barn and letting them add living quarters on the back for their families. Their *pueblito* was torched, you know?"

"Are your patrols stopping the vandalism?" Evelyn asked. "Have there been any more problems of that nature?"

"No, my men have stopped that ugliness. Should have put them on that sooner." Luis walked them toward the barn door as he talked.

"*Gracias*…ur, thank you." Flora said.

They waited to discuss their meeting with Luis until they were in the automobile and on their way.

"Well," Flora said, "so much for our great theory."

"You think we're completely off base with that idea?"

"I do. I think it was a brilliant motive with no evidence whatsoever to support it."

"So we need to reassemble the puzzle, you think?"

"Yes. Let's go back to what Lil Bird told us. We might be skeptical about his motives but it would be unwise, in my view, to discount his message entirely."

"As always, we need more information," Evelyn said, and sighed.

"Which means whatever we can learn from Francie today about the personalities involved will be even more important."

Evelyn nodded slowly. "Might even be the end of our investigation if we can't learn something useful from her."

"Just think, Evelyn, we're going to sit down for lunch in a bit with an actual trollop."

Evelyn smiled with half her mouth. "It would probably be best not to let her hear you refer to her in that way. I imagine even she has her pride."

"Yes, I know you're right, and she does seem to be quite a nice person, whatever else she might also be. I'll mind my manners."

Evelyn steered the Chevrolet around to the back door of the Carnegie library in Walnut Creek where they had been instructed to meet Francie. They arrived at precisely eleven-thirty, but their new friend was nowhere in sight.

The park itself, stretching to the creek along its far perimeter, was equally empty. However, no sooner had Evelyn switched the ignition off than a full-figured bottle-blonde slipped out from between the thick shrubbery at the rear of the building. Flora hopped out and started to climb into the back seat, but the woman gestured her aside, indicating her own desire to sit in the back. Francie climbed gracefully inside, preceded by a cloud of musky perfume.

"Very clandestine!" Flora whispered to Evelyn. She leaned over the seat. "Good morning!" she said to Francie. "How are you this morning?" The daylight highlighted Francie's heavy make-up, and the front of her bright red blouse gaped where it stretched across her bosom. Despite the obvious efforts to hide her wrinkles, crows feet creased the skin at the corners of Francie's eyes. Evelyn glanced in the rear view mirror, noting that Flora's friend was older than she had previously assumed.

"Go on ahead, here," Francie pointed. "If you turn right, that'll take you out the Clayton Road. I'm fine, thank you. How are you girls?"

"We're fine," Evelyn said, "and so glad you're willing to talk with us. I'm Miss Evelyn Winslow, by the way."

"Yes, and I'm Flora, Miss Flora Fitzgerald."

"I remember you," Francie said. "Did you enjoy your little gambling adventure?"

Flora looked over the seat back. "Oh, very much so. I've never tried anything like that before. It was grand fun."

"And you are Miss...?" Evelyn said, glancing in the rear-view mirror again.

"Davies. Frances Davies, if you want to be formal about it."

"Ah," Evelyn said, not sure what would be the appropriate level of formality under the circumstances. "And where are we headed?"

"Oh, sorry. I thought we could go out to the Clayton Cafe. It's not fancy or anything, but the food is passable. I grew up out there, so folks know me, but not exactly the way people know me in Walnut Creek."

"Hmm," Evelyn said. "The Clayton Cafe you say? I don't believe I've ever heard of that place."

"I shouldn't wonder," Francie said. "It's just far enough out of town for couples who don't want to start tongues waggin'. And right next door to the hotel for convenience sake, if you get my drift."

Evelyn squinted and tipped a glance to Francie through the mirror. "So, if I get your drift, you're suggesting that twosomes engaged in private affairs they wish to keep secret, romantic liaisons, as it were, might come out here to Clayton to protect their secret?"

"Yes, isn't that what I said? You might be surprised who you run into way out here," Francie said, and she gave Flora a wink.

"I imagine we would," Flora said slowly, turning to stare at the empty landscape through which they passed. "Given that it doesn't take much to surprise Evelyn and I when it comes to romantic liaisons."

Francie gave Flora a skeptical expression. "Now don't sell

yourselves short, my friend. I'll wager not much gets past you girls."

Flora straightened the hem of her skirt while Evelyn negotiated some bumps in the rapidly narrowing road and got them safely across a one-lane bridge over a dry gully.

"Gosh," Flora said, gazing out the window again. "It's rural out here, nothing but rolling hills. What did your family do here?"

Francie didn't answer right away. Evelyn wondered if, without intending to, Flora might have asked an awkward question. After all, not everyone had a father who was a wealthy shipbuilder or a brilliant businessman. Given how Francie supported herself, her roots were likely humbler than theirs.

"I was born out here in Nortonville," Francie finally said, gesturing at the road they were traveling. "Where the coal mines used to be. Now those are sand mines."

"Coal mines in California," Evelyn said. "Imagine that."

"Okay, up ahead. That's the town of Clayton and up here on the right, just past the Rhine Hotel, there's the cafe. You can leave the auto anywhere, only don't block the hitching posts right up front."

"Are those for horses?" Flora said, in a tone of wonderment.

"You've got no need to tie your auto down, now, do you?" Francie said with a laugh. "City girls."

They were the first lunch customers in the cafe, although a pair of disreputable-looking cowboys sat at the long counter against the far wall, hunching over tumblers of some cloudy liquid. Their eyes slid sideways to take in the new arrivals, but beyond that, they didn't look as though they had moved in a very long time.

"Where are their horses?" Flora said in a whisper as the three women took seats at a distant table.

"We'll have three beefsteak sandwiches," Francie called to the bald cook bustling behind the counter.

"Hiya, Francie. Comin' right up," he called back.

"Beefsteak's about all they have here," Francie said. "Delicious, too, you know, because the meat comes right off the cattle ranches here in the Clayton Valley. He'll bring us a tin of peanut butter, too, if you want somethin' on the beefsteak."

"Yes, that will be lovely, I'm sure," Flora said, not sounding at all sure about the prospect.

"Shall we talk while we're waiting?" Evelyn said.

"Knock yourself out," Francie said, "but I gotta tell you, it's like I told your friend here, I need to be discreet. I need to keep secrets in my line of work. If it gets around that I don't keep secrets, the work dries up, you understand? I'm not going to tell you anything that's been told to me as a secret or that might risk my future business."

"Sure," Evelyn said as both she and Flora nodded solemnly. "We understand. How about this…if we ask you a question you can't answer without revealing a secret, you just tell us and we'll move on to something else?"

"Gimme an example."

"Well," Evelyn said, "for example, we've heard rumors that Joaquin Pacheco was something of a rascal." She cut a quick look to Flora, who stared, fascinated, at Francie. "We heard he may have been romantically involved with someone he shouldn't have been. And so naturally we're wondering if his murder might have had something to do with that."

"Yes," Flora said. "Perhaps he was killed by a jealous husband? That sort of a situation."

"And your question is…"

"Well, do you know if Joaquin was romantically involved with anyone?"

Francie stared through the dusty and fly-specked window for a moment. "I can tell you Joaquin was a busy boy," Francie said. "He's dead now, so I can tell you that much."

"But you can't tell us who he might have been involved with?"

"Nope. That would be telling tales on someone who's still with us, least as far as I know." Francie closed her lips tightly.

Evelyn sat back and thought about her question for a moment. "In other words, you might very well know who he was seeing but you can't tell us?"

"The only thing I can tell you, honey, is like I said, that young man was a busy boy. I can also tell you he was never interested in my services. I didn't really know him, if you know what I mean."

Evelyn was not entirely sure she did know what Francie meant. It could have gone a couple of different ways. "Let me see if I'm clear. You're saying Joaquin was romantically involved with a person—"

"or persons," Flora interrupted.

"Yes, possibly more than one person, and that person—"

"or persons."

Evelyn gave Flora a sharp look, and Flora put one manicured hand to her lips, not quite hiding a smile.

"is still alive," Evelyn finished her thought.

"As far as I know, there is only the one dead person," Francie said. "And to be perfectly clear, I never said I did know Joaquin was romantic with anyone."

Francie tightened her lips closed again and Evelyn feared that might the end of her disclosures.

Chapter Thirty

At the risk of offending Francie, Evelyn knew she had to try another question. She exchanged a glance with Flora, who made an agreeable-sound. She certainly had not heard about any other bodies turning up. Although now Francie had mentioned it, Evelyn supposed it wasn't impossible Joaquin's partner had also died and the body just not been found...yet. Especially given Dr. Whitley's report that Joaquin's body had been moved from the place where his death occurred. The body of the other half of Joaquin's romantic entanglement might yet be found. Her body could be hidden anywhere.

At long last, the heavy-set and completely hairless cook emerged from behind the counter bearing three solid white earthenware plates. He dropped one plate in front of each woman and wiped his hands on an already grease-stained apron. The contents of each plate were identical: two thick slices of bread with a beefsteak slopping over the edges between them. Flora dipped her head quickly, hiding her aghast expression as she adjusted the angle of her plate.

Evelyn decided to take a break from questions about the murder until they'd finished their meal.

"Oh," the cook said, "you're gonna need that tin a' peanut butter. Lemme get that."

"And knives and forks," Francie called, "and...er...soft drinks? The whole shebang. Where's your usual hash-slinger anyway?"

"Polly's off," he said when he returned with their silver-ware, napkins, and a half empty tin of peanut butter, a knife jabbed into the top. "She's havin' another baby, you know."

"Gosh! That must be number four. Or is it five?"

"Beats me," he said. "Bridey was out here too, oh last Sunday I think it was. I'll be right back with those...ur...soft drinks." He stepped over to take orders from a table across the room where more customers were getting seated.

"You'd think I'd know how many babies Polly has," Francie said. "She's my sister, one of 'em anyway."

"How many sisters do you have?" Evelyn asked politely, while cutting one bite-sized end off her sandwich with the sharp knife.

"Had four sisters. Now we're down to three. Third sister, Bridey, works in the sheriff's office. As for the boys, my broth-ers, one of them died in The War, in France. Owen died in a mining accident up in Nortonville. He was only fifteen. And then Selwyn died from the flu. We lost my aunt, my brother, and my own little boy all in one month back in 1919 from that flu."

"Oh, I'm so sorry, Francie," Flora said, giving Francie a sympathetic look. "You had a little boy? I'm so sorry. You must have been heartbroken."

"Yeah, well, what're you gonna do? That flu went through those mines and folks were dropping right where they worked. It's not like we had a doctor to come all the way up in these hills. The rest of us are lucky we didn't all die."

"To lose a child, though, that must have been so hard. What was his name?"

"He wasn't even two. We'd hardly got a chance to know him. His name was Dylan." Francie swallowed a bite and gazed through the window again. "We buried him on the hill up there with everyone else."

"Was he your only child?" Evelyn asked.

"Yeah, well, you know. You have to be darned careful about that sort of thing in my line of work. Can't make any money when you're laid up having babies." Francie brought her focus back to her plate and sliced into her sandwich again. "Now I let Polly do all the baby-making, and I drop in for a visit now and then." She turned to Flora, who was sawing at one end of her beefsteak. "How's your lunch, hon? You wanna put some peanut butter on that?"

Flora had freed the bite and stuffed it inside. Her mouth was too full to reply. She shook her head and held up one palm toward the peanut butter.

"Hey, Cookie?" Francie called. "Those drinks?"

When Cookie arrived with three glasses of foamy amber liquid that looked, and as it turned out, tasted, a lot like beer, Francie held onto his apron for a moment.

"You have any idea how Polly's doing?" she asked. "Or Bridey? I haven't seen either of them in ages."

"Good, as far as I know," Cookie said. "Haven't seen much of Polly, what with the baby, but like I said Bridey was in here just last Sunday. She was having a long heart-to-heart with the Catholic priest, Father Bertrand, over at the corner table. No idea what that was about. I got steaks on the grill." He hurried away.

Evelyn sent Flora a long look while Francie made serious progress on her beefsteak sandwich.

They continued to eat mostly in silence until Francie's plate was clean, and Evelyn and Flora had eaten their fill, both succeeding in making respectable in-roads into the meal.

"I have another line of questions," Evelyn said, "if you're ready?" She dabbed at her lips with her napkin and sat back. "The coroner identified what type of gun was used to kill Joaquin…"

Evelyn caught a horrified eye-roll from Flora, which had also not escaped Francie's attention. Evelyn guessed discussing such topics so casually over a meal had offended Flora's delicate sensibilities.

"Oh, here," Francie said. "Let me get some of this out of your way." She moved the peanut butter tin and her empty plate to the next table, then glanced doubtfully at Flora and Evelyn's still unfinished sandwiches.

"Thank you." Evelyn said. "Now then, as I was saying, we know the weapon used was a .38 Special, a revolver. The deputies all carry .38s, but pistols. Do you know anyone who owns a .38 revolver?"

Francie shook her head slowly, at the same time using the nail on her pinky to pick at a stubborn piece of meat stuck between her teeth.

"No...I sure don't. These days a lot of the guys carry their guns with them everywhere, but I sure don't remember anyone carrying a revolver. That's the gun with the round thing on the side, isn't it?"

"Yes, the cylinder."

"Sorry, nobody springs to mind."

"Too bad," Flora said. "Well, it was a long shot anyway."

Evelyn sent her friend a sharp look, hoping Flora's unfortunate turn of phrase wasn't intended to be amusing. Francie either didn't notice or chose to ignore the ill-timed remark.

"It used to be the case," Evelyn said, "I guess possibly two years ago or more, all the deputies carried those revolvers. So it's possible the owner of the revolver is a retired deputy, an older man. Do you know any retired deputies?"

Francie squinted in thought, still working on the trapped bit of meat. Finally, she said, "I am acquainted with quite a few older gents, you know, in my line of work. Even one or two retired deputies. But I'm thinking about one fellow... He's not retired, but he used to be a deputy, and now I'm thinking about it, he does sometimes carry one of those revolver-type guns."

Acutely aware that blurting out the question on the tip of her tongue would likely result in Francie locking her lips closed again, Evelyn struggled with how to get the woman to reveal the name she wanted.

"And this man you're thinking about, the man who used to be a deputy and owns a revolver, was he one who…who was interested in your services?"

Francie finished with her post-meal dental cleaning and gave Evelyn a stare. "That particular former deputy was not, as you say, interested in my services, but that's the last question I'm going to answer about who might be a customer or who never was. You're skatin' pretty close to the line with that last one."

"I understand," Evelyn said. "As long as he was not a customer…and lots of folks would know a man who used to be a deputy, would you be willing to tell me his name?" She held her breath, waiting.

Francie narrowed her eyes again, then took a brief look at Flora. "Oh, well, you know him anyways, or know about him. Remember Flora, that day you met us all behind the fruit shed? You remember Olive? The fellas were asking her where her husband Hank was? Hank, that's the fellow. Used to be a deputy. Got let go a few months back."

"Oh, yes! I do remember that. Hank. He wasn't there though, right? Olive called him a dewdropper. And one of the fellows called Hank a nellie. What is a dewdropper, anyway?"

"That's right, Hank wasn't there. He's gets jobs doing private security ever' so often. Hasn't really been able to find a steady job since the sheriff let him go. Porter is the last name. Hank and Olive Porter." Francie stopped, then answered Flora's question. "A dewdropper is a lazy man. A man who doesn't want to work."

Evelyn was still trying to put the pieces together. "This Hank Porter is Olive's husband, you say?"

Francie nodded.

"And Hank Porter owns a revolver? And Olive was at the gambling game the other day, but Hank wasn't? Do you know where Hank was that day?" Evelyn tried to catch Flora's gaze.

If this Hank owned the revolver used in Joaquin's murder and Hank had gone missing, Evelyn found that highly suspicious.

"If I'm remembering right," Francie said, "Olive called Hank a dewdropper, then later she defended him. Seems like Hank musta been working that day, although I couldn't tell you where."

"Do you know where the Porters live?" Evelyn said, going for a more straight-forward approach. "And have you seen Hank Porter anywhere lately?"

Francie described a white house at the end of a long drive-way off Mt. Diablo Blvd. "Just after you make that turn at the stop sign," she said. She couldn't recall having seen Hank anywhere in the last few days.

"Why are you asking?"

"Here's what I'm thinking," Evelyn said. She took a deep breath and forged boldly ahead. "Possibly Olive was having extra-marital relations with Joaquin Pacheco. Hank caught them at it Saturday night, and he shot Joaquin. Then Hank moved the body into the orchard and took off, you know, to avoid getting caught. Although just because you haven't seen Hank lately doesn't necessarily mean he's gone on the run."

Flora nodded and tipped her head thoughtfully.

Francie just scowled. "I see what you're saying, and it sorta makes sense, but you know, as far as I know, Olive Porter is not a tramp. I've sure never heard anything about her playing around with Joaquin or anyone else."

"That sort of thing wouldn't really be common knowl-edge though, would it?" Evelyn said. "If an otherwise respect-able lady was doing something she should not have been, one would assume she would be discreet about it." Evelyn gave that idea some additional thought and continued. "And even if she wasn't doing anything, that wouldn't necessarily stop her hus-band from believing she was carrying on."

"Right. I get what you're saying," Francie said. "It's not impossible Hank shot Joaquin only because he had a wild thought the boy was…having relations with his wife. Although they say Joaquin was shot late on a Saturday night, so I gotta say you might be right about Hank catching 'em in the act."

"That's a good point," Flora said.

"And another thing," Francie said. "Hank mighta killed Joaquin 'cause he was making whoopee with the wife, and if he did, those deputies stick together. Even though Hank was let go, those other deputies would probably look the other way, and not waste too much energy makin' sure Hank got caught. They're so close with each other, they might even help Hank cover it up."

"For example," Evelyn said, "they might help him carry the body out to the orchard? And then crush Joaquin's face with a rock to steer the coroner off?"

"And," Flora added, "they might also believe Joaquin got what was coming to him."

Francie pursed her lips and nodded slowly. "Mighta happened exactly that way. Who am I to say?"

Flora lifted her chin. "On the subject of illicit liaisons..." When she had Evelyn and Francie's attention she lowered her voice and went on. "What do you suppose Father Bertrand was doing out here on Sunday afternoon with your sister Bridey who works for the sheriff? Any chance those two were carrying on and Joaquin was shot because he found out about it?"

Evelyn's eyebrows shot skyward and she listened for the answer. This single piece might bring the whole puzzle into focus.

Francie threw her head back and laughed loudly enough to draw the attention of everyone in the cafe. She finally choked out a few words. "Oh, my! One problem, you know, with bein' investigators is you girls see mysteries everywhere you look." Francie lowered her voice and leaned in. "Bridey's been trying to keep it on the qt, but she's been wantin' to join a convent ever since her husband left her. I'm sure Father Bertrand is only helping her find a place, 'cause I can assure you, Bridey is not one to be foolin' around, and certainly not with her priest.

"You know what else, and I'm only saying this 'cause I like you girls. If Hank killed Joaquin and even one deputy helped cover it up, the two of you are gonna wanna be a lot more careful than you have been up 'til now. Those boys stick together. Even though Hank was let go by the sheriff, those guys are gonna watch his back. Might be you should go on home and keep your noses outta this business, you know? For your own good, is all I mean."

Chapter Thirty-One

Evelyn gave Francie a long stare. She was trying to think of a polite way to say that she had no intention of keeping her nose "outta this business."

"Yes, Evelyn," Flora said in her quietest voice. "Perhaps we should. Remember what happened the last time someone told us to mind our own business?" She turned to include Francie. "Miss Winslow was almost drowned in that incident."

"Yeah?" Francie didn't appear to be overwhelmed with shock or concern. It was clear she'd seen a lot in her lifetime, and very little surprised her.

Evelyn shook her head. "Just to finish up," she said, "would you be willing to tell us, that is, if you know, why Hank Porter was 'let go' by the sheriff. For what reason was he fired?"

Francie stared into space again for a few seconds, then glanced at Evelyn. "Guess you'd better get that outta someone else," she said. "Maybe someone connected with the sheriff." She sent quick but shrewd glances to both her companions. "That is, if you're not already gettin' the drift."

Evelyn blinked few times, then made eye contact with Flora. This would have to be a topic for discussion between them at a later time.

Flora leaned in close to Francie. "That one old man at the counter keeps staring at you. Do you know him?"

Francie did not turn to look. "He's just perusing the merchandise, honey. Cookie will let me know if I got a customer."

Flora gazed at the man while pretending to read the short menu painted on the wall. After a few seconds, she leaned back and shuddered.

Francie tipped her glass and drained the last of her drink. "This has been swell, ladies, but I gotta get goin'. You ready to go?"

Both Evelyn and Flora had half their beefsteaks remaining.

"Do you think we could get some newspaper to wrap these up?" Flora said. "We have a couple of little friends at home who would really appreciate our leftovers for their dinner."

Francie waved at Cookie, who brought over a slightly used brown paper bag, and Flora packed up what was left on their plates.

Before returning to his post, Cookie said to Francie, "Don't leave without you come talk to me." Francie wrinkled her nose for less than a second and nodded.

"I'm gonna stay out here in Clayton" she said to her companions. "I oughta take this chance to go look in on my sister, and maybe see if that new baby has arrived yet.

"Now, when you make that right turn onto the boulevard in Walnut Creek, go a half mile or so and look to your left. You'll see the Porter's house down that long driveway. Sometimes when Hank's off work, we play our gambling games in his old barn there just before you get to the house. You want I should call you next time we play?"

Flora's eyes widened. "Oh, gosh! I don't think so. I wasn't very good at it."

Francie laughed. "As Mae West would say, 'Good's got nothing to do with it, honey.'"

"Can I ask you something, though?" Flora said, then continued without waiting for an answer. "I thought those dice games were illegal in California, but there were at least three deputies at the fruit shed that day. One of them even played a few rounds. Why didn't they arrest everyone if gambling is illegal?"

Francie gave Flora a wondering stare. "Honey, there's a lot that's illegal. Doesn't mean it doesn't go on, and right under the eye of the law, too. Speaking of which, I'd better go see if this old man's gonna make it worth my while."

Evelyn slipped four dollar bills across the table to pay for their three beefsteak lunches with some left for Francie, who quickly slid the money into her pocketbook. She leaned in close to Evelyn. "Four dollars is enough to cover the steak dinners and a quick roll in the hay, should you be so inclined."

Evelyn pulled herself upright, carefully keeping her face an unreadable blank, and said, "Thank you, Francie, I mean, for answering our questions." She took Flora's elbow and they hurried outside.

Once on the sidewalk, Flora pulled them both to a stop. "Evelyn, did she just offer to—"

"Hop in the automobile, Flora. We have a long drive home."

Flora did as she had been instructed, but left the smirk on her face. Evelyn was reaching for the ignition when Flora stayed her hand. "Hold the phone a minute, Evie. I have another question. If we're looking for someone who has access to one of those old revolvers the deputies used to have, and Francie's sister Bridey works at the sheriff's office, don't you think it might be reasonable to assume she could have had access to one of those guns?"

Evelyn turned to Flora, trying to imagine why Bridey might need a gun and what the devil Flora was getting at.

"Well," Flora continued, "I'm only trying to fit these new pieces into the puzzle. Perhaps Bridey had a clandestine meeting with Father Bertrand way out here to discuss her plans to join a convent, or perhaps she had another reason to meet with the Father. Remember, that Sunday was the day after Joaquin was shot and killed, and if Bridey had a revolver…"

"Ah. I see what you're suggesting now. You think Bridey was having an affair with Joaquin and they had a falling out?"

"That seems a bit unlikely, but perhaps. She's about our age, early thirties, wouldn't you say? And well, not to put too fine a point on it but she's not all that attractive, especially not to an adorable young man like Joaquin. He might have, well, had his way with her in a reckless moment, then wanted to end it, or cheated on her."

Evelyn was nodding along with Flora's reasoning. She was making sense. "What if...what if Joaquin tried to force himself on her and she shot him in self-defense?"

"Well, that would be ugly, wouldn't it?" Flora gazed out the window. "That would fit with Lil Bird's comment about how Joaquin got what was coming to him, and especially with Bridey's connection to the deputies." She drew a deep breath. "I'm going to need to give these ideas more thought," she concluded. "Do we have other errands? Or are we going directly back to Walter's?"

"We could stop at the jail and try to get the name of the detective you told me had been assigned to the investigation. Or possibly even have a word or two with Bridey, who turns out to be Francie's sister."

"Yes, and if the detective seems capable and cooperative, perhaps we could give him the information we've learned thus far and let him take over from here," Flora said.

"And if we did that, we'd likely lose our hard-earned fee."

"That would be a shame."

"Besides that," Evelyn said, "Where would be the fun in letting someone else solve the puzzle?"

Flora gave her friend a brief scowl. Not much of what they'd been up to lately really fit their usual definition of fun.

Evelyn was concerned this new investigator, the sheriff's detective, might have the same prejudices and axes to grind as the other employees of the sheriff's department. He might be just as likely to try to pin this murder on one of the other farmworkers. No, Evelyn was going to keep asking questions and seeking answers until she was satisfied the real murderer had been identified and apprehended.

As she steered the automobile back toward the hamlet of Walnut Creek, Evelyn gazed around them at the passing countryside, dotted here and there with farmhouses and small outbuildings. Any of the places she saw could fit the bill as a remote place where a single gunshot would have gone unheard.

If Francie was correct about the hotel and diner in Clayton being a place where folks brought their illicit affairs, Joaquin could have been anywhere, even out here, the night he died. And most likely Rafael would never have found his brother this far out. Her mind went back to thinking about the apparently missing Hank Porter.

"We might consider stopping by the Porters'," Evelyn said. "I'd really like to set eyes on that Hank."

"Because?"

"For one thing, if he has gone on the lam, that might be evidence he was the one who shot Joaquin. And I wonder how much Olive Porter knows. She married Hank so she must have once loved him but she might be willing by now to finger him if he killed her lover Joaquin."

"My, now look who's talking like a gangster."

Evelyn laughed. "It is our summer vacation, Flora, and there are no schoolgirls here to learn bad habits from us."

"True. Okay, I can understand why you'd like to see for yourself whether or not Hank has gone on the run. What I don't get is how stopping at the Porters' house is going to give us that information. Unless you intend to simply walk up and ask his wife if you can see him. If he doesn't come to the door, or isn't working in the yard, you know, you won't likely lay eyes on him."

"I follow what you're saying. We'd have to come right out and ask whoever answers the door, and that doesn't seem like it'd be a successful endeavor if his wife is covering for him."

"And what do you say if he's the one who comes to the door? 'Oh, we only wanted to make certain you hadn't gone on the lam after shooting Joaquin.'"

"Good point. Very well. We won't stop, at least until we can come up with a credible story."

Flora smiled and shook her head slowly, despairing for the soul of her friend. "Another fib, Evie, another fib." She was quiet for a few moments, not unlikely thinking up a fib her friend could realistically use. Then she said, "Are we going to have to come out here again tomorrow to take Marisol back to the ferry?"

"Not unless we want to. Marisol said Rafael can take her in his truck. I thought instead we could take Pearl's roadster out for a spin tomorrow."

"Ooh, that sounds like fun! Perhaps we could even give me a driving lesson?" Flora squeezed Evelyn's arm, pleading. "That little roadster is so cute."

"We'll see," Evelyn said, laughing.

They made the turn in Walnut Creek. A short while later, sure enough, they spotted a mailbox on the left with the Porter name painted on it in red. At least if they decided in the future to pay the Porters a visit, they would know where to go. Evelyn slowed and pulled onto the shoulder opposite the mailbox as they both peered at the house and barn, several dozen yards out the gravel driveway.

"Uh-oh," Flora said. She'd seen a sign half buried in brambles a few feet from the mailbox. "Public Auction," she read. A date and time were listed.

"Oh, dear," Evelyn said. "It looks as though the bank is taking the Porters' house and property like so many others. Hank lost his job, and now they're losing their house. It's no wonder Olive was snippy when you met her at the gambling game. She must have a lot on her mind." They both gazed at the driveway, the faded white house at the end of it, and the ancient barn to the side. A Model T sat to the left of the kitchen entry, its glass windows gone, and one door tied shut with twine.

"Does that look like the tail-end of a pickup truck to you?" Evelyn pointed. "See? There, tucked in by the side of the barn?"

"Could very well be. You want to go look? If it is, then at least we know Hank has not taken his truck on the run."

"I think we'd better not. That Model T likely means someone is at home."

Evelyn pulled back onto the road and cruised the twists and turns of the highway like the practiced expert she had become. They rode in silence, both lost in thought, brooding about what they had learned, and what it all meant. Both leaned first to the left, then to the right, and back again as the curves unfurled before them. On one of the left leans, Flora slid across the seat and snuggled close to Evelyn.

"Hmm?" Evelyn murmured.

"Just feeling grateful." Flora dropped her head to Evelyn's shoulder. "I shouldn't like to have to be in Francie's line of work."

"Um-hmm, nor I. Nor would I like to be in Greta Werner's shoes, or, for that matter, in Olive Porter's."

Later, Flora ground the leftover beefsteak along with last evening's potatoes and other vegetables for the dogs. "Gracious!" she said to Spritz, "Now we've got meals for you and Spike for several days. Good thing, too, because I certainly don't feel like fixing food or eating again today." She stepped to the kitchen door. "Evie? Are you going to want supper?"

Evelyn put down her newspaper and joined Flora in the kitchen.

"We don't want much, do we?" Flora said, peering into the refrigerator. "We could have buttered string beans, and bread with peach jam…though I'm not seeing any butter…"

"There's a package of oleomargarine. There, on the middle shelf, with the packet of dye on top."

"Oh, phooey. I don't want to be bothered mixing in that dye. Here," she said, plopping the package in front of Evelyn. "Will you do it, please? Without the dye, that oleomargarine looks too much like lard. Tastes like lard, too. I'm going to put that little sign on the porch tonight and see if we can't get the milkman to leave us a pound of real butter in the morning."

Evelyn got busy tracking down a small bowl and a spoon. "Oh," she said in mid-task. "What do you think about taking in a movie tonight? The theater on Webster Street, The Alameda, is opening with something called *Night After Night*. It features Mae West."

"Mae West? That actress with those naughty plays in New York? I didn't know she acted in movies."

"This is her first. I don't think she's the main star but she's in it."

"Yes, let's do go. And Pearl told me if we go to that theater they give a dish away with every ticket. She said she could always use more cereal bowls."

Chapter Thirty-Two

They both enjoyed the comedic movie, and the evening of escape from their worries and concerns. On the stroll home, Flora announced that henceforth, they would try to see all the movies featuring Mae West. She feigned throwing a feather boa over one shoulder and in a husky voice and using the words of Oscar Wilde, she paraphrased her new favorite movie star. "I generally avoid temptation unless I can't resist it." As they came in the door, Flora executed a sudden change of topic. "Are there advertisements in today's paper for automobiles?"

"Certainly," Evelyn said, offering Flora part of the newspaper. "Automobile makers are desperate to sell cars in this economic depression. They're even lowering their prices, trying to keep the assembly lines running. Look in there, you'll see." She tapped the newspaper. "Walter says we can buy a new automobile now for the same price as a used one." She'd gotten distracted with the advertisements. "See this one here, the coupe? That's what I'm thinking. Much smaller than Walter's big sedan, but with a rumble seat for when we want to give someone a ride."

"Not one of these sporty roadsters?" Flora said, pointing out a different picture.

"If we get a roadster, we could never take anyone else along. And Spritz would have to ride in a closed basket. She'd jump right out, otherwise."

"Won't our passengers in the rumble seat get cold and wet in San Francisco?"

"Yes... You're right about that. Well, possibly we can find a smaller sedan with a rear seat. There has to be someplace to carry luggage, anyway."

"And boxes of peaches. And it has to be a Chevrolet?"

"They're manufactured right near here in Oakland, and we're not going to get a Ford."

"Aren't Fords built in Richmond?"

"We're not buying a Ford, Flora. That Henry Ford is not getting our money. He's been pushing those lies about an international Zionist conspiracy for years. Do you know, every new Ford that's sold comes with a copy of that rag he calls a news-paper, the *Dearborn Independent*, chock full of articles that make those horrible lies sound like facts. Why, I read just the other day Henry Ford sent piles of money to Adolf Hitler to support his election in Germany. He's also one of those trying to get colleges to institute limits on the number of Jewish students admitted, just because they're Jewish. No siree, we are not buying a Ford."

In a quick search of the telephone directory Sunday morning, Evelyn located the nearest Congregational church and pro-posed they attend the service. She felt the need of some spiri-tual guidance, and she knew Flora would love the singing. The church was a mile and a half from the house, but it was flat all the way, and the pleasant morning called for a good walk.

Flora hummed through the hymns again for half the walk home.

"Sounds as though you enjoyed the service," Evelyn said.

"Hmm? The service? Yes, that was a lovely large choir. How did you enjoy it?"

Evelyn hadn't really paid much attention to what was going on around her, but used the time to think deeply. "Well, not to change the subject too dramatically, but I've been thinking more about Joaquin's death. Between Hank Porter being one who owns that type of revolver, and his not having been seen lately, I find myself becoming more convinced that Joaquin's death had something to do with the Porters."

"You've entirely given up the hypothesis that the motive may have been to gain control of the labor contracting business?"

"I'm beginning to. That motive for killing Joaquin and framing Rafael only makes sense if the killer was Luis, the foreman, and the Pachecos do appear to trust him. I'm inclined to let that idea go in favor of a romantic liaison gone wrong."

"What about this possibility Bridey had something to do with Joaquin's death? Don't you think if she shot him when he tried to force himself on her, don't you think her coworkers would come to her rescue and dump the body for her? That fits with what Lil Bird told us, right?"

"Possibly. We don't have any evidence at all that Joaquin was that sort of a man. Remember, Francie said Joaquin was a 'busy boy' which I took to mean he had no trouble finding lady friends. Let's leave that on the back burner for now. I certainly would hate to see Bridey accused if she, in fact, had nothing to do with Joaquin's death, and even if she did, if she shot him in defense of herself, I might be inclined to drop the whole investigation and look the other way. However, as I said, I can't let go of this feeling the Porters are involved."

"The pieces do seem to be coming together in just that way, don't they? If we've met anyone who fits the bill for a dissatisfied wife, it would be Olive Porter, thus throwing suspicion on Hank as the aggrieved and jealous husband. Does this mean you want to go back and see the place again? Perhaps look for evidence, or suspicious circumstances?"

"I'd certainly like to get a look at the bed of that pickup truck. If it was used to transport Joaquin's bleeding body, there might be signs on the truck, but…" She stopped, lost in thought.

"Does this mean I don't get my driving lesson, or even a ride in Pearl's roadster?"

Evelyn smiled. "Yes, dear, you'll get your lesson. Now that Rafael is home, nothing is so urgent it can't wait another day. At least I hope that's the case. Anyway, Monday will be a better day to make that trip. Folks will be at work and busy. Not so many eyes about if we decide to pay the Porters an unannounced visit.

"Tell me, how do you see this puzzle coming together?" Evelyn asked.

"I do agree that we can let go of a couple of ideas for sure," Flora said. "For example, the idea that Francie's sister Bridey had something to do with Joaquin's death. Perhaps she was having an affair with Joaquin, or perhaps he might have seen the priest doing something he shouldn't have been doing with Bridey, but given what Francie told us about Bridey wanting to join a convent I think those ideas are out the window."

Evelyn chuckled. "Yes, that hypothesis came down like a flaming balloon, didn't it?"

Walking, and still a few blocks from Walter's, they linked arms and bent their heads, going over again how the various clues they'd uncovered might form a picture that explained Joaquin Pacheco's sad death.

Evelyn backed Pearl's bright yellow roadster carefully out of the garage and revved the engine, trying to get it to run smoothly.

"I think," she said, "it would be best to take her out for a spin around town first, before we try your lesson. The choke, this knob here? It regulates the amount of air the engine is getting and when the engine is cold the choke needs to be adjusted. Let's just let her warm up a bit." She pressed the accelerator again, eager to drive the roadster herself.

"Yes, let's." Flora gave the knob a doubtful look. "I hope I can do this."

"Do you want to learn to drive?"

"Yes, of course I do."

"Well then, you will be able to learn."

Ten minutes later, Evelyn pulled the roadster to a stop in the middle of the wide avenue in the vacant industrial area. She left the engine running and stepped out, gesturing for Flora to take her place in the driver's seat. Evelyn began her instruction by explaining the use of the pedals by Flora's feet.

With a jerk and a sudden stall, they were off for six feet or so. Half an hour later and with numerous more jerks and stalls, Flora was beginning to get the hang of keeping the vehicle going while shifting gears, and had even successfully steered around a couple of pot holes.

"You've been saying all along I have to learn to drive before we can get our own automobile," Flora said. "Now that I know how to drive, is it time?"

Evelyn laughed, hiding a twinge of misgiving. "I should say it's getting close. We'll have to wait for Walter to return, you know."

"Oh, phooey! It's always something."

"You know, Flora, I've said all along that when we get our own auto, we must pack it up and go camping in the mountains. Here we are in California and we've still not seen Lake Tahoe or anything of the Sierra mountains except from the windows of the train."

"Camping? You mean sleeping in the dirt?"

Evelyn laughed. Flora did not.

"In a tent, dear, and possibly we can get army surplus cots. You'll love it! Waking up in the fresh mountain air, gazing out over the scenic lake."

Flora gave a her a skeptical expression. "There are lodges and hotels at Lake Tahoe, you know."

One thing both Flora and Evelyn had learned to do in their years together was to know when to stop discussing a difficult subject that did not need to be resolved in the moment, although sometimes that took more effort than others. Evelyn mumbled something under her breath about "buckets of money" but beyond that she let the topic drop.

Later that evening, Evelyn interrupted a quiet reading time to say, "I've been giving this some serious thought."

Flora pulled her nose out of her latest novel. "I'm sorry, what's that?"

"We've convinced ourselves that Olive Porter must have been having an affair with Joaquin."

"Right, and her husband Hank caught them in the act and shot Joaquin."

"Yes, using his old six-shooter."

"And then Hank took off to avoid getting caught. You're having some second thoughts about that story?"

"I am, and I'll tell you why."

Flora folded her book closed. "Do tell."

"That was the tail-end of a pickup truck we saw tucked beside the barn at the Porters' house, I know it was. And it only makes sense that it was Hank's pickup. I don't think Hank has gone anywhere."

"So, Hank shot Joaquin, and instead of running he's only lying low inside the house?"

"That's one explanation."

"That's not going to be a practical place to hide for long. And isn't Olive going to be angry that her husband shot her lover? She'd be so angry she'd likely give Hank's location away. Instead, she seemed to be covering for him. At least she was when I met her at the gambling game."

"Hank only has to hide until someone else is arrested for the crime," Evelyn said. "And Olive needs Hank to be working, not lounging in jail. They're about to lose their house."

"You're thinking Hank's gone into hiding at home?"

"Or at least he's not on the run. And you saw Olive at the gambling game several days after the shooting. She was fine, wasn't she?"

"She wasn't shot, if that's what you mean." Flora tapped her lip and squinted. "How about this version of what happened? Hank shot Joaquin en flagrante delicto. Olive must have been terrified if she was with Joaquin when he was shot. Then she got mad. She grabbed the revolver and shot Hank. And the reason his truck is still there is because he's lying dead somewhere."

"Possibly," Evelyn said, shaking her head and marveling at Flora's vivid imagination. "In that case, how did Joaquin's body get out to the orchard? You said Olive is a small woman. Could she have dragged the body into the truck herself?"

"Hmm. Unlikely. Anyway, why would Olive hide Joaquin's body if Hank was the one who shot him? Wouldn't she just call the sheriff and have Hank arrested?"

"Possibly, but as I said before, Hank is Olive's meal ticket, however unreliable. It's not going to save their house or do her any good to have Hank locked up even if he did commit the murder. And if she shot Hank dead herself she's not likely going to call the sheriff."

Flora stood and began pacing around the parlor. "Well, then, how did Joaquin's body get to the orchard?"

"Here's one idea. Olive let Hank live and made him take the body to the orchard in the pickup to eliminate suspicion from herself. Could Hank have moved that body by himself?"

"Perhaps. How about this? Hank shot Joaquin for what Lil Bird told us was 'a good reason.' Also, Francie said the other deputies might help cover up what they regard as a justifiable crime. It's not unreasonable to assume Hank had help disposing of Joaquin's body."

"So far, so good," Evelyn said. "Where is Hank now?"

"Perhaps when Hank got home from dumping the body, Olive was lying in wait with his revolver."

"Olive shot Hank in revenge for killing her lover?" The subject was not amusing, but Evelyn couldn't contain a smile. "And now she's got Hank's body just laying around the house while she goes off to gambling games? We have to assume the other deputies would not help Olive get rid of Hank's body, if only out of loyalty to their former colleague."

"Precisely," Flora said, "and now she's stuck with Hank's body. How about this? Hank came home after dumping Joaquin's body, got in the tub to wash up, and that's where Olive nailed him. Blam! That's where we'll find Hank's body, still lying in the Porters' bathtub."

"Very creative, Flora. How does Olive wash-up now, with Hank occupying the tub?"

"Bird baths, Evie. Splash a little here, a little there, you're set to go. Anyway, not everyone washes up as often as we do. It's only been a week since Joaquin was shot."

Evelyn sighed and scrunched her lips, puzzled. "I can't see how we'd get a look into the Porters' bathtub, but I sure would like to take a gander at that pickup truck. Dollars to doughnuts we'd find Joaquin's blood in the bed of that truck, or evidence of his body having been there at one time."

"And while we're there gaping at the truck, we could climb in a window and take a peek at the bathtub." Flora smiled.

"Eight days after the fact, I'd think the smell alone would attest to the presence of a body."

"Eew!" Flora plopped back into her chair.

"In any case," Evelyn said, "the point I wanted to make was, although I have no idea where Hank is now, I am beginning to wonder if we've got this story right. I do think the Porters hold the key to this mystery if only because they have possession of the revolver we're hoping to find. I'm just not sure about the motive or about who pulled the trigger."

Flora put the fingers of her left hand to her forehead imitating a fortune teller. "I see another trip to Walnut Creek in our future. I suppose we should go sooner, rather than later."

"That only seems prudent."

Chapter Thirty-Three

Mid-morning on Monday, Evelyn appeared downstairs in a dark navy day dress and matching brimmed slouch hat. From her chair in the parlor, Flora lowered her novel and regarded her friend. "You should wear something less severe," Flora said. "Something that will allow you to blend into the background more."

"I'm hardly going to blend into the background if I get caught in the Porters' bathroom."

Flora smiled. "That's true. I was thinking more about when we're sneaking down the Porters' driveway. You don't want to be seen from the house as you're trespassing, do you? Or were you planning to drive right up? Oh, I know! You drive right up and park. While you're distracting Olive at the door, I'll climb up the side wall of the house and get a peek into the bathtub."

"Ixnay on that plan, dear. Not hardly." Evelyn sighed. "Very well, what do you suggest I wear? And while we're on the subject, when are you planning to get dressed? I'm not taking you in that peignoir set, no matter how alluring."

"I've already laid my dress out, and even chosen my hat. Come upstairs and I'll help you find something suitable. Pearl probably has something that will work."

It being closer to noon, traffic was light through downtown, and they made good time getting to the tunnel. As she often did, Evelyn felt a grip of alarm as they entered the narrow opening.

Strictly for entertainment, earlier they'd driven to where they could look down on the site designated for a new and much longer tunnel. The survey work appeared to be at a standstill, probably due to the same lack of funding that was slowing down many other projects. That new tunnel didn't look as though it was going to be completed any time soon, even though the benefits were many.

Emerging safely from the old tunnel, Evelyn decided to tell Flora what she'd been puzzling over. "You know," she said, "I'm thinking we might have this whole story wrong."

"Again? How so this time?"

"Lil Bird pretty much told us Joaquin was killed because he was having a romantic liaison with someone he shouldn't have been, don't you think?"

Flora shifted to face Evelyn and nodded.

"And then," Evelyn continued, "we learned Hank Porter owned the type of weapon used to commit the murder. From there, we leapt to the conclusion that Joaquin's liaison must have been with Hank's wife, Olive. We made that assumption because that's the way things usually are, or that's the way we think things usually are, not because we had any evidence to support that theory."

"Uh-hum?"

"Well, you know what our friend Sherlock Holmes has to say about making assumptions without evidence. And I'm of the opinion that what evidence we do have does not point toward Olive being the one having the affair with Joaquin. And, if we are headed out to spy on the Porters' pickup truck—"

"or their bathtub."

"Yes, or their bathtub, it would be better if our observations were not clouded by assumptions not based in evidence."

"Yes. although I do have to admit, dear, you lost me right there at the end. It would help if you'd explain what evidence you're talking about."

"Good point. For starters, what do we know or rather what have we heard about Joaquin?"

Flora thought for a moment and said, "Rafael told us Joaquin came home that night to wash up and put on a clean shirt, so we're assuming when he left he was headed for a romantic engagement. Although Rafael also told us he'd asked Joaquin to keep watch that night at the barn. It is true that when Rafael went to the barn at two in the morning looking for his brother, Joaquin wasn't there. So perhaps he really was off with a lover."

"Yes," Evelyn agreed. "And Francie said Joaquin was a 'busy boy,' implying that he had numerous of those types of, shall we say liaisons. Francie also said Joaquin had no need of her services. We might assume that to mean Joaquin had women falling all over him, but we have no evidence of that."

"What else could it mean?"

"Well, let's keep looking at the evidence we do have, however meager. For example, both Tia Rosamaria and Rafael implied disapproval of Joaquin's activities."

"They kind of curled their lips, but then neither of them wanted to talk about what they meant," Flora said. "My father used to curl his lip at me in precisely that way."

"I don't know as I've seen your father often enough to judge, but yes, we've both seen that expression of distaste before, too many times."

"You're thinking Joaquin might have been a nellie? And we know who else people called nellie. The same man who owns the revolver, Hank Porter."

"Yes. And that's where looking at the evidence puts us."

A pause followed, then Flora said, "Are you suggesting that while Hank may have shot Joaquin, that might have resulted from a lover's quarrel between the two of them and not because Hank caught Joaquin with Olive?"

"Possibly Hank became concerned that Joaquin might make their relationship public. Bad feelings are rife among the farmworkers, and the Vigilantes, including Hank's buddies in the sheriff's department. Possibly Joaquin got angry about the labor strife and threatened in fury to reveal their...liaison."

"Don't you think most everyone already knew about Hank's...ah...proclivities? We've already discussed the fact that everyone says Hank was 'let go' from the sheriff's department, but no one says why. The point being, Hank could hardly have been angry or scared enough to shoot Joaquin if the facts were not so secret to begin with."

"That, my dear, is an excellent point."

"I almost feel sorry for Hank," Flora said. "We've not heard anything to indicate he wasn't a perfectly good deputy. What a shame if he was let go for some completely irrelevant reason. Why can't people simply let others live their lives in peace? And now look what's happened. Hank lost his job and the Porters are about to lose their house."

"True, too true. Even so, Hank can't be permitted to go around shooting people. This only increases my interest in inspecting that pickup for evidence that a bloody body may have been recently transported in it."

After a long moment of contemplation, Flora spoke again. "You know what I find curious about our hypothesis that Joaquin was shot in some way related to a romantic encounter, en flagrante delicto?"

"What's curious?"

"That list of Joaquin's personal effects Dr. Whitley showed us included all of Joaquin's clothes, even his boots. Whitley also mentioned the blood found on the collar of the shirt. Don't you think that means Joaquin was fully dressed when he was shot? If he was killed in the middle of...making whoopee, wouldn't he have taken at least some of his clothes off?"

Evelyn's eyes narrowed and she nodded slowly. "Yes, I do see your point. Another clue."

Evelyn maintained highway speed until just past the Porters' mailbox, then slowed suddenly and pulled under the cover of a copse of valley oaks. Once she was sure the Chevrolet was not visible from any window in the house, she parked. They walked to where they could survey the Porters' driveway, mapping out a route that would minimize the likelihood of being spotted from the kitchen window as they made their approach. The end of the pickup, Evelyn's main target, was still visible where it had been a few days before, poking out from the side of the barn. The Model T still sat out front, moved under the shade of a tree.

A high shrub of blackberry vines lined the front of the property, covering most of their approach to the drive. Flora's slate-blue dress and straw boater faded nicely into the background. The floral print she'd chosen for Evelyn, borrowed from Pearl's closet, would have been too flashy for church but tended to melt into the greenery and black-eyed-susans along the roadside nicely.

Scuttling across the driveway opening, they stopped behind a bush at the corner. They peered intently at the only window visible in the house, searching for movement.

"Are you sure you want to try this?" Flora said in a whisper. "You know, if Hank is really here, and Olive did him in and still needs to dispose of his body, she may be doing it piece by manageable piece. There may not be enough left in the bathtub to even identify him."

Evelyn gripped Flora's arm, giving a nervous chuckle. "Honestly, dear, I think you should write those serialized horror stories they print in the true crime magazines. You have quite the knack. In any case, it's really only the pickup truck I want to get a look at."

"Yes, very well. If nothing else, that'll be another piece in the puzzle."

Slowly, they started along the far side of the driveway toward the small barn. That would take them past the door to the barn and within easy viewing distance of the pickup truck, while staying mostly out of view from the house. When they reached the corner of the barn, Flora whispered.

"You go on ahead. I'll back you up." She fell in line behind Evelyn and they tiptoed around the corner and across the front of the barn, both noticing the door was ajar by about four inches.

Evelyn reached the far corner, the pickup immediately in front of her. She checked for faces at the window in the house, saw none, then peered over the side of the truck bed. Somewhere behind she heard a solid "click," but was so close to achieving a view into the bed of the truck she hardly noticed.

"Ah!" she said, quietly. A frying-pan-sized dark brown stain marked the wooden floor of the truck bed and long streaks of brown led toward the tailgate. She turned to point the stains out to Flora but her friend was nowhere in sight.

Evelyn's heart stopped. For the briefest moment her mind was a complete blank. She stepped away from the truck and gazed the length of the driveway. Flora was absolutely gone. She could not possibly have made it all the way back to the Chevrolet in the time it had taken Evelyn to peep into the pickup bed. The only other possibility was that Flora had stepped or been taken without a sound, into the barn. Evelyn's feet moved before she'd even formed a complete thought. She ran to the previously open barn door and found it not only closed, but locked tightly, unyielding to her frantic tugs.

"Flora! Flora, come out of there at once!" Evelyn slammed an open palm against the wood of the barn door, heedless of anyone who might be watching her from the house. Beyond a whisper of shuffling, Evelyn got no reply, increasing her fear. Trying not to panic she searched the wall of the ancient barn. Dirty windows were located high on the wall, useless in helping

Evelyn see what might be happening inside. "Flora!" she cried again in an angry but increasingly helpless tone.

Stepping to the corner of the barn, she searched the wall on that side. One batten flopped loose, opening a slot between two boards at about eye-level. Not thinking about splinters, she grabbed the rough wood of the batten and broke it off. Cupping her hands against the light, Evelyn peered through the gap. What she saw frightened her into silence.

Shafts of sunlight streamed through the high windows, swirling with motes of dust and bits of straw. One ray fell on Flora's wide-eyed and terrified face and revealed her raised arms with hands held palms open. Her straw boater had become dislodged and chose that moment to fall to the floor. A movement caused Evelyn to shift focus and she saw what had triggered Flora's terror. A shorter figure, a woman, but hardly more than a shadow from Evelyn's perspective, crept forward toward Flora. She had a gun pointed at Flora's face.

"One sound," the woman said in a voice that was audible, but only just so. "One peep, and I'll blow your brains out." She pressed the point of the revolver to Flora's forehead for emphasis. "Turn around." The woman spun Flora with a shove to her shoulder and pushed the gun into her back, urging her toward the dimly lit rear wall.

Flora shuffled one foot, then the other. As she moved, Evelyn could see another figure revealed in the pale light. The nearly naked torso of a man came into focus. He moved and a chain rattled. His eyes opened and he whimpered once, the noise barely human, the sound of a trapped rodent. What Evelyn could see of his body was filthy. His face was dark with many days' growth of beard. He could easily have been there for more than a week. His mouth was bound with a frayed and soiled bandana. This had to be the missing Hank.

The shadowy figure of the woman, presumably Olive, stepped to the side, taking a coil of soiled rope from where it hung on a nail. Evelyn could see where this was going. Yelling for help would only bring Flora into more danger and would do nothing to rescue her.

Olive answered almost as though Flora had spoken. "Don't you worry, your friend isn't going to help you. She's next." Evelyn realized Olive must surely have lost her mind.

She stepped away from her peep-hole, scanned the side wall, and dashed to the rear corner of the small barn. There she clambered over a post and rail fence and gazed at the back wall trying desperately to think what to do. She had to do something, and fast. Barns always had more than one door. A narrow and rickety wooden ladder was attached to the back wall and led to the open bay of a hayloft. Evelyn threw herself at the lowest rung. She could hear the sound of a chain clanking and a heavy body thrashing, banging uselessly against the wall inside. She hoped the noise would be enough to mask the sound of her progress.

She scampered in silence up to the loft opening. From there she could only see the floor of the hayloft and several bales of straw. Cautiously, she leaned inside, waiting for the shot that would blow her head to pieces. As she moved, her view widened to include more of the floor below where Hank stood shackled to the wall. Adjusting to the dim light inside, she saw the chain holding Hank looped through a pair of handcuffs, binding him. If he'd looked up, he could have seen Evelyn, but his stare remained directed steadfastly forward as he jangled the chain again.

Evelyn could just barely see over the edge of the hayloft, where two hands reached into the air. She would recognize those hands anywhere. By stretching to gaze over a bale of straw, she could just make out the top of Olive's head. Olive and her gun were so close, Evelyn knew Olive would hear if she made a move and that might mean the end of Flora.

Chapter Thirty-Four

Evelyn saw thin hair draped limply across Olive's head as she peered over the bale of straw teetering at the edge of the hayloft. Without allowing herself time to think twice, Evelyn braced her feet and threw her athletic body at the bale, giving it a good push. The straw bale was much heavier than Evelyn imagined it would be, but she'd put everything she had into that thrust. The ponderous bale slid over the lip and dropped. One shot rang out as it fell, reverberating in the ominously still air of the barn. A small fountain of straw burst upward. The bale landed hard. Evelyn scrambled forward, seeing only that she'd scored a direct hit and flattened Olive. In spite of that, the other woman squirmed under the bale, clearly alive and conscious, and probably still gripping the revolver. Evelyn had to get Flora out of that barn before Olive struggled free of the bale and could aim another shot. She threw her arms over the edge of the hayloft, reaching for her friend.

"Flora! Here!"

Flora stepped on top of the fallen bale and its still-thrashing victim, and jumped, grasping Evelyn's hand and securing one elbow over the edge as Evelyn pulled with all her strength. Working together, they got Flora into the hayloft.

Holding tight to Flora's hand and without stopping for a second, Evelyn propelled herself backward. If she'd stopped to think about it, she would have turned and used the ladder nailed to the wall to get closer to the ground before dropping Flora's hand and leaping through the hayloft door, but there simply wasn't time.

From the ground, Evelyn saw her friend's head emerge. Flora made a quick assessment of the situation, turned, and availed herself of at least two of rungs on the ladder. Her feet churned the instant they hit the ground, following Evelyn around the far side of the barn.

Her hands around Flora's waist from behind, Evelyn boosted her friend over the fence. Encumbered only slightly by the billowing day dress, Evelyn vaulted over. A ripping sound accompanied her hurdle, heralding the probable end of Pearl's flowered dress.

Being squashed by a weighty bale of straw had not slowed Olive down nearly as much as they might have hoped. They still had thirty feet of driveway to run before they could take cover behind the brambles and get to their automobile. Olive's threatening voice called out. Flora shrieked in panic and they threw themselves forward, spurred even faster. They turned onto the gravel highway shoulder, running. The Chevrolet came into view up ahead.

A few seconds later, Olive also reached the junction of the drive with the highway, waving the revolver. She took aim, not seeming to care who saw her shooting at the two ladies. She fired and a bullet thudded into the trunk of a tree to their right.

Evelyn yelped in terror and they kept going. Another shot rang out and Evelyn dropped, one leg crumpled beneath her. She screamed in pain. Flora leapt back and seized Evelyn's arm as another shot whizzed just over their heads.

Summoning strength she didn't know she had, Flora hoisted Evelyn by one arm and a shoulder. With a good deal of whimpering and moaning, Evelyn was able to get her good leg under her. They hobbled frantically toward the automobile, Evelyn crying out with every step.

"I can't drive, Flora, I can't drive!" Evelyn gasped in pain. Flora steered her toward the passenger door and helped her inside.

"Where are you hit?" Flora said. "I don't see any blood." She slammed the door, raced around the front of the automobile and got in behind the wheel. "Put the key in the ignition, Evelyn."

"What are you doing? You don't know how to drive!"

"I do now!" Flora engaged the ignition, depressed the clutch, pulled the choke, and nudged the gas pedal like a pro. The automobile lurched forward just as another shot slammed into its rear. Something shattered.

Evelyn moaned again. Walter wasn't going to be happy about that.

Flora goosed the gas pedal and released the clutch enough to make fits and starts of forward progress, putting at least some distance between themselves and the deranged woman with the revolver.

"Where's the hospital, Evelyn. I have to get you to the hospital! Where are you hit? I don't see any blood? Oh, good gracious, is it internal? Do you have internal injuries? Where's the hospital?"

"Calm down, dear. You're hyperventilating. I'm not shot. It's this dratted shoe. It's fallen apart again. I tripped on it and must have twisted my ankle. Oh, no, look..."

Flora did not look, intent as she was on driving and in any case, not wishing to see her friend's injury.

Evelyn moaned in despair. "The entire shoe has come apart."

"Yes, that is a shame," Flora said in a distracted tone. "All I can think about are those gunshots!"

"Oow, my ankle really hurts. I can't put any weight on it at all."

They'd left Olive and the revolver well behind them as they drove around a curve and the automobile continued in a jerky fashion into the town of Walnut Creek.

"Do you even know which one is the brake pedal?" Evelyn said. "Because that's a stop sign up ahead at the intersection."

Flora rolled to a cautious halt. She forgot to disengage the gears at the last minute, causing the auto to lurch and the engine to stall, but they had made it safely that far. Flora resisted, but Evelyn prevailed and slid behind the wheel while Flora trotted around to the passenger side and got in.

Evelyn whimpered whenever she had to depress the brake. Even so, they made it the next block and a half to the soda fountain. Flora dashed inside and procured a bag of ice to pack around Evelyn's ankle. As Flora worked, Evelyn grew woozy with pain.

"Shall I get you something to drink?" Flora said. "You don't look so well."

"No. I don't feel so well. Just hurry and telephone the sheriff. Olive might make a run for it. Who knows who else she might hurt in her frame of mind."

Flora made a hurried second trip inside to telephone the sheriff and secure his deputies' assistance in rounding up Olive Porter. Wide eyes from those seated at the soda counter followed her every move, but she wasn't concerned with their interest. She had more important matters on her mind.

Several minutes later, three sheriff's vehicles approached coming south down Main Street. The cars looked like any other black Fords on the road, except the word 'Sheriff' was stenciled on both the front and rear windows and small decals adorned the driver's side doors. One man's job apparently was to lean out the side and honk the horn. Other motorists looked confused and appeared to have no idea how to respond to the honking. They mostly waved gaily and continued on as they had been. The sheriff's vehicles passed the Chevrolet, still parked in front of the soda fountain, and disappeared around the turn at the stop sign.

"You saved my life, you know," Evelyn said, leaning her neck on the back of the seat. "I would have died right there in the gravel, gunned down by that unhinged maniac if you hadn't pulled me to safety and driven us away."

Flora turned and gave Evelyn a long stare. "Have you already forgotten? I wouldn't have been there to drive you if you hadn't rescued me from that same maniac inside the barn. In any case, I think you saved yourself when you fell. Didn't you hear that bullet whiz past right where your head would have been if you hadn't collapsed?"

Evelyn managed a smile. "Thank goodness for small graces. Anyway, as much as I'd rather not, we'd best go back and tell our story to the deputies." Evelyn did not relish the prospect of returning to the scene of such recent terror. "Before we go, would you mind stepping out to survey the damage? One of Olive's bullets did hit Walter's automobile."

Flora climbed out and went to the rear of the Chevrolet. "Oh, dear," she said, one hand over her mouth.

"How bad is it?"

"Well…it's not so bad it can't be repaired, but I am afraid she blew Walter's right taillight clean off. It looks to me like, if one could mail order that part, it would be possible to simply remove these two screws…" Flora's voice faded as she leaned over to determine the placement of the screws in question. "Yes, it should be possible to replace this part and all will be as good as new, almost."

"Almost?"

"Well, very nearly. There is this one scratch…but I think even that can be disguised with a bit of paint. We won't need to tell Walter about this, will we?"

Evelyn gave a shaky laugh. "I think we do need to tell Walter, dear."

"Hmm. Perhaps he'll be placated when we tell him, better a scratch on his new automobile than a bullet in his dear sister."

Evelyn wasn't so sure. "Pearl isn't going to be happy about this dress either," she said, waving the flap of flowered fabric torn up the side of the skirt.

A minor disagreement followed Flora's pronouncement

that she would drive them back to Alameda. Rather than argue, Evelyn started the engine and reversed out of their parking spot. "I promise," she said, "I'll give you another driving lesson every day until you're proficient. You're absolutely correct. If we're going to travel anywhere by automobile, and given the trouble we seem to get ourselves into, it's essential that both of us be able to drive."

The three sheriff's vehicles were parked in front of the Porters' house, and uniformed officers fairly swarmed the barn. Evelyn pulled the Chevrolet next to the mailbox and was immediately accosted by a young deputy.

"No parking here, ma'am. Sheriff's department business going on here. This is not a sideshow."

"I am aware, young man. Miss Fitzgerald here and I are the ones who called this situation to the sheriff's attention."

The deputy gaped once or twice before regaining his authoritarian attitude. "Nevertheless, you may not park here."

"Excuse me," Flora leaned to the window and cooed. "Might we speak to Deputy Calhoun, please?"

"Yes," Evelyn added. "Deputy Calhoun will wish to speak with us, I can assure you."

The young officer narrowed his eyes, shrugged, and said, "I'll see if he's available." He strode the length of the driveway and vanished inside the barn.

Evelyn gazed pensively while they waited. "She had one more bullet, you know."

"What do you mean?"

"The cylinder in a revolver holds six bullets. If she reloaded after the night she shot Joaquin, she had one bullet left when we drove away. I hope poor Hank made it."

A few moments later a bustling of activity around the barn door indicated something was about to happen. Two large deputies emerged flanking a tiny woman between them. Olive looked like someone who had been bearing a heavy burden for far too long and had finally been crushed under the weight of it. She could hardly put one foot in front of the other. The deputies lifted her into one of their vehicles and closed the door, then one turned to stare at Walter's Chevrolet.

"Look who I see," Flora said, tipping her head in the direction of that officer.

"Is that...is that Lil Bird?"

"Yes, I do believe it is. And do you know what's more? If my guess is correct, I believe Lil Bird knew as much as he told us only because he was someone who helped move Joaquin's body and divert suspicion away from the Porters."

"You may be correct, dear."

Standing at the end of the driveway, Deputy Calhoun gazed at Evelyn and Flora, waved to the officer they'd nicknamed Lil Bird, and the two of them approached the Chevrolet. Something about the slump of their shoulders told Evelyn all was not well inside the barn.

"You girls want to follow us down to the office? We need you to tell us the whole story, how you came to be here and what all happened. My pal here..." and Calhoun gestured with his thumb at Lil Bird. "He says you told him over the telephone Olive Porter shot at you?"

"Yes, sir," Flora said. "She did indeed. Several times."

"Five, to be precise," Evelyn added.

Flora leaned closer to the window and peered up at Calhoun. "But we'll give our statement later. Miss Winslow suffered a serious injury, and I need to get her to a doctor."

"You're shot?" he said, his voice rising in concern.

"No, no," Evelyn assured him. "It's only a twisted ankle, but it hurts like the devil."

Calhoun watched the passing traffic, which was starting to back up with folks hoping to get an eyeful. "Okay, then. I'll have someone telephone you to set up an appointment. Give the officer here your telephone number." He waved at yet another deputy and pointed at the stalled traffic, then started toward the barn.

Evelyn could see the third vehicle back was a white Nash wagon with a red cross painted on the side. An ambulance. Who here had need of an ambulance, Evelyn wondered.

Chapter Thirty-Five

"Oh, Deputy." Evelyn called out to Calhoun. He returned to their window and she hesitated. "What about Hank? Did you find him in the barn? He's there in the barn, chained up."

Calhoun stepped back and glanced away again.

"He helped us," Flora said to Lil Bird. "He made noise so Olive couldn't hear Miss Winslow coming to save me. I hope he's okay."

"Yes," Evelyn agreed. "Although Olive had that one last bullet..."

For the first time Evelyn noticed the revolver Lil Bird was holding. Gazing at the gun without looking up, he pulled the cylinder release and spun the cylinder to show one bullet remaining in a chamber. Evelyn stared at the flat end of that single bullet. She couldn't help but imagine the damage that bullet could have done should Olive Porter's aim been better controlled.

"She couldn't do it," he said. "She told me she was gonna shoot him, but then she jus' couldn't do it. Said he was still her husband in spite of everything. He's in bad shape after bein' chained up for a week, but at least he's not shot."

"Oh," Evelyn said. "Thank goodness for that."

"You girls need to move your vehicle," Calhoun called. "I got to get this ambulance in here. And where's that fella who went to get a hacksaw? Hank's still chained to the wall and we can't find a key anywhere. Olive swears she doesn't know where it is either. She says that's why she left him hanging there all this time."

"Oh," Evelyn said. "I believe your Dr. Whitley has that key, you know, the coroner? He showed us the list of items found in Joaquin's pockets. That key is among Joaquin's effects."

Evelyn winced when she stepped on the clutch and whimpered a good many times as they completed the return drive to Walter's. Other than the whimpering, they rode in shocked silence. The bag of ice Flora had so thoughtfully acquired had melted all over the floor of Walter's Chevrolet by the time they got to his house. As Flora helped Evelyn hobble up the stairs and onto the sofa they noted the injured ankle was visibly swollen and had turned red and hot to the touch.

"I think that means it's only sprained, not broken," Evelyn said. "We'll pack it in more ice. I'll be fine with a little rest."

"We'll see," Flora said, her tone filled with doubt. "In the meanwhile, I'll get busy with totaling our expenses and prepare an invoice for the Pachecos. How much should we charge them for the injury to your ankle? And what about repairs to Walter's Chevrolet? Do those go on the invoice also? We should charge for a new pair of walking shoes at the very least, don't you think?"

With one hand over her forehead, and not in the mood to think about serious questions, Evelyn did not answer.

Flora hacked loose a few chunks of ice from the Frigidaire's freezer compartment, found a small rubber mat on the back porch, and packed the twisted ankle. She came downstairs a few minutes later carrying a dark brown bottle. "I found this in the medicine cabinet. It looks like something Pearl might give the boys." She read the label. "Nyalgesic? I think it's a liquid aspirin. Let me get a spoon and we'll give it a try."

Evelyn was feigning sleep when Flora returned, something she occasionally did when she wasn't in the mood for an argument. For Evelyn, pretending to be asleep often had the added benefit of leading directly to actual sound sleep. Flora laid a crocheted throw over her friend, left the bottle and spoon on the side table, and curled up in Pearl's chair for a watchful rest.

Given what they'd been through, they both needed the nap. Over an hour had passed when Flora returned to consciousness. Evelyn still snored lightly on her sofa bed.

Flora jumped up to change Evelyn's ice pack again, noting as she did so that her friend's ankle was looking decidedly better. She brought their supper into the parlor on a tray and adjusted the radio dial to Evelyn's preferred news program, beginning soon. Several times a week the station featured journalist Dorothy Thompson's report direct from Berlin.

While they waited, Flora said, "I'm trying to get my mind off Hank and Joaquin and all the bad news, and I've had an idea, something we might do for fun." Evelyn was busy chewing, having discovered a ravenous appetite.

Flora continued. "We never really had our day at Neptune Beach amusement park, you know, and I'm wondering if we might invite Jaing to come stay with us here for a day or two, and bring her son along. Don't you think he's just the right age to have fun at such a place? With the rollercoaster, and the mini-golf, and all of that decadent food, don't you think he'd love it?"

"That is indeed a swell idea, dear, and I'm sure you're right about how much fun we'd all have…"

"But?"

"I might be wrong, but I fear Jaing and her son might not be allowed into the park."

Flora flopped back in her chair, a scowl clouding her face. "You mean because they're Chinese?"

Evelyn nodded in sympathy with Flora's scowl. "It seems as though there's always another battle to fight doesn't it?'

After the news, and Dorothy Thompson's report that the government in Berlin was descending into a swirling shambles of rumors and intrigue, Flora finally managed to get Evelyn to swallow a spoonful of the Nyalgesic. They waited for it to take effect before attempting the climb upstairs.

Feeling drowsy, Evelyn said, "You know, the minute I realized you were gone, locked in the Porter's barn, I suddenly knew the whole story, what must have really happened. It was as though we had all the pieces of the puzzle, but they didn't fall into place until that moment."

"You even knew Olive Porter had killed Joaquin?"

"I did, and when you look at the whole picture, well, I know this is a strange thing to say, but it's not hard to comprehend how Olive might have come to that end." As she spoke, Evelyn realized that talking, putting her thoughts together and telling the story, was helping distract her from the pain in her ankle. When Flora asked her to explain what she meant, Evelyn was grateful.

"Well, there Olive was, we may assume, having a reasonably good life. Her husband had a secure position as a deputy with the sheriff's department. He was making enough of a salary to get a loan on a nice little house and a bit of land. Even as the economic situation in the rest of the world crumbled and people all around them were losing jobs and moving into shantytowns, Olive and Hank Porter were doing relatively well. Then Hank was let go from his job with the sheriff."

"For no good reason," Flora said.

"Yes. And one has to wonder if Olive knew why…"

"Oh, but surely she must have done."

"Yes, one would assume she did know. And it's also obvious why finding Hank and Joaquin in the barn together would infuriate her."

Flora nodded. "After Hank lost his job he probably promised her he would never do that again. That he would behave himself and somehow get his job back, or another one."

"Precisely. And then, a week ago Saturday night she caught her husband carrying on with Joaquin in their barn. She must have thrown a fit knowing the financial plight they were in, the bank foreclosing on their house, and all because Hank couldn't behave himself. She didn't stop to think what she was doing. She saw Joaquin, and in that moment, he looked to her like the cause of everything that had gone wrong in her life. Olive simply flew off the handle with rage."

Flora gave a sad nod. "She probably thought if Joaquin was gone, everything would go back to the way it had been before."

"If she thought anything at all, given the intensity of her outrage."

"She got Hank's old revolver and shot Joaquin in the back of the head."

"Yes," Evelyn said.

"You know, when she had me cornered in the barn, when she had that revolver pointed at my head, her eyes, the way they lit up, and they rolled," Flora rolled her eyes, letting the whites show wildly, conjuring up the face of the woman who had confronted her. "She was insane. Perhaps insane with fury or frustration, but quite literally completely out of her mind." Flora let out a deep breath and held Evelyn's arm. "In that moment, I really thought I was going to die."

Evelyn didn't want to say so, but she had suffered the very same fear as she'd peered at the scene through the gap in the barn wall. "Your fear is not surprising," she said, "considering Joaquin had already been killed and Hank was, for all intents, being held prisoner."

"And again for no good reason," Flora said. "Only because of their love for one another." Flora buried her head in her hands while Evelyn patted her friend's back gently. "None of this had to happen, Evie, if people would just leave each other alone. If the sheriff had simply ignored Hank's 'liaison' with Joaquin, none of this would have happened."

"That may be true, but the problem goes deeper than that. What Joaquin and Hank were doing is against the law. How can the sheriff be expected to retain a deputy who regularly violates the law?"

Evelyn's comment did nothing to sooth Flora's despair. She shuddered.

A moment later, Flora said, "One thing I still don't really understand. You described Joaquin and Hank as 'carrying on.' They weren't asleep on that bale of straw, right? So how did Olive shoot Joaquin in the back of his head? Didn't he see her coming with the gun? And if he didn't, then surely Hank must have. Why didn't Hank stop her?"

Evelyn gave that question some consideration, or rather, she gave some thought to a way to frame the answer so as not to shock her friend. Evelyn suspected she knew the answer, but she wasn't sure her less worldly-wise friend really wanted to know the details. She caught Flora's gaze and said in a quiet voice, "Well, it would have been relatively easy to shoot Joaquin from behind if Olive snuck up on the two men embracing."

Understanding appeared in Flora's eyes. *"En flagrante delicto?"*

"Well, possibly not entirely. After all, we know both men were still dressed, or mostly so."

Flora gave a bleak nod. "And then how did Olive get Hank chained to the wall? He's not going to let her chain him to the wall, and using his own handcuffs, too."

Evelyn blinked several times. It was not impossible that Hank had already been chained to the wall when Olive came upon them but that hardly seemed like something Flora would understand.

"Well," she said, "Olive did have the gun and she'd just shot Joaquin. Possibly she chained Hank up herself."

"She just happened to be carrying Hank's old handcuffs with her?"

"Well, possibly..." Evelyn said, letting her voice trail off. "Or possibly Hank had let himself be handcuffed by Joaquin. You understand? As part of the...?"

"Handcuffed?" The tone in Flora's voice shifted to a higher note. "Is there no end to the shenanigans people will get up to, *en flagrante delicto?*"

Evelyn didn't know whether to laugh or moan. "Apparently not, my dear. You know, you remind me of something Mama once told me. She said when she was a girl, her mother said she didn't care what any two people might get up to, as long as they didn't do it in the street and frighten the horses."

The End

Dear Reader,

Thank you for reading *An Unforeseen Motive*. I hope you enjoyed it, and the other books in the *Winslow & Fitzgerald Investigations* series.

Please consider posting reviews for these books on your favorite book-related websites. If you liked this story, your friends would probably enjoy hearing about it. I am most grateful for any help in spreading the word.

To be among the first to learn about new releases please subscribe to my private list on my website at www. cherieoboyle.com. You may also send me questions or comments on that site. I would love to hear from you!

Thanks again for your support! – *Cherie O'Boyle*

Early in her working life, Cherie O'Boyle made a living as a carpenter while finishing her bachelors degree. She next entered graduate school at the University of Oregon, where she earned a PhD in experimental psychology and then became a university professor at California State University, San Marcos, retiring as a Professor Emeritus. Shifting gears again Cherie next took up a variety of artistic pursuits. She spent several years completely distracted with racing flyball and sheep herding with her border collies. Thus, writing award-winning mystery fiction is only one of the ways she currently spends her creative time. Cherie is a native Californian and lives in Northern California.

AUTHOR NOTES

Today the former site of the Giant Powder Company provides a peaceful walk along the shores of San Pablo Bay near San Francisco with stunning views of the city. In 1932 it was a bustling explosives manufacturing company. Armaments for both World Wars were made here and shipped to the Pacific Theater out of nearby Port Chicago. At about 10:20 PM on the night of July 17, 1944 the loading dock at Port Chicago exploded in a colossal blast, sending fire and smoke over two miles into the air. Shock waves were felt as far away as Boulder City, Nevada. Three hundred and twenty enlisted men assigned the dangerous duty of loading munitions were killed and another four hundred wounded. Of the men killed, two hundred and two were African-Americans. This one event accounted for 15% of all African-American casualties in World War II. Lolly, her husband, and their son Steven are fictional characters, of course, but I can't help but wonder if they survived the blast, especially Steven who might have been loading the ships at that time.

In 1933, the year after *An Unforeseen Motive* takes place, Adolf Hitler ordered the complete rearming of Germany in violation of the Treaty of Versailles. As in The Great War, certain American manufacturers profited from prohibited trade with Axis countries right through the end of the Second World War.

In 1924 after the conclusion of The Great War, Congress voted to provide each returning veteran with a lump sum bonus, payable in 1945. In the spring of 1932 at the depth of the Depression, unemployed and destitute veterans began demanding immediate payment of this promised bonus. More than twenty thousand of them traveled to Washington, DC and set up an encampment on the Capitol Mall. Public support for the Bonus Army was widespread. On Wednesday, June 15, the House of Representatives voted to provide swift payment to the veterans. The bill was then forwarded to the Republican-controlled Senate which promptly rejected it. President Hoover had promised to veto the bill, and ordered troops use tear gas and bayonets to drive the Bonus Army from their encampment. Four years later, in 1936, the veterans did finally get their bonus, when Congress voted to pay the money over President Franklin Roosevelt's veto.

In December 1932 Pan American World Airways announced plans to provide commercial airline service to Hawaii. Amenities covered in the price of the ticket included fine dining options, pillows, blankets, and luxurious space to stretch one's legs. All the stewardesses on board were registered nurses.

ACKNOWLEDGEMENTS

I owe debts of gratitude to more people than ever for their contributions. Several dedicated mystery writers and readers provided valuable feedback about numerous iterations of this book. Michele Drier, June Gillam, Linda Townsdin, Cathy McGreevy, Dänna Wilberg and T T Thomas collaboratively provided hours of critique for the first draft. Special thanks to Nancy Flagg, Ian Wilson, and Ana Brazil for their generous beta reads.

Thank also to Shireen Miles for joining me on one wild day of research exploring what's left of old Chinatown, even though most of it was closed due to that nasty virus.

And thank you to everyone else who has crossed my path and left bits of knowledge and humor to enliven and populate these pages. If I thanked everyone who helped, the acknowledgements would be longer than the book.

Made in the USA
Las Vegas, NV
30 July 2023

75435677R00163